Neena Lee Is Seeing Things

Sheila Athens

Chapter One

Neena Lee could tell something was amiss.

She sat in the lobby of *Coastal South Travel* magazine, trying to determine why the normally friendly receptionist wasn't making eye contact with her. She and Tammy knew each other well. Had even gone to lunch together a few times over the years.

The magazine's editor, Frank McDonald, had hired Neena as a freelance travel writer so many times that *Coastal South Travel* had represented the bulk of her income each of the last three years—an income she desperately needed to get back on track.

But today, the receptionist looked nervous. Her eyes stayed on her computer monitor, though her hands lay in her lap, away from the keyboard. She hadn't invited Neena to go on back to Frank's office like she had every other time Neena had visited.

Was Frank keeping Neena waiting to make a point? To get even with her for not completing her last assignment a month earlier?

A gust of wind shook the single picture window as sheets of rain pounded the old one-story brick building. She startled, then tried to cover it up by rearranging her body in the standard office-waiting-room upholstered chair. She did *not* want to alert Tammy—or anyone else here, for that matter—about the anxiety that had so often crippled her these last few weeks. She closed her eyes and drew in a long, hopefully calming breath, just as her therapist had taught her to do.

"Looks like the outer bands have arrived," Tammy said.

Neena's eyes popped open at the receptionist's words—her first bit of small talk since Neena's arrival. "Yeah, I was pretty sure they were chasing me down the street on my way here."

Tammy chuckled. Her gaze flashed briefly to Neena's, then returned to her monitor.

Though the latest tropical storm was supposed to stay offshore, Jacksonville would get several inches of rain over the next twenty-four hours. Neena had considered postponing this meeting, but she needed to make sure she was still in Frank's good graces. She hadn't talked to him in a month.

Tammy's head snapped up as a gangly man-boy entered the reception area from the direction of Frank's office. He had close-cropped brown hair and wore slim-cut khaki pants and a light blue oxford.

"Ms. Lee?" he asked.

Neena stood. "Yes?" He looked to be maybe in his late twenties, about five years older than her daughter.

He held out his hand. "I'm Justin Reid."

She glanced to Tammy, whose gaze was once again suspiciously unmoving from her computer screen, then back to Justin. Who was this guy? She shook his hand. "Neena Lee."

"Lee is your last name, right?" he asked. "It's not a two-part first name—Neena Lee? Like Billy Bob or something like that?"

"No. You got it right. Neena's my first name, and Lee is my last name." She smiled, though his tone had seemed to mock the Southern culture of this region near the Florida/Georgia border. His nondescript accent didn't tell her where he might have grown up.

"Shall we?" He motioned toward the hallway that led to Frank's office.

She followed him past a row of offices, three of which now looked strangely vacant. The desks held no picture frames or other personal me-

mentos. Whiteboards were wiped clean. Name placards next to doors stood empty, as if the writers she'd known for years had been erased.

The two offices that *did* look occupied were now labeled with the names of recent college grads she'd met only once, at the summer picnic Frank had thrown for the staff and freelancers to celebrate the magazine's fifteenth anniversary.

A buzz of anxiety skated through Neena's body. She willed herself to stay calm. She didn't have enough information to know what was going on here yet. But then whatever part of her body had been delivering these attacks lately didn't seem to care about logic.

She followed Justin into the office at the end of the hall—Frank's office, except that it no longer held her editor's perennially messy stacks of paper, photos of his grandchildren, or the gator skull that had sat on his bookshelf for years. Instead, the surfaces were immaculate. Devoid of paper and any personal belongings. There wasn't even a pencil holder or stapler in sight. It was as if the entire office had been sterilized.

"What happened to Frank?" she asked as Justin motioned for her to have a seat at the four-top table in one corner of the room. She swallowed, forcing her fear back down her gullet as best she could.

He sat in the chair across from her. "I've been sent by the corporate office to get the financials of the magazine more in line with the projections."

But that didn't answer her question. She leaned toward him, her heart ricocheting in her chest. "Has Frank been fired?" *Oh, God.* He'd been her main source of income and her primary hope for getting her life back on track after her recent hospitalization.

Justin spread his long skinny fingers across the tabletop in front of him. "We've...had to make some changes in order to move the needle a bit. To change the trajectory of our financials."

"So Frank's gone? And Nancy and Lori and Jeff?" Those were the names that had been missing from beside the office doors. All talented, experienced writers who'd worked for the magazine for years. Each middle-aged, like her.

She sat back and tried to imagine how Justin might see her—a white woman in her fifties, still slightly overweight, though her bohemian-inspired skirt and blouse now hung loosely from her frame, thanks to the lack of appetite she'd had since Kevin's death. A smattering of coarse gray hairs infiltrated the brown in her straight, shoulder-length style. People had always complimented the combination of dark hair and blue eyes, but she didn't suspect that was something Justin would notice. He likely just saw someone his mom's age—or maybe even older—sitting across from him.

"We've retained a small number of staff writers and will focus on acquiring freelance articles written on spec," he said.

So they'd kept the recent college grads and would buy articles from people who'd already paid for their own travel expenses? That business model wouldn't work for her. She had enough money in the bank for maybe three months of mortgage payments, but that didn't take into account the bills she'd racked up during her recent hospital stay. And she was already out a thousand bucks, thanks to her brother's cremation, a process which—amazingly—she'd been able to handle completely online. "So you're letting me go, too?"

"You're not an employee, so I can't technically do that."

But not giving her freelance assignments would be the same thing as firing her. Both meant no money in her pocket. She looked him in the eye, determined to be as strong and direct as possible, despite how vulnerable she felt. "Do you foresee any assignments for me in the near future? I've been a regular contributor for years."

"And the rest of the staff had to really scramble to cover your last story."

She set her jaw. "There were personal reasons for missing that deadline." Like finding her only sibling dead from an accidental overdose. She'd invited Kevin to move in with her four months ago—an attempt to get him far away from his dealers in Charlotte. She'd tried to figure out how to best support him. Tried to create a normal, loving environment. And still, he'd managed to OD in her guest bedroom. How had this happened to the little brother she used to push around in a stroller? The one who once dipped all her Barbies in bright blue house paint to turn them into Smurfs? How had she *let* it happen?

For the second time in her life, a family member had died on her watch.

And shortly thereafter, she'd been hospitalized for chest pains. She'd been sure she was having a heart attack, but a battery of tests had determined otherwise. Her heart was fine, but Kevin's death had set off a maelstrom of panic attacks. The episodes had come often, but inconsistently. She never knew what would set her mind off.

But Justin didn't need to know any of that.

"There's a difference between being late for a deadline and not even writing the article," he said.

She stared at him, unsure what to say. Even if she hadn't been in the behavioral health unit at the local hospital, she'd been too fragile to do any kind of work. Hell, most days, she wasn't certain she could make a phone call without hyperventilating. But she wasn't going to discuss the death of her only sibling with this...stranger, much less her mind's inexplicable reaction, so she remained silent.

He continued. "I'm sorry to have to say this, but most people bounce back more quickly after a death in the family."

So Frank—or someone—had told Justin about Kevin's death. Still, she wasn't going to say much. She needed to channel the strong, capable reporter she'd been for thirty years, not the unpredictable, vulnerable woman she'd been the last month. "Are you the permanent editor?"

"I'm not sure any of us are permanent." His cheekiness was infuriating.

Frank and Nancy and Lori and Jeff *should* have been permanent. Their hard work had made this magazine a well-respected publication over the years. Neena's own article on southwest Florida's recovery after Hurricane Ian had won three different travel writing awards.

He continued. "But I'll be here for as long as it takes to get the magazine back on track." He took off his hipster glasses and cleaned them with his shirttail. He looked even younger without them on.

She glanced around the sterile, tidy office, thinking how a kid thirty years her junior had discarded all the middle-aged writers like piles of unwanted clutter. She now saw her surroundings from a new perspective. "Are you working from corporate? It doesn't look like anyone's working in here."

"I don't allow paper. Digital files only." Another nod to a generation that had grown up with computers in their hands? Or perhaps some lame attempt to be unique?

Either way, she apparently had nothing to lose. "Look, I'll be honest with you. I really need the work. Is there a local festival or something I could cover?" The magazine was based there in Jacksonville, but her mind scanned the Atlantic coast from Charleston to Key West, then up the gulf side toward Destin, Mobile, and beyond. "Surely there's some new hotel or golf course or event for us to feature. Anything?" She wanted to believe she could be trusted with a new assignment, though her trademark confidence and verve had yet to return. In the three weeks since she'd gotten out of the hospital, even little tasks like taking the garbage can to the street sometimes threatened her calm.

Her outpatient therapist had given her exercises to help overcome her anxious feelings. Said she'd learn how to manage them over time, but Neena needed to get out into the world *now*. If she didn't get her income flowing again, that pile of extra hospital bills on her kitchen table would remain unpaid.

A gust of wind howled outside. She gripped the edge of the table like it was a life raft.

Thank God Justin didn't seem to notice her reaction. He shook his head. "I'd like to help you, but all the current articles have been assigned to other people."

Like the twenty-somethings who now had offices down the hall? She forced herself to smile. "I've loved working for *Coastal South Travel* ever since Frank sought me out to write for him. He'd seen my article about how important the mangroves are to the South Florida ecosystem and he—"

"It doesn't matter what happened five or six years ago," Justin said. "I'm interested in good writers who meet their commitments in the present day."

"That last deadline was the only one I've ever missed. That situation was a onetime deal." She didn't have any other siblings with lives that could spiral out of control. And God forbid anything like that ever happened to Rosie. Her daughter's current boyfriend was problematic enough. But Neena had raised Rosie to be savvy and smart, so hopefully that relationship would peter out as soon as the pair graduated with their master's degrees in a few weeks.

Justin rose, an indication that the meeting was over. "I can't make any promises."

She rose, too. *Damn it.* She should have spent more time brainstorming about other magazines, other sources of income. She should be on the phone calling those people this afternoon.

His eyes narrowed as he seemed to really see her for the first time. "Here's a random question for you."

"Yes?"

"Do you know who John F. Kennedy Jr. was?"

A random question, indeed. And of course, she knew the answer, but she got the impression maybe Justin didn't. "He was the president's son. He died in a plane crash off Martha's Vineyard. July 16, 1999." She remembered that day vividly. She'd been seven-and-a-half months pregnant with

Rosie. She'd had some issues, so the doctor had her on total bedrest—the only other time in her adult life when she hadn't been strong and independent. She'd spent the entire day watching on TV as search planes circled over the Atlantic. Remembered the feeling of hopelessness when they'd finally located the wreckage on the ocean floor.

Both John and his father had held such promise but hadn't lived long enough to carry it out.

"You know the date he died?" Justin's eyes widened. "Off the top of your head?"

"We've always had a connection to that family. My mother and father met when they both worked for his father."

Justin cocked his head to one side. His eyebrows bunched together, like he was trying to figure out the players and the timeline.

"John F. Kennedy was running for president," Neena said. "My parents both worked on his campaign here in Florida." But like so many Americans, they'd viewed the Kennedy family like royalty, even years later.

A crash of thunder rattled the windows, momentarily moving her attention to the palm trees whipping in the wind outside, but Neena needed to stay focused on what was going on inside. "My daughter, Rosie, is named after the president's mother, Rose Fitzgerald Kennedy."

He frowned. "So you think the average person would know the difference between the president and his son?"

She did her best not to look appalled. He clearly didn't think most people would know. *Really?* He'd even asked the question with a straight face. "I guess that depends on who you consider the 'average person' to be."

He looked thoughtful. "This magazine's current readership *does* skew older. We're going to have to work to appeal to a more vibrant, edgier demographic."

Code words for *younger*. "I really am open to any story you could assign to me," she said to his back as he headed down the hall.

But instead of replying to her, he pulled his phone from his pocket and punched at the screen. By the time they'd reached the lobby, he'd already moved on to a conversation about advertising revenue with someone on the other end of the line. He raised his chin in a half-hearted goodbye, dismissing her.

Neena nodded to Tammy as she left, not trusting herself to speak in her current agitated state. Plus, it felt like Tammy had somehow betrayed her, though Neena didn't fault her for keeping her mouth shut. For protecting her own job as much as she could.

Neena's phone buzzed as she trudged through the deluge to her car. The ringtone for Rosie. Neena quickly climbed inside, turned on the engine, and waited for the Bluetooth to engage, though the pounding rain would make it difficult to hear. "Hey, honey."

"What is that *noise*?"

"I'm in my car and it's raining really hard."

"Yeah. I was hoping the storm would make it to Gainesville and close everything down, but no such luck. Not yet, anyway," her daughter said.

"Why? What's wrong?"

"Just the usual. I'm overworked. Underpaid. Flunking my research course."

"I thought you were going to ask your boss to cut back your hours so you could study more."

"Yeah, well, that was before the new girl no-showed during her second week there. We haven't seen her since, so I'm having to pick up her shifts."

At least someone in the family was making some money. Rosie had worked in the same Gainesville coffee shop—right near the University of Florida campus—for a couple of years. "Well, hopefully they'll hire someone soon."

"I can't *wait* for this semester to be over." Rosie sounded like a disgruntled teenager, even though she was twenty-three and finishing her master's degree.

"What is it? Five more weeks?"

"Speaking of which…" Rosie's tone lightened. "There's this guy Caleb's dad knows who owns an apartment in Paris and he says he'll rent it to us…"

Neena closed her eyes, willing herself to find some patience. Each time she'd met Rosie's boyfriend, she found more about him to dislike. From what she could tell, he'd moved right into the graduate program after undergrad so he could stay in the college town party scene. When she'd asked him what he planned to do after graduation, he'd acted like he'd never even contemplated having a life as an adult.

But the most damning thing was that he didn't treat Rosie with the respect a woman deserved. On three different occasions, the pair had planned a weekend getaway to the Keys, only for him to cancel at the last minute with some lame excuse, despite the fact that Rosie had rearranged her entire work schedule and life each time.

And both times Neena had spent time with them, he'd talked down to Rosie—criticizing her outfit and her taste in music and the fact that she didn't pick the table he would have picked when they'd all met for lunch in Gainesville.

Neena had had a boyfriend in college who talked to her like that, but each time she challenged him on his tone, he claimed that she was "reading into it" something he hadn't meant. That he couldn't be held responsible for how she interpreted his words. Only after they'd broken up had she realized what a bully and a manipulator he'd been. If Rosie was in the same kind of relationship, Neena wanted to do everything she could to save her daughter from that kind of toxicity.

Rosie prattled on. "Anyway, we can stay there until the end of April, when the guy has already promised it to another friend and—"

"No." Thank goodness Neena was still in the parking spot. Her hands shook as she held the wheel tightly. The pounding of unrelenting rain made it difficult to concentrate.

"What?" Rosie's tone was sharp.

"I don't want you to go to Europe with him."

"Just because you don't like him doesn't mean that—"

"You don't have the money for a trip like that anyway."

"I would if you'd give me Grandma's money."

The five thousand dollars Neena's mom had left for each of her grandchildren, though Rosie hadn't been born until several years after Mama had died. Kevin had never had any children. "Her will specifically says that money is to help you buy your first home. You know that."

"So Paris will be the first place I live after college. My first home." A smirk came across in Rosie's voice.

"That's not what she meant." Though she had to give Rosie credit for her creativity.

Her daughter huffed. "You don't think I deserve a little vacation after *eighteen* years of school?"

"That money wasn't intended for a vacation. It was intended to help pay the down payment on your first home." Which, God willing, would not be with the current boyfriend. "To help build the foundation for your life moving forward, not fritter it away on some jaunt to Europe."

"God, Mom. Just because you never have any fun doesn't mean I have to live like that, too."

Time to move on to a less contentious topic. "Did I tell you the new people next door have a *goat* instead of a lawn mower? Mrs. Ferguson is having a fit." She had to shout over the sound of the rain that battered the roof and windshield.

"Nice try, Mom."

The phone went dead—Rosie's doing as opposed to storm-related. Neena was sure of it. That venomous tone had been all too common from Rosie in recent months.

Neena rested her elbows on the steering wheel and cradled her head in her fingertips. Her body shook as the magnitude of it all overtook her. Limited money in the bank, because she would never touch that five thousand dollars Mama had left for Rosie. No prospects of an income. A daughter who hated her—the daughter Neena had brought into the world by herself because there'd been no prospects of a man in her life as her thirties came to a close. The entire time she was going through the IVF process, she'd dreamed of how she and her child would be close, a bonded pair as they took on the world together.

But now Neena was alone. Her only companion the unreliable brain that could hijack her with another anxiety attack at any moment.

She wondered if this was how Mama had felt in the days leading up to her suicide—like she had lost control and might never regain it. Granted, Mama had suffered from depression for years. Neena realized that now. Whereas her own anxiety problem had started just weeks ago, after Kevin's death.

And though her brain had now turned against her, like Mama's had, Neena would never kill herself. She wouldn't do that to her own child, regardless of how Rosie treated her. No way would Neena risk making Rosie feel what she felt every day: that she should have done more to save her mother. And now her brother, too.

The anxiety might be new, but she'd learned over the years that the only thing to do was to keep marching forward. To keep doing what had to be done to survive. She'd done it after Mama had died. She'd done it as a single mother for all those years. And she would do it now.

And for now, that meant finding a way to make money. She hadn't been this hard up for assignments in decades. Not since she first started out as a freelance travel writer. But she would *not* lose the little bungalow she'd been so proud to finally buy for the two of them when Rosie had been in elementary school. As a single mom, Neena had worked hard to buy that house. It was where her best memories lived, and not even the fact that Kevin had taken his last breath there could change that.

She'd lost so much over the years—her mom, her brother, and for a while now, maybe even her sanity. She'd be damned if she would lose her house, too.

Rivulets of water ran down her windshield. She glanced at Justin's window as she put her car in reverse.

Yes, she would march forward, just as she'd always done.

Chapter Two

That ever-present undercurrent of unease still seethed within Neena four days after her visit to Justin's office, despite every-other-day sessions with her outpatient therapist.

Each day, Neena would buzz about the house—a flurry of nervous activity that sometimes accomplished useful things, sometimes not. While the rest of the neighborhood was still carpeted in leaves and limbs from the recent tropical storm, Neena's need to keep moving meant her yard was immaculate.

When she felt calm enough to interact with others, she forced herself to reach out to magazines all over the Southeast, offering her services. She pitched stories to any publication that would take them. She even touched base with former colleagues she hadn't talked to in years, though she felt like a schmuck for contacting them only because she needed something. She tried to make her point that she needed any assignment she could get, but without sounding too desperate. She was fairly certain she failed at that.

She knew she should touch base with the two or three girlfriends who'd checked in on her periodically since Kevin's death. She'd appreciated their conversations, but she'd always been a fairly solitary creature. She wasn't yet ready to open up about everything she'd gone through, even to the small circle of women she knew would support her. They'd been together through Regina's divorce and Julie's mastectomy and Wendy's cross-country move. They came together when necessary and gave each other space as needed—an attribute Neena valued greatly.

She was scrubbing her kitchen grout with a toothbrush when the ringing of her cell phone jolted her. She jumped and spilled the cupful of cleaning solution all over the floor. *Frank's old office number.* She threw the dishtowel over the puddle and took three deep breaths, trying to chase away the nerves that now bubbled up her throat. "Hello."

"I may have a story for you," Justin said.

So much for small talk. But then she didn't want to be his friend. She wanted him to give her work. And this was the first assignment she'd received, even after all her time spent drumming up business. "You do?"

"I tried to kill it, but the editorial board really wants a feature on the twenty-five-year anniversary of John F. Kennedy Jr.'s death. Personally, I think it's a snoozer of a story, but what do I know? I'm just the guy they hired to turn this magazine around."

So his question the other day hadn't been so random after all. Maybe her age was finally working *for* her instead of against her. "And you're assigning it to me?"

"I am if you can get on a ferry tomorrow morning and have this story ready to turn in when you get back to the mainland Monday afternoon. That's the drop-dead deadline. We go to print on Wednesday."

"I can and I will."

"You've heard of Cumberland Island?"

Ahhhh. Yes. Florida's Amelia Island sat just north of Jacksonville, and Cumberland was the next island up from there—the first off the coast of Georgia, right across the Florida/Georgia border. Though it was only an hour north of her, she'd never been there, mainly because it was accessible only by a ferry that had to be scheduled in advance.

But Neena had researched it a bit over the years, thinking she'd visit one day. Maybe take Rosie there for a day trip during one of the cooler months, when it wouldn't be so hot and sticky. From what Neena remembered, the island had once been primarily owned by the family of the famous industrialist Thomas Carnegie for use as their winter getaway. Several of their mansions still stood, though one was in ruins from a fire decades ago. The island had no restaurants or retail stores, so Neena surmised it must be a unique blend of opulence and remote wilderness. Most of it was now a National Seashore run by the National Park Service and known primarily for the feral horses that ran wild along the shoreline.

But she knew it wasn't the horses that Justin was interested in. "It's where John F. Kennedy Jr. got married," she said. "In a tiny white church, with no paparazzi around. They pulled off a secret wedding before the media even knew about it." Like so many things Kennedy, it had been a fairytale wedding. The few pictures the family had released after that weekend showed a tiny candlelit church with the beautiful couple in the doorway. America's most eligible bachelor had gotten married. Neena's heart—and likely the hearts of thousands of other young women—had broken a little that day.

Justin scoffed. "That kind of thing would never happen today. Someone would be snapping photos for social media or flying a drone overhead, taking footage of the whole thing."

"I guess that makes it all the more special," she said. She wasn't going to let him downplay the magic of the event. She moved to her computer, ready to begin her research the second this phone call ended.

"Not my idea, but the editorial board has decided this will be the cover story," Justin said. "So much for listening to my input about attracting younger readers."

She swallowed. Writing the cover story meant even more pressure, especially with such a tight deadline. And even more money for her dwindling bank account. "Will I get to go inside the church?"

"You'll connect there with a guy named Hiram Edwards. He's some kind of local historian. His family has lived there for generations. He'll take you all over the island."

"Including the church?"

"Including the church. You'll be staying at a place called the IvyLena Inn."

She managed an affirmative sound, though her mind was reeling. There were only two hotels on the island—the IvyLena and the Greyfield—both historic mansions that had been turned into inns back in the 1960s. She'd looked them up on the internet a few years ago as she'd dreamed of a weekend getaway for her and Rosie, but each cost several hundred dollars a night. *Way* out of her budget, even in the best of times.

"Both inns are usually booked months in advance, but the IvyLena had a last-minute cancellation. A member of the editorial board was able to pull some strings and get you in."

"Okay. Thank you." She hated the note of panic creeping into her voice. She really was appreciative of the assignment, but what did one wear at such an exclusive resort? Given that the remote island was primarily a national park, surely guests didn't show up in sequins and heels. Or did they?

And what about the fact that it was accessible only by ferry? What if she had some kind of setback while she was on the island? What if she required a mental health professional? Was there enough cell phone coverage to allow her to reach her outpatient therapist if she had some kind of crisis? What if something happened to Rosie? Would they bring her back to the mainland only on a certain schedule?

Justin's voice broke into her thoughts. "Tammy's coordinating the details now. She'll email everything you need."

Neena made a mental note to thank Tammy for her help. They were in this new world of Justin together, after all. And with him giving her an assignment, she'd do her best to try to like him, too. "Sounds great."

"And Neena?" He paused. "I may have fought the board on this, but this story is important to them, and we got lucky getting you into one of the inns. Don't let me down on this."

Her gaze rose to the reflection in her computer screen. Her shoulder-length hair was stringy and in need of a wash. Her eyes had dark circles both below *and* above them. She hadn't slept well in days. No, *weeks*. Behind her, the parts of a broken table lamp lay spread across the kitchen counter—a project she'd started, then abandoned. Beside it, the books she'd checked out of the library that had gone untouched for days.

If Justin knew what a mess she was, there was no way he'd be giving her such an important assignment.

"You're good with this?" he asked.

She sat up straight, hoping the posture would give her a confidence she didn't really feel. "I'm good."

"I mean it. Are you sure you can handle this in your...present state?"

"I can handle this. I'm good."

She was also a liar.

***

Sixteen hours later, Neena stood at the dock in St. Marys, Georgia, a travel mug full of coffee in her hand. She'd had two cups at home, too, but since she hadn't seen 6 a.m. in months, she needed extra caffeine. She'd made the hour-long drive from Jacksonville in just enough time to make the mid-morning trip aboard the *F.A.R. Away.* The vessel was the IvyLena's private passenger ferry, named after industrialist Frederick Andrew Richards, who'd built the mansion as his family's winter residence back in 1905.

Because no cars were allowed on the seventeen-mile-long island except those owned by the few who lived there, she'd left her car in the private parking lot reserved for guests of the inn. Other people milled about waiting for the ferry contracted by the National Park Service to take them to the island, but guests of the IvyLena had a special covered waiting area, apart from the others. Neena wondered if this was how first-class airline passengers felt, though she'd never had the privilege of flying in such luxury.

The St. Marys River stretched as far as she could see from her left to her right. Beyond it, an expanse of chartreuse-colored grasses gave way far in the distance to a stand of wind-twisted trees. White egrets waded along the shoreline below her while other birds squawked overhead. The dashboard of her car had already read 89 degrees—hot for this early on an October morning, even on the Florida/Georgia border—but at least the slight breeze made it seem cooler at the dock.

Only two other people waited nearby—two fifty-something men who looked suspiciously alike, each tall and lanky with a full head of dark wavy hair, both graying at the temples. They, too, each had a suitcase, which further set them apart from day-trippers to the island. When the one in the red shirt smiled and nodded at her, she quickly looked away, embarrassed that she'd been caught studying them.

Her phone ringing provided a welcome distraction. Rosie's ringtone. Finally, her daughter had seen fit to return her call from the night before.

"I was getting worried about you," Neena said, turning her back and walking away from the two men for privacy during her call.

"You're headed to some island off the coast of Georgia. Accessible only by ferry." Her daughter's voice was filled with boredom as she repeated the words Neena had left on voicemail. "You think your cell phone will work over there but won't know for sure until you get there. I know. You said all that in your voicemail."

"It's not just *any* island. It's the one where JFK Jr. got married." Neena's body thrummed with excitement.

"Oh, God. You're going to tell everyone you see about how your parents met when they both worked for JFK—the original one."

Neena grunted. "Why would you say that?"

"Because that's what you tell everyone. Any time the subject comes remotely close to that family, you tell people about it."

It *was* kind of a cool story, but apparently her daughter didn't appreciate it. "Just be careful. Don't get in any car wrecks or have appendicitis or anything like that while I'm gone. I'm not sure if they'll take me back to the mainland except at the scheduled times for the ferry."

"I'm twenty-three years old, Mom."

"Which has nothing to do with car wrecks or appendicitis. Those can happen at any time."

"Well, I appreciate the update on your travel plans." Rosie's tone had become more businesslike. Either she was eager to get off the phone or she'd realized how bratty she was being.

Neena's heart ached for the days when she was more a part of her daughter's life. When Neena would set up a sprinkler in the yard for little Rosie to run through on hot summer days. When they'd brown marshmallows on tinfoil in the oven so they could eat s'mores any night of the year. When they'd go for walks in the nearby Timucuan Preserve, pretending they were members of the Native American tribe that had once lived on the land.

Neena wished she was still the most important person in her daughter's life.

"And I'm glad to hear you're back at work," Rosie added. "You were kind of scaring me there for a while. You weren't, like, the capable mom I've always known."

"Well, I'm feeling better now." Maybe if she said it enough times, there wouldn't be any backsliding. "I didn't mean to frighten you."

"I'll talk to you later, Mom. I'm heating up an English muffin and there's smoke coming out of the toaster oven."

Neena tensed at the thought of a fire at Rosie's apartment while she was gone. "I love you," she said as the phone clicked off on the other end. She hesitated a few seconds, bolstering her resilience, then turned around and headed back toward the awning.

"You're headed to the IvyLena?" the man in the red shirt asked when she returned to stand beside her suitcase. His deep voice had the distinctive drawl of the South—upstate South Carolina, if she had to guess. Or maybe the North Georgia mountains.

She smiled. "I am."

"It's our first visit." He pointed to himself, then to the other man and back to himself.

"Mine, too."

He held out his hand. "I'm Dwight. And this is my brother, Carl."

A pang of grief swept over her. She would love to be vacationing with her brother, too, but that was no longer possible.

The other man gave a quick lift of his chin but seemed uninterested in engaging with her. His gaze quickly returned to his phone.

She shook Dwight's hand. "I'm Neena."

They both turned at a sound behind them. One of the two young men who worked aboard the *F.A.R. Away* approached, pushing a two-wheeled silver cart that looked like a fancy wheelbarrow.

"Ms. Lee?" the young man asked when he'd reached them.

Neena nodded.

He turned his attention to Dwight and his brother. "Mr. Leggett? And Mr. Leggett?"

"Leggett squared," Dwight joked.

"Welcome to the *F.A.R. Away*. Y'all can make your way on board. I'll bring your luggage for you."

Dwight stood aside and motioned for Neena to go to the end of the dock first. When they reached the *F.A.R. Away*, he held his hand out to help her up the three steps and onto the boat.

"Thank you," she said, feeling flattered, but then reminded herself he was just being polite. He would have likely done the same for any female.

The boat was a bit larger than the typical watercraft she'd seen on the intracoastal waterway and along the shoreline of the Atlantic. It had a covered area for the driver, but the back was open with several long wooden park-bench-type seats. She chose one that faced backwards so she could watch the water as they headed up the St. Marys River toward Cumberland Island.

She turned in her seat to take in her surroundings. Dwight and Carl each chose a bench behind her. The young man guided his cart full of luggage down to the boat and slid the suitcases under some empty benches.

She turned back toward the water and took in a deep breath. Perhaps this ride would do her good—lots of sunshine, fresh air, and time for contemplation. She rummaged through her bag for the baseball cap she'd packed there, pulled her ponytail through the hole in the back, then settled the cap low on her head. Her already fair skin had gotten even paler during the weeks she'd spent wallowing in her house after Kevin's death, too uncertain to go out in public. Too afraid another anxiety attack might overcome her.

Maybe outings like this would have reminded Kevin of the beauty outside the seedy world where he'd spent so much of his last few years. Maybe they should have gone places together, like the two brothers aboard the boat now. There were so many things she might have said or done with him that could have saved his life. She snuck her index finger under her sunglasses to wipe her tears away, hoping the brothers wouldn't notice she was crying.

She could hear their deep voices during the trip to the island, but the sound of the boat's motor, the wind, and the slap of the waves against the hull made their words indistinguishable. Just as well, as she needed time to sit with her own thoughts.

This trip should feel like a fresh start. She was outdoors, back at work, and about to explore a new-to-her location. But the confidence she'd built over the years now seemed like a distant memory. Sure, she had the same journalistic experience she'd had two months ago, but now it was coupled with the knowledge that an anxiety attack could derail her at any moment.

She took a deep breath, sat up straighter, and forced herself to focus on the beauty of nature. Palm trees stood majestically against a perfect blue sky on a shoreline in the distance.

Dwight touched her shoulder and pointed to a school of dolphins that frolicked off to the right of the boat. She smiled and nodded—a thank you for his kindness. He returned her smile and settled back into his seat.

About forty minutes into the trip, they passed a large dock with a cabin nearby. Perhaps the National Park Service building? A few people milled about onshore as if waiting for a ferry that would take them back to the mainland. A few minutes later, they passed a dock marked Private. It might belong to one of the few residents of the island but could also belong to the Greyfield Inn, which—according to Google Maps—sat a couple of miles south of the IvyLena.

Finally, the boat slowed as they entered a third No Wake zone. She turned to see another dock up ahead. Two large brown pelicans awaited them on pillars as the boat reached their destination. But the wildlife she really wanted to see were the wild horses that roamed the island, descendants of those left by Spanish explorers four hundred years earlier.

A forty-something woman stood on the dock, waiting for them. She was clad in khaki shorts, tennis shoes, and a long-sleeved shirt that appeared to be one of those that protected a person's skin from the sun. Her casual attire made Neena feel better about what she'd packed.

"Welcome to Cumberland Island and the IvyLena," the woman said as each of the passengers stood to disembark from the boat. "My name is Jennifer. Please meet me up on the shore. Don't worry about your luggage. We'll have it delivered to your rooms."

The two brothers were closest to the exit of the boat. Carl was first to step onto the dock, then Dwight, who turned around to offer his hand to Neena as she stepped over the edge and onto the wooden planks.

They walked off the dock and around a white pickup truck that had been backed up nearby. They met Jennifer on a little rise above the water.

"I'm going to give you a quick tour of the grounds before we make it to the inn," she said. "Frederick Andrew Richards built the mansion for his wife in 1898. He'd learned about the island from his good friend, Thomas Carnegie, whose family owned much of the land here by that time. Ivy and Lena were the daughters of Mr. and Mrs. Richards, thus the name of the inn."

This matched the research Neena had done online in the brief time since she'd gotten this assignment. Richards and Thomas Carnegie had gone to school together. After the death of her husband, Lucy Carnegie had built several homes on the island so that her grown children would stay close to her. The Greyfield Inn—the only other inn on the island—had been one of them.

"Each morning, you'll have a chance to sign up for tours of the rest of the island where you can see Plum Orchard—one of the Carnegie mansions—and Dungeness, the ruins of Lucy Carnegie's own home. There are also nature hikes, tours of the garden, the beach, all kinds of things for you to see."

"How did Dungeness burn?" Dwight asked.

"If I tell you everything now, what will they tell you on the tour tomorrow?" Jennifer winked at him, then turned to walk up the dirt road toward an expansive lawn about the size of two city blocks. Before them, a single gigantic live oak draped in Spanish moss anchored one end of a large white mansion. Neena recognized it from the IvyLena website, though the setting was even more beautiful than she'd imagined. The building's long, wide second-floor veranda faced the river, which was rimmed in palm trees and palmettos.

But Jennifer focused on other parts of the grounds first. "There are a couple of important buildings on the far side of the lawn." She looked to Dwight and Carl. "You two will be staying in the carriage house, which is the one farthest to the right. The suite is on the second floor, above where the carriages were kept. The stairs are on the left side of the building."

The men nodded.

Jennifer continued to walk. "Beyond those trees over there is an open-air barn. That's where you can get bicycles anytime you want to go for a ride. My only caution is to check the seat before you go. Make sure it's not wobbly. This salt air is really bad on everything, and you don't want to be somewhere out on the island if something goes wrong."

Neena's research had told her that the island was about seventeen miles long. The far end included the church where JFK Jr. had been married. The IvyLena sat in about the middle. Guests at the Kennedy-Bessette wedding had stayed at both the Greyfield and the IvyLena, as both exclusive inns had a small number of rooms available. Friends and family had reportedly moved freely from one inn to the other as they enjoyed a rare, private getaway. The few photos from the weekend included pictures of John on the porch at the Greyfield Inn and in the dining room at the IvyLena, where he was kicked back having a drink with two of his cousins.

Neena still couldn't believe she'd be sleeping at a place where the Kennedy family had once stayed. She felt like such an imposter. She was almost certain that everyone she'd meet there—staff and guests alike—would know she didn't belong at such a high-end hotel. Surely something—her dress, her mannerisms, her lack of worldliness—would give her away as an interloper among the rich and well-heeled.

The rest of the island was wilderness, with a few houses scattered in. The few families there—including descendants of Asa Candler and his Coca-Cola fortune—had been on the island for decades.

"Another caution is about the horses," Jennifer said. "They may look docile when they're grazing nearby, but remember they're wild animals. Don't get too close. They'll spin and kick you right in the head or chest before you even know what happened. And, believe me, they've got some powerful hindquarters. The mamas are especially mean if they think you're getting too close to their foal or yearling."

Neena's gaze met Dwight's. He raised his eyebrows in mock fright of being kicked by a wild mare. She smiled at his silliness, careful not to let their guide see.

Jennifer then angled their walk toward the back of the white stucco inn. While the long front veranda had sweeping, open views of the river, the back sat ensconced in a forest. It appeared as if the large live oaks had wrapped their Spanish moss-covered branches around the building over the last hundred-plus years. One corner of the back of the building held a large, glassed-in room—perhaps an observatory of some kind?

Jennifer answered Neena's unasked question as they continued around the building. "The glassed-in room is the sunporch, which is a bit of a misnomer given how it's surrounded by trees. But in a hot climate like this one, guests usually welcome the shade. It's kind of like sitting inside a treehouse. Most people love it."

They'd arrived back at the front of the inn, and Jennifer led them up the wide staircase to the second-floor veranda. The few guests in rocking chairs on the long covered veranda smiled in greeting. Had it not been for one guy sporting earbuds, Neena could pretend she was back in the early

1900s, hosted by Frederick Andrew Richards himself, at a soiree for rich snowbirds seeking to escape the harsh Northern winter.

The entire veranda had a tropical feel. Several ceiling fans circulated the humid air. Large, big-leafed plants stood in massive ceramic planters. At each end, a long porch swing filled with pillows invited guests to relax. The navy blue, shutter-like front door held the largest wreath Neena had ever seen—a beautiful mass of twisted vines and delicate lavender flowers.

Jennifer turned and faced the river, as if she wanted the new guests to appreciate the magnificent view before stepping inside. Neena, Dwight, and Carl each did the same. That setting—that view—had a calming effect, even though Neena was eager to see inside the inn.

Jennifer took three deep breaths, then turned and held the massive front door open so her guests could step inside. A wide entry hall ran from the front of the house all the way to the back. A sweeping staircase—like something from *Gone with the Wind*—filled the left side of the entry hall.

Jennifer led them into the living room, which sat on the righthand side of the entry hall. The large space boasted several seating areas, a massive fireplace, an antique chess set, portraits of several members of the Richards family, and a collection of gator and sea turtle skulls. "Hors d'oeuvres are served in here at six every evening. They'll ring the bell when it's time to go to the dining room."

She then led them across the entry hall to a large parlor that held a display of tasteful gifts monogrammed with the IvyLena logo, as well as cookbooks, prints of local scenery, and other local goods for sale. Neena made a note to come look at the items later, though she was certain she couldn't afford anything they sold there.

A young woman sat at a desk working on a computer on the other side of the room. She looked up, welcomed each of the new guests by name, then went back to her work. So perhaps that wasn't the registration desk?

Maybe Neena's expectations were off. Maybe she shouldn't assume that an upscale place like this operated like a Marriott or Hilton.

Jennifer slid open a pocket door at the far end of the room to reveal what might have once been a butler's pantry. Glass shelves were lined with goblets, highball glasses, and twenty or thirty bottles of liquor. The Honest John Bar, Jennifer explained, was so that guests could help themselves to any kind of liquor, wine, or beer they wanted at any time of day. Ice and chilled beverages were kept in the refrigerator under the counter. She showed how each guest should record on a little sheet of paper each time they poured themselves a drink. Their drink tally would be added to their final bill. Everything else on the island was included as part of the nightly charge.

The entire vibe of the place made Neena feel fancy, though her bank account said otherwise. She tried to imagine sitting in the mansion's living room, sipping a martini while laughing with the wealthy socialites who wintered on the island. She'd sit by herself later, trying to conjure what that life might be like.

For now, though, Jennifer led them out of the parlor and up the sweeping staircase in the entry hall. "The library is the only public room up here, but many of our guests enjoy it." She'd reached the top of the stairs and escorted them into a large room that looked out over the river. The three walls that weren't glass were lined with old leatherbound books, though an assortment of the day's newspapers sat on a table—a mix of old and new. Lamps with glass globes that were undoubtedly older than Neena sat beside massive leather chairs and couches.

"And Ms. Lee? This is your room." Jennifer smiled as she pointed to the single door at one end of the room. "The Magnolia Suite."

Neena smiled and nodded, though her nerves jumped to high alert. In any other hotel, announcing to strange men where a single woman was staying would be a serious security violation, but Jennifer didn't seem to think twice about it. Perhaps with the small number of people staying at the IvyLena at any given time, this place was safer than most?

As Jennifer told the newly arrived trio about some of the artifacts in the room, an elderly man with a stooped back plodded into the library and walked straight toward the door to Neena's bedroom. Her suitcase was in his hand. He stopped, as if sensing her presence, and held her gaze for several long seconds. He had an air of wisdom about him, like a village elder who had seen everything that had happened on this remote island over the past several decades.

Jennifer and the brothers didn't seem to realize someone else had entered the room. It was as if the man and Neena were the only ones there. Alone and taking each other in.

Finally, the man turned slowly, walked the few remaining steps to her bedroom door, and placed her suitcase just inside the room. He then closed the door softly, returned his gaze to Neena, and then exited the room. She heard his slow, methodical footfalls on the stairs as Jennifer talked about some of the leatherbound volumes the library held.

In a different place, this interaction might have seemed creepy, but here, it felt...mystical. Almost magical. Like she and the man had a connection she couldn't explain.

She rushed to catch up as Jennifer led the brothers back down to the main floor and toward the remaining rooms at the back of the inn. A long communal table with about twenty seats dominated the large dining room, dwarfing the three four-tops that sat along one wall.

"Most guests prefer to dine with the other guests, though sometimes people want something a little more private," Jennifer said. "That's why we ask you during the reservation process how you'd like to take your meals. We want to make sure everyone's wishes are met."

Neena wondered where she was supposed to sit, given that she hadn't handled the reservation herself, but Jennifer had already moved on to the sunporch, which was as magical as Neena had imagined. Rays of sunlight dappled the comfortable couches and rocking chairs, creating cozy corners for a cup of morning coffee or a nice reading nook.

A small open room near the back of the entry hall held a coffee station where guests could help themselves at any time. A narrower, more utilitarian staircase—probably designed for servants of the Richards family—led from that room down to the first floor. Neena, Dwight, and Carl followed as Jennifer descended the stairs.

"Guests should feel free to walk right into this part of the kitchen." Jennifer motioned to a pair of glass-fronted refrigerators. "Your picnic lunch will be in here every morning by 10:30 in a basket with your name on it. And there will always be hibiscus lemonade, water, and iced tea in these big urns." She pointed to a tub of reusable sports bottles underneath the counter. Neena assumed that plastic water bottles were especially problematic here. Not only were they bad for the environment in general, but then someone would have to haul them off the island.

By the time the tour had ended, Neena was eager to see her own room, which turned out to be an airy hideaway tucked among the moss-covered branches of the live oak tree outside her window. She wouldn't need the fireplace during this stay, but she could imagine how cozy it might feel if the weather outside was cold and the wind off the water made it even chillier. The large room held a queen-size bed, two comfortable chairs, and a dresser. Her private bath—complete with a clawfoot tub—was near the entrance to her room.

She didn't want her clothes to get any more wrinkled than they already were, so she quickly unpacked, hanging some items in the closet and placing some in the dresser.

The only problem with her room was that the bottom drawer of the dresser wouldn't open. It wouldn't even budge. Well, it *was* an antique and they were close to the ocean. Perhaps the salt air had gotten to it the same way it got to the bike seats.

She finished unpacking and headed to the place that had caught her attention the most during the tour—the inviting front veranda. She took the first rocking chair she came to and settled in, ready to take in her surroundings. She loved this porch, and she loved people-watching. It would be an ideal location to get a feel for the place and to plan the research she'd do while she was here.

But her eyes homed in on the stooped old man who'd delivered her luggage to her room. He now watered an elephant ear in one of the large planters on the porch. As he finished with that plant, his gaze rose to hers. He moved on to the next one without breaking their connection to one another.

Now that he was closer, she could see his silvery-blue eyes more clearly. They shone brightly against the canvas of his tanned, sun-spotted skin. Deep wrinkles created channels across his face, like the many tributaries that weaved their way through the nearby marshes. His full head of white hair made it hard to guess his age. Seventies? Maybe even eighties?

But it was his eyes that fascinated her most. His gaze was both comforting and enigmatic at the same time. It was like he had secrets to tell her.

Like he'd been waiting for her to arrive.

Chapter Three

Neena exited her bedroom the next morning with one thought in mind: to have a conversation with the elderly stooped man she'd seen the day before. His wise, all-knowing eyes had gotten her journalist's intuition flowing again. Some of her best stories had been based on interviews with people like him—seemingly unimportant figures who knew what went on behind the scenes. People who could tell the *real* stories that upstart journalists didn't even think to ask about. Writers like the young interns who now made up the staff of *Coastal South Travel* relied too heavily on the curated information dished up by PR firms. But this man was old enough to have been on the island during the Kennedy wedding, assuming he'd worked at the IvyLena that long. People from his generation tended to stay with one employer. If that was the case, perhaps he could give Neena information that others hadn't uncovered—information about this place, the Kennedys, about the way the entire island had kept the wedding a secret.

And besides, the old man's eyes had held her in their grip, as if she couldn't look away. She wanted to learn more about him. About what made him so bewitching.

He'd gone inside shortly after she'd seen him on the veranda yesterday, and she hadn't been able to find him again after that. His disappearance yesterday made her even more determined to talk to him today.

But first, she needed breakfast. She made her way to the main floor of the inn and got herself a cup of coffee at the coffee station off the back of the entry hall, near the dining room. She'd just joined a few other guests at the long communal table when a young server appeared with a small glass filled with a creamy light orange liquid.

"A bit of peach smoothie to get you started," the young woman said. "For breakfast, we've got crispy bacon and a cheese omelet with vegetables grown in our garden, but if that's not to your liking, the chef can make you just about anything else you'd prefer."

Neena looked at the plates of the other guests who had already been at breakfast for a bit. The food looked delicious. "The omelet is fine, but I have a question for you first."

The young woman smiled. "Absolutely. I'll answer if I can."

"You have an employee, an older man. He delivered my suitcase from the dock yesterday, and then I saw him watering the plants on the veranda."

"Kind of a stooped guy?" The server hunched over, mimicking the older man's posture.

Neena nodded. "And a full head of white hair."

"That's Gus. He's the longest-term employee here." The young woman frowned and looked off in the distance for a second, thinking. "But I don't think I've seen him today. Maybe he finally took a day off."

Ahhh. So Neena's intuition had been right. Maybe he *had* been working when the Kennedy wedding took place on the island. She smiled, happy to know her journalistic instincts were returning after the unsettling weeks she'd spent following Kevin's death. "Does that mean he'll be off for a couple of days, or might he be back tomorrow?"

The server shrugged. "I don't know. You want me to check the schedule?"

The stylishly dressed couple across from her had leaned forward, as if curious why Neena would be so interested in one particular employee.

"I'm a journalist here working on a story," she said to the server, knowing the nosy couple would overhear. "I'd love to talk with him, if I can. Maybe you could let me know when he works next?"

"Let me see what I can find out. Your breakfast will be right out," the server said as she bustled toward the stairs that led down to the kitchen.

The brothers from the ferry entered the dining room and sat at one of the private tables along the perimeter of the room. Like before, Dwight gave a smile and a friendly nod when his eyes met hers. She smiled and held his gaze for a few seconds.

Were they *flirting*? She hadn't flirted in two decades, maybe more. Once she'd decided to have a child on her own, Rosie had become her focus. Though Neena had had a couple of relationships since then that lasted a year or so, nothing had stuck. But now that Rosie was becoming an adult—or rather, *was* an adult—perhaps Neena should start thinking about men again…?

Neena had just finished the small peach smoothie when the server returned with a delicious-looking omelet. The plate was adorned with orange slices and sprigs of some kind of fresh herb.

"Gus isn't here today," the young woman said as she set the plate down. "But he'll be back tomorrow."

Neena's tour of the island was scheduled for today, so maybe that was just as well. She'd plan to connect with Gus tomorrow. She thanked the server, who then moved on to wait on other guests as they arrived in the dining room.

Neena was finishing her omelet when another staff member rested a hand lightly on her shoulder. "Ms. Lee?"

Neena turned to acknowledge the young woman. "Yes?"

"Hiram Edwards is here for your tour of the island." She nodded toward an older Black man sitting in one of the cushioned chairs on the sunporch. "I offered him breakfast, but all he wanted was a cup of coffee. I'll pick up your picnic lunch while you finish up. The kitchen prepared extra for him, too."

Neena smiled and thanked her. The staff of the IvyLena Inn seemed to think of everything.

She quickly finished her breakfast and went over to introduce herself to Hiram.

He stood as she entered the sunporch. He was in his sixties or seventies but still tall and stocky enough to make her wonder if he'd played some college or maybe even pro football when he was younger. "Good morning, Ms. Lee."

She shook the hand he offered. "Please, call me Neena. If we're going to spend all day together, we might as well be on a first name basis."

He dipped his chin in agreement. "Neena it is. And you can call me Hiram." He picked up the picnic basket that had been delivered to a nearby side table and motioned to two sports bottles that sat beside it. "The girl said those are filled with hibiscus lemonade."

"Then we're all set." She smiled and headed toward the front of the mansion.

Once they were outside, he led her to an old jeep—the only vehicle in the front circle drive. "It's not fancy, but it's all we need here. There aren't many places to go."

"It's perfect," she said as she climbed into the passenger seat. She was eager to see what the island looked like beyond the protected privacy of the grounds of the inn.

Hiram drove between two stone pillars that marked the entrance to the IvyLena, then took a left onto a long straight dirt road. "This here is called Main Road. Pretty original name, huh? There was a proposal a few years back to pave it, but most of the residents fought against it."

She could see why. This place was like a throwback to earlier times, when life was simpler. Before "progress" intervened. And with the canopy of trees overhead, it seemed like it wouldn't take much to tip the entire island back into its once all-natural state, when there were no human inhabitants.

He tapped a cooler that sat between the two front seats. "I've got plenty of bottled water, so let me know when you need one. We'll stop every hour or so for a restroom break and to walk around to see the sights."

What she really wanted was a second cup of coffee, but Hiram didn't seem to have any caffeine onboard. "Thank you. How often do you give tours like this?"

"Not often. Both the IvyLena and the Greyfield offer two- or three-hour tours of various parts of the island a couple of times a day, so folks staying at the inns go on those. There's one concessionaire who's licensed to give van tours for day-trippers who come over to the National Park. But you're a big fancy journalist who needed to see the whole island on your first day here. I get brought in sometimes for the professionals." He turned and winked at her.

She laughed at his humor, grateful he hadn't seen what a mess she'd been just a month ago as she'd quivered in her bed in the behavioral health unit. Or later, when she'd passed out during her first trip to the grocery store. It was nice to be treated like a competent professional, like someone whose work could inform and influence others. She squared her shoulders against the seat of the jeep. Maybe this was the week when she would finally feel like her old self again. "Well, I appreciate your time today," she said. "Is this like...a job for you?" When Tammy had emailed Neena's travel arrangements, they hadn't said anything about needing to pay him at the end of the tour. A bolt of panic shot through Neena. Maybe she'd missed that detail?

"Nah. I've just lived on the island most of my life. I only went away for college and a couple of years after that working in Atlanta. My family has been here for more than a century."

"Two years in the big city were enough for you?" she teased.

"It sure enough taught me how lucky I was to live in a place like this."

Neena nodded, trying to imagine what it might be like to grow up here, but her thoughts were soon interrupted by Hiram.

"Let's get some facts out of the way first," he said as the jeep jolted its way through the thick subtropical undergrowth. "Less than fifty people live on the island. The National Park Service allows a maximum of three hundred visitors a day here—a combination of campers and day-trippers—but we aren't likely to see many of them. Cumberland is the largest of Georgia's barrier islands at more than thirty-six thousand acres—one-third larger than Manhattan. About half of those acres are marshes, mud flats, and tidal creeks."

He soon turned from numbers to tales of life on the island, from the Timucua Native Americans to the arrival of Europeans to the establishment of plantations that grew sea island cotton and, finally, the Carnegie era. Hiram was not only knowledgeable, he was the consummate storyteller, going so far as to leave her with a cliffhanger as he pulled into each stop where she could get out to explore.

Their first sighting of the island's wild horses was on what had once been a huge cotton field. A few minutes later, another gathering of them grazed on what used to be a golf course outside one of the historic homes.

Hiram chuckled. "Most people can't wait to see some wild horses. They don't believe me when I say that by the end of their stay, they'll be tired of them."

"They *are* a cool part of the island," she said. But the thing she really wanted to see was the tiny church where John F. Kennedy Jr. and Carolyn Bessette had been married. Yes, it would be a key part of her article, but her interest in the church was also personal. "John-John," as he'd been dubbed by the media when he was younger, had been about three years older than she was. She'd first seen the iconic photo of him saluting his father's casket when she was in middle school.

Her mom had always said that the ghost of JFK would never be able to rest, having left behind two children like that—both John Jr. and his older sister. Mama had been a big believer in the idea that unfinished business here sometimes kept the departed from the hereafter.

Neena had never given her mother's fixation on the Kennedys much thought until she'd hit her teens, when John Jr.'s handsome face and lean, athletic body graced the pages of magazines. Like so many other girls, she'd wondered what it would be like to date this American prince.

Hiram interrupted her thoughts. "Luckily, there are three herds of horses. They each pretty much stick to their own part of the island. When the females go into heat, the males move from herd to herd, which is a good thing. If that weren't the case, there would be too much in-breeding and they wouldn't have survived here for so many centuries."

He continued his storytelling as they made their way from one end of Main Road to the other. At one point, he slowed the jeep and motioned with his chin toward a small stone house—the only structure that sat right on the dirt road, hugging its edge. It looked more like a decrepit gatehouse than an actual residence and had obviously been there for many years.

"I'm going to speed up as we go past this house...and you should do the same, especially if you hike or ride a bike past here."

She turned and gave him a questioning look.

Hiram continued. "Boone Calhoun was a prodigy who created some kind of hardware that went inside computers back when they were first being made. Sold the patent for millions of dollars when he was in his early twenties. You can find articles on him on the internet. But then he...got a little eccentric. Convinced a great uncle who'd owned this property for decades to let him buy it so Boone could get away from everyone. But now he's convinced that the people who come here are only posing as tourists to spy on him."

Neena wondered why they needed to speed past his house. "Is he dangerous?"

Hiram gave her a side-eyed glance, then returned his gaze to the road as his foot mashed the gas pedal to the floor. "Less than he used to be. He's about seventy years old now and doesn't look very healthy, but he's been known to stop people along the road and hassle them. A couple of 'em even said he pulled a gun on 'em."

Dangerous, indeed. Neena hadn't planned on getting shot during this tour, but she definitely wanted to learn more about Boone Calhoun. Maybe even interview him if she could, assuming it was safe to do so. The guy sounded pretty unstable, but then again, who was Neena—a recent patient in a mental health ward—to judge someone else for their mental illness? People like Boone Calhoun needed help and understanding, not judgment.

By midafternoon, she'd learned about Robert Stafford, a man who had employed his former slaves after they were emancipated, including providing them with housing, education and bank accounts. "They built houses in what was called The Settlement. That's where we're headed next."

Neena sat up a bit straighter, a renewed interest in their tour. She'd seen on a map that the First African Baptist Church was in The Settlement.

"Remember that fact," Hiram said. "He set up bank accounts for them so they could save their money. That helped them prosper later, including some of my ancestors."

Neena was grateful to hear that someone had helped the newly freed slaves. Like many Southerners, she wrestled with the shameful parts of the region's complicated history.

As the jeep made its way through the foundations of what was once The Settlement, Hiram told her about Beulah Alberty, who'd been the schoolmistress and mayor of the "town" for many years. Beulah's was the only house still standing in The Settlement, though another, newer house sat next door. Its owner—a committed environmentalist—worked to keep Cumberland Island wild. A banner sporting the name of her nonprofit organization flanked the side of her house.

But as Hiram pulled his jeep behind the mayor's historic home, Neena didn't focus on the occupied house next door. There, in the grassy lot behind Beulah's home, was a building about the size of a one-room school-house. Though simple and unassuming, the tiny white clapboard church stood out like the holy grail Neena had been seeking. She sat in awe as the jeep slowed to a stop.

"Legend has it that John F. Kennedy Jr. came to Cumberland Island with some of the Carnegie cousins when the boys were in their early twenties. It was the first place he'd ever been where the paparazzi didn't follow him everywhere he went. He remembered that years later when he and Carolyn were looking for a place to get married, and he asked Mitty Ferguson and his wife, Mary, to help him. They run the Greyfield Inn. Mitty is Thomas Carnegie's great-great-grandson." He turned and smiled at Neena. "And that's how our little island came to host one of the most famous weddings of the century."

He pulled two large laminated photographs from beside his seat and handed them to her. One showed John F. Kennedy Jr. and his bride in the doorway of the church. Candles lit the interior behind them. The other photo showed a group of fifteen or so Kennedy men gathered in a group. Neena had seen both of these pictures before. They'd been among the few released by the Kennedy family to the media after the wedding had taken place.

She looked up at the church, trying to imagine John and Carolyn stand-ing at its entrance. "Can we go inside?" Her voice was involuntarily quiet. Almost reverent.

"Of course," Hiram said as he exited the driver's side of the jeep. "You want a picture on the steps before we go in?"

A staff photographer would be here in a few days to take the official photos for the magazine, but she *did* want some photos for herself.

"Go stand up there and give me your phone. I'll take a couple of you in front of it," Hiram said.

Once she'd posed like a tourist, he opened the wooden double doors. Sunlight streamed into the otherwise dim one-room church. Four rows of wooden pews faced a small raised pulpit at the other end. The entire place was about the size of a large living room. She loved that she and Hiram were the only people here so she could take it all in without having to be distracted by others.

"Sorry it's so hot in here," Hiram said. "There's no electricity to cool it off."

"What time of day was the wedding?"

"Around dusk."

So that would explain the candles in the picture.

"Go on." He nodded toward the front of the church. "Look around all you want."

Her hand grazed the back of each pew as she made her way to the front. A Bible lay open on a tall table in front of the pulpit. First Corinthians 13. *Love is patient and kind...* Though her family had never been churchgoers, she'd seen that verse many times over the years.

"Stand behind the pulpit." Hiram still had her phone. He raised it in front of him, ready to snap a picture.

She did what he'd asked and smiled for the photo, but as she did, her attention snapped to a man seated in the back pew. Other than when she and Hiram had entered, no footsteps had echoed on the wooden plank floors. Where had this man come from? When had he arrived?

Her eyes widened as he nodded a greeting. She recognized him. A nervous buzz thrummed through her body. *Oh, God. Not another panic attack.* She couldn't move. Her limbs felt as if they were encased in concrete.

How the hell was John F. Kennedy Jr. sitting in the back pew of the church where he'd been married?

He disappeared for a couple of seconds, fading out like a hologram losing focus, then returned to existence, as bold and solid as a real person sitting there. He raised a hand as if waving to her. His other arm, clad in a white oxford rolled up to the elbow, rested casually along the back of the pew.

She snapped her eyes closed and squeezed them tightly, willing the hallucination to go away. She'd finally, *finally* ventured out into the world and now this was happening…? Why had the doctors and nurses not warned her something like this might happen? Why had they not prepared her for hallucinations or backsliding or whatever the hell this was?

She focused on breathing deeply. Forced herself to visualize a peaceful meadow filled with butterflies and songbirds. Herself, sitting on a shaded bench with a light breeze in her hair.

Maybe she *was* going crazy. Her therapist had told her that thousands of happy, productive people live with panic disorder every day. But maybe Kevin's overdose had unearthed some far worse mental illness than the onetime crisis she'd told herself she'd had a few weeks ago. Maybe some defect had lurked just below the surface of her psyche all along. The same self-destructive DNA that had coursed through Mama's body, waiting to be brought to life by the right set of circumstances. A cold electric current shot down her spine. Did she give in to this genetic goblin? Or fight it?

"You okay?" Hiram asked.

Her eyes shot open, and she forced herself to focus on him, despite the man still sitting in the back pew. "I'm fine. Just soaking up the feel of the place." She hoped her nervous smile didn't look as fake as it felt. But—*thank God*—this no longer felt like a full-blown panic attack.

Still, behind Hiram, America's onetime prince motioned for her to come toward him.

She forced herself not to shake her head, to rebuff him, because of course a person can't communicate with someone who isn't even there.

Besides, Hiram would witness every movement she made and every word she said in this room. And whatever was going on inside her head was a very private matter. One she would share with no one except maybe her therapist.

But there was only one door leading in and out of the church. The narrow center aisle was her only means of escape.

She would have to pass within a couple of feet of this ethereal John F. Kennedy Jr. in order to get out of this place.

Chapter Four

Neena stepped down from the pulpit, purposefully keeping her attention on Hiram and away from the back pew. The heat and humidity in the church were now stifling—a combination of her own nerves and the lack of air conditioning. "Did the pictures turn out all right?" she asked, trying to pretend everything was normal and that she was *not* seeing a hallucination. There was no way John F. Kennedy Jr. could be there.

Hiram held out her phone. "Make sure you're okay with them. We can take more if we need to."

She took the phone from him and turned to face the front of the church, away from whatever or *whoever* it was sitting in the back pew, just to the right of the center aisle. She scrolled through the photos as slowly as she could, not really seeing them. The longer she took, the more time she had to steady her breath. Long breath in. Long breath out. Long breath in. Long breath out. Finally, she turned toward Hiram. "They're good. Are you ready to go?"

"After you." He stepped aside and held his arm out to the back of the church, inviting her to go ahead of him.

Neena wished he wasn't such a Southern gentleman. Her going first was like walking *toward* an attacker, rather than running away. Not that the man at the back of the church seemed menacing in any way. He was, after all, America's Golden Boy. He just wasn't *there*. He couldn't be there. He had died almost twenty-five years ago.

She had to act like there was nothing out of the ordinary. Maybe if she won this battle, there would be no more hallucinations. No more underhanded tricks from a brain that needed to focus on healing.

Her legs shook as she moved down the aisle toward the one door leading to the outside. She moved her hand from the back of one pew to the back of the next, steadying herself while at the same time trying to hide her distress from Hiram.

She was two rows from John F. Kennedy Jr. when he spoke. He leaned forward, bracing his hands on his knees. His words came out in rapid-fire succession. "Only you can hear me. I *have* to talk to you."

Oh, God. He was talking. Her level of crazy had just gone up a notch.

She turned to look at Hiram, a deliberate attempt to shut down any conversation with the man her broken brain had created. "Where do we head next?" she asked with as much false pep as she could muster.

"Dungeness," he said. "The original home of Thomas and Lucy Carnegie."

"He can't hear me." The hallucination's voice had even more urgency than before. "Make an excuse to get away from him for a few minutes. We have to talk."

She had to concentrate on moving her rigid legs, one after the other, as she came within two feet of the first and only illusion she'd ever seen. She walked as close to the pews on the opposite side of the aisle as she could.

"You're the only one who can help me," he said as she came beside him. He reached across the narrow aisle to touch her. She felt a slight breeze on her wrist, but nothing more.

She somehow made it out the door, down the three weathered wooden steps, and into the yard. "I need to sit down." She pulled her sweaty shirt away from her sternum, fanning herself.

Hiram looked at her face more closely. "You look a little peaked." He cupped her elbow with his hand, steadying her.

"I just need to rest for a bit. It was so hot in there." She hoped he bought the excuse for her discomfort, though he didn't look like he was sweating at all.

He opened the jeep door and helped her inside. "I'll crank up the AC and get you some water."

"Neena!" The other voice called to her from the doorway of the church. He—or it—knew her name? This had to be some kind of personal hell, brought on by her recent mental collapse.

She closed her eyes and let her head fall against the headrest as she wished for Hiram to drive away from this place as fast as he could.

But the problem was: since John F. Kennedy Jr. was in her mind, would she really be able to escape him?

***

During dinner at the communal table that night, Neena asked as many questions of her fellow diners as she could without drawing too much unwanted attention to herself. Had any of the Kennedy family been to the island in recent weeks? Were there any other stories about JFK Jr.'s stays here that Hiram might not have told her?

But neither the other guests nor the staff gave her any answers that would indicate they'd seen anything out of the ordinary. And certainly not that they'd seen some hologram fading in and out at the back of the church.

No, they seemed more interested in swapping stories they'd heard about Boone Calhoun, the man who lived in the little stone house that Hiram had sped past—a friend of a friend who'd gone to MIT with Boone years ago, how much money Boone had made by selling the patent for his computer hardware, how much that windfall translated to in today's dollars, how he got his groceries and other supplies since he never left the island.

Just as Neena had resigned herself to the fact that no one else had seen John F. Kennedy Jr. that day, Gus, the elderly steward, stepped into the doorway of the dining room. He stood stock still, making no attempt to enter the room.

He was about a living room's length away from her, but his blue eyes shone bright against his tanned skin. An unsettled feeling washed over her as she met his gaze. Her senses sharpened. The clinking of silverware grew louder. The scent of the basil on the roasted vegetables grew stronger. She sat still, taking it all in. Wondering what it all meant.

Three times over the course of dinner that night, Gus stepped into the opening and stayed there for a minute—maybe two—before one of the waitstaff needed to bustle past him, causing Gus to step aside.

Finally, the fourth time this happened, his hands rose slowly from his sides and interlocked, fingers on the inside, near his palms. When he turned his hands up and wiggled his fingers, an old chant Neena hadn't thought of in years sprang to her mind:

Here is the church and here is the steeple.

Open the door and see all the people.

He closed his palms, trapping his fingers inside. Then he raised his forefingers, creating the steeple. The sign of a church.

Slowly, he nodded.

Her heart pounded in her chest. What was he trying to tell her? Did he know what she'd seen in the church that day? Why did it always feel as if he could see right inside her soul every time their eyes met?

She swept her napkin off her lap and stood. Thank goodness it was already time for dessert. "Excuse me. I have to go." When she looked back toward the opening, Gus was gone.

"Is everything okay?" asked the elderly guest sitting to her left.

"I'm just tired," she said, doing her best to get out of the room before she had a panic attack. Before her body announced to the world that she was not at all the stable person she pretended to be.

She raced through the wide entry hall, up the wide staircase and through the library, toward her guest room as fast as she could. Though the adrenaline coursing through her body made her want to slam the door shut, she made herself close it gently before she perched on the side of the tall bed. She worked to catch her breath, which she knew was more from her agitated state than from running up the stairs.

What would she do? She needed to get off this island before her brain had a total meltdown. What was the earliest ferry in the morning? How could she arrange to be on it?

No, she couldn't leave. She had to write her article. She had to get her income flowing again. She'd gotten a good overview from Hiram today, but a respectable journalist wrote an in-depth story. And she had to rebuild her credibility with Justin in order to get more assignments from him. No way could she drop the ball for *Coastal South Travel* a second time.

She squeezed her eyes closed. She could do this. She could stay on the island and face whatever she needed to face. Her future—and Rosie's—depended on it.

Gradually, her breathing began to slow.

"No rush, but let me know when you're ready to chat."

She gasped at the sound of a male voice. She jumped off the bed, turned around, and backed against the wall, her arms spread wide—her body's innate reaction to surprise. To danger. Had JFK Jr. been sitting in that chair near the window when she'd entered the room? Or had he just "appeared" there, a product of her addled brain?

He crossed one ankle over the opposite knee, like he was settling in for a while. A sliver of bare skin showed between the leg of his faded jeans and his running shoes. "For the record, you're not going crazy."

She stared at him, unable to say anything. She wasn't sure her throat still worked for either talking or breathing.

"And you need to think of me as 'John.' 'JFK Jr.' is way too long." He gave a teasing smile. "And way too pretentious."

"What do you want from me?" Her words came out in a choked whisper.

"I have a favor to ask."

"Of me?" What the hell could she do to help him?

He leaned forward, his expression more serious. "I can't find Carolyn. I've been looking and...you're the only one who can help me find my wife."

Neena studied him, certain her skepticism showed on her face. It was one thing to see a hallucination. It was another thing to get involved in whatever misguided escapade he was trying to drag her into. "I'm so, so sorry about what happened to y'all. You definitely have my sympathies. I know what it's like to lose a loved one, but I can't help you."

He sprang to his feet. "Why not?"

His sudden movement startled her. She glanced at the door as voices entered the library. She didn't want anyone to hear this conversation when it was clear she was traveling alone. "I have an article to write. I've only got a few days on the island, and I've got to make the most of them. I'm on a tight deadline." *My editor wants to fire me.*

He ran his fingers through his hair as he paced in front of the window. Frustration rolled off of him like he was really there, in her room.

"Can't you just get someone else to help you?" She slid over to the lamp and switched it on, hoping some illumination would prove that he wasn't really there.

Instead, his aura got more solid. Less like the wisps of clouds she'd seen settling into a valley in the Blue Ridge mountains and more like a real live man.

He stopped his pacing and turned to face her. He had the musky scent of a man. "Don't you get it? A couple of other people have seen me here over the years, but you're the only one who can hear me. The only one who's *ever* heard me." He punctuated his words with his hands.

"In twenty-five years?" Surely there had been someone else. Surely there would be someone else in the future.

"There must be something I can offer in exchange for your help." His voice sounded desperate.

"Can you pay my mortgage for me? Maybe my medical bills? Add a few grand to my bank account?"

He stood silently but gave no response.

She scoffed. "Yeah, I didn't think so."

"It's been tough since your brother died, huh? I get it. I've been through a lot, too."

The sincerity in his voice made Neena tear up. He, too, had lost several family members, including his father. But still, she had to stand her ground. She had to protect her sanity at all costs. "I can't help you. Please just go away." She cradled her head in her fingertips, hoping he'd be gone when she looked up again.

He took a few steps forward and stood right in front of her. The closer he got, the more human he seemed. The faint scent of a musky aftershave grew stronger. She looked up at his handsome face. How tall had he been? The way her mother had followed the Kennedys, she should know the answer to that question.

"It can take ages—years, even—to deal with your grief, but you've got something even deeper to deal with. Like a...spiritual difficulty. A burden on your soul...and you definitely don't want to die with that inside you. Believe me—I know." His gaze fell to the floor.

She stepped away from him before he sucked her right in. "Look, my friend—"

"John," he said. "Please call me John."

"I just got out of a hospital where I had nothing to do most of the day but sit around and think. If I had something wrong with my soul, I would have realized it then. And besides, I can't go traipsing off with you, doing God knows what. People already think I'm unstable. And I've got an article to write."

He paused as if taking her in more fully. "You definitely have a soul burden."

She rolled her eyes. "I have a *bank account* burden. And at the moment, a *Kennedy* burden, but I do not have a soul burden. And if you can help me with my 'spiritual difficulty,' then why can't you go find your own wife?"

He shook his head. "It doesn't work that way."

The second he finished his sentence, someone knocked at the door of her guest room. She and John both stiffened. She moved toward the door and cracked it open a bit. One of the female staff members stood on the other side.

"Can I help you?" Neena asked.

"I'm sorry to disturb you, but you left dinner so quickly. We wanted to see if you were okay. Is there anything I can get for you?"

Neena smiled. "No. I'm fine. That's sweet of y'all to check on me."

"You missed the peach cobbler for dessert. We left a dish of it for you in the fridge. On the shelf where we normally put the picnic lunches. Feel free to help yourself if you decide you want it."

She tried to look calm, though it was entirely possible she looked like she was in shock. "Thank you."

"Good night, then." The young woman nodded her farewell.

"Good night," Neena said as she closed the door, eager to convince "John" that he needed to leave her alone.

But when she turned to face the room, he was gone.

Chapter Five

Neena grasped the doorframe of her guest room and held it tightly as her brain tried to convince her shaking body that, logically, there hadn't been anyone else in her guest room with her. She closed her eyes and focused on her breath. *In, then out. In, then out.* Once she felt steadier, she opened her eyes and made her way to sit on the four-poster bed. The overstuffed chair near the window was still empty. No JFK Jr. No apparition. No one. Though she was certain she'd seen him just moments ago.

Why would her grief over Kevin's death make her brain play this kind of trick? And why now instead of a month ago when she'd first found him, one arm hanging awkwardly off the twin bed, his pillow covered in vomit? Sure, the Kennedys had long been important to her family, but why John Jr. when her mother and father had once worked for his father?

It must be because she was on Cumberland Island. Since this was the place John and Carolyn had been married, he was fresh on her mind. Yes. That had to be the explanation. But why had the doctors not prepared her for these...hallucinations?

The jangle of her phone caused her to jump. Rosie's ringtone. She rose slowly and tested her stability before crossing the room to her purse. "Hello."

"Are you okay?" Rosie sounded worried.

"Yes. Why?" Neena made her way back to sit on the bed.

"It took you a long time to answer and your voice is shaky."

Neena's mind raced for a little white lie. She would *not* tell Rosie anything that would worry her. "This is a historic inn, so no elevator. Those couple of flights of stairs are a bear."

"I'll bet it's a cool place."

"It's lovely. I can definitely see why the rich people come here."

"Have you seen any wild horses yet?"

Neena hesitated. It had been a long time since Rosie took this kind of interest in her mother's work. She was up to something. "I took a tour of the island and saw them several times while we were out and about."

"What's the hotel like?"

"Why are you asking me all these questions?"

"Can't a girl be interested in the places her mother gets to visit?" Rosie's tone was light and playful.

Neena was still suspicious, but if Rosie wanted to have a pleasant conversation, then she would play along. "It's a really cool place. You feel like you're staying at someone's home as opposed to an inn. It's very intimate. You dine together at a big communal table. You walk right into the kitchen and open the fridge to get your picnic lunch. You pour yourself a cocktail whenever you want."

"The drinks are free?"

Neena chuckled. "No. You write down what you drink on a little slip of paper. An 'Honest John Bar' is what they call it." She let a beat of silence fall between them. "And how's your week going?"

"I crammed with a study group and got a B on the test in my research class, so that will bring my grade up a lot."

"Enough to pass the course?"

"I'm seven points away, but we have a couple more tests, so I think I can do it."

"Good. Stick with that study group."

"Oh, for sure. And, Mom?" Rosie's hesitation seemed to foreshadow a change of topic.

Neena waited, eager to see what this call was really about.

"Caleb found some super cheap plane tickets to Paris." Rosie's voice was almost apologetic, like she knew she shouldn't be asking this. "The dates are perfect, but the price is only good for a couple more days. We could save eight hundred dollars if we buy them now."

"Sounds like quite a deal. Are you going to go for it?"

Rosie let out a puff of air. "We can't. Not without Grandma's money."

"Is Caleb paying anything for this trip? Or is it all on you?" That sounded like something he would do.

"Yes, Mom." Her daughter's voice dripped with impatience. "He's paying half of everything. This is about him, isn't it? I know you've never liked him."

Neena had always tried to toe the line between supporting her daughter and being too overbearing about who she hung out with or dated. But maybe it was time to share her specific concerns. "It's primarily because that's not what Grandma intended for that money. But while we're talking about it, I don't think Caleb treats you with the kind of respect you deserve."

"Because he doesn't open my car door and old-timey stuff like that?"

"He talks down to you. It's condescending."

"People our age aren't all nicey-nice like they were when you were in college."

They weren't all nicey-nice then, either. A jagged pain sliced through Neena's chest, even all these years later. It was the same one she'd felt when her roommate told her that Rick, her longtime college boyfriend, had been sleeping with another girl every time Neena went back home to care for her mother. "And what about the times Caleb has lied to you?"

Rosie let out an angry grunt. "God, Mom. I wish I'd never told you those things. We've worked through them, okay?"

But Neena couldn't forget that Rosie had run into him at a bar in Gainesville on a weekend he'd told her he was headed home to South Florida. Or how Rosie had seen him with his arm around another girl at a Gator game, something he denied later when she confronted him about it. "It's just that Caleb treats you like my old boyfriend, Rick, used to treat me. In hindsight, Rick wasn't a nice guy."

This bit of her mother's history seemed to pique Rosie's curiosity. "What happened with Rick?"

"Last I saw him was at a party the last semester of our senior year. A bunch of us were standing around the keg in the backyard of this house when his new girlfriend—the one he'd cheated with when he was dating me—came around the corner, all upset. He'd just pushed her up against a chain-link fence and caused this big snag in her brand-new sweater."

"So you saw her, not him."

"He came around the same corner and grabbed her by the arm, pulling her back behind a shed so they could 'talk about it.'" Neena still remembered the look of fear in the other woman's eyes. The sudden realization that it could have been her.

"So Rick was an ass."

"And probably an abuser."

"Good story, Mom, but Caleb's not like that. Besides, I'm old enough to decide who's right for me."

That was enough sharing for today, especially since Rosie wasn't listening anyway. Best to get back to the matter at hand. "That may be true, but it doesn't mean I have to fund your trip."

"*Grandma*. It would be *Grandma* funding the trip."

"I've given you my answer on that topic."

Rosie's voice was impatient. "Look, I know you're all messed up about Uncle Kevin and Grandma and whatever, but nothing's going to happen to me. You've been so paranoid since you got out of the hospital. Aren't you still going to counseling or something?"

It wasn't paranoia, but that was a conversation for another day. "I see my therapist once a week." If nothing else came of all this, she wanted Rosie to understand that there was no shame in seeking help for mental health issues.

"Then stop projecting all your fears onto me," Rosie said.

Neena closed her eyes and swallowed. How had Rosie figured out so much when it had taken Neena years to understand how much her mother's death had impacted her?

Rosie continued. "I'm not going to kill myself, and I'm not going to OD like Uncle Kevin did."

"I appreciate that." But there was a myriad of other ways that something bad could happen to Rosie, including a condescending boyfriend who could rob her of her sense of self-worth. She wanted Rosie to be strong and empowered, not beat down and unsure of herself.

Neena hadn't saved her mother or her brother. That regret would live with her forever. But she wouldn't let it happen again. Maybe she was being overprotective with Rosie. Maybe not. The only thing she knew for sure was that she would do everything she could to save her daughter.

***

Neena savored the next morning's delicious breakfast—eggs Benedict with crab meat instead of Canadian bacon, along with fresh berries tossed in honey and fresh-squeezed lemon juice. She also enjoyed the conversation with the other guests around the communal table. One couple told stories of their recent African safari. Another couple boasted about their twin grandsons who'd been born a month earlier. This lingering at the table felt luxurious. Neena wondered if this was how these people lived all the time. Did they ever scrimp and scramble and worry like she had to on a daily basis?

The ringing of her cell phone interrupted her extravagant dallying. "Excuse me. I've got to take this," she said as she stood. "It was nice having breakfast with y'all."

She hurried out of the dining room and up the wide staircase that led to her room as she answered her phone. She definitely needed privacy for this conversation. "Carla. Thank you so much for returning my call." She'd placed a call to her therapist early that morning but wasn't sure when she might hear back. This whole having-a-therapist thing was new, and she didn't know the protocol.

"Good morning," Carla said. "Sorry about all the car noise, but I'm on my commute in to the office. I wanted to get back to you before my appointments started for the day."

Neena tried to imagine what kind of car Carla drove. Funny how Carla knew so much about her, but Neena knew so little about her therapist.

Neena reached her room and shut the door behind her. "I appreciate the call back. I won't take much of your time, but I want to ask about a potential side effect of my medicine."

"What kind of side effect?"

Neena sat on the edge of the bed. "I'm...uh...seeing things. Things that aren't there. Is that normal?"

"Tell me what you're seeing." Carla's tone was cautious.

"It doesn't happen all the time. Just every now and then." Neena realized she was babbling. Trying to put off the inevitable admission. "I see, like, people. Well, one person in particular."

Carla hesitated. When she did speak, her words came out slowly. "That's not a common symptom of panic disorder, so you may have something else going on. Give me some specifics."

Neena closed her eyes and willed herself to move forward. She'd called Carla for help, after all. She needed to be honest with her. To tell her the whole story. "I'm writing an article about the twenty-five-year anniversary of John F. Kennedy Jr.'s death. And I've...seen him a couple of times."

"Anything else?"

Neena admired Carla's attempt to draw more information from her. Journalists did the same thing with their interview subjects. "I've also talked to him." She winced when she said it, knowing how outlandish it sounded.

"You're seeing the ghost of JFK Jr.? And you're conversing with him?" Carla sounded alarmed, though Neena could tell she tried to hide it. "Do you see other people, too? Hear other voices?"

"No. Just him. He wants me to help him with something."

"Neena." Carla's tone was calming, but insistent. "You need to come see me as soon as possible. I've had a cancellation for tomorrow afternoon. Does two o'clock work for you?"

"I can't. I'm on Cumberland Island. It's where John and Carolyn were married." She rushed to cover up the fact that she'd just admitted they were on a first-name basis. "I'm here until Monday, and there aren't any ferries—"

"At this stage of the game, you need to make your mental health your first priority."

The sternness of her therapist's voice startled Neena. "But I've got to get my story written, especially since I've missed so much work already. You and I are scheduled to meet on Tuesday anyway. Can't we talk about it then?"

"I don't think that's a good idea. This could be serious."

"I know." Neena hesitated. "But it's weird—I'm not scared of him. I think I can manage."

Carla let out a long breath. "I'm not a bit happy about waiting, but promise me one thing: if the visions get worse, or if this...hallucination...asks you to do something dangerous, you've got to get to a hospital immediately. Make sure whoever has a boat on that island gets you back to the mainland ASAP. You hear?"

Neena crossed her fingers, a trick of deception leftover from childhood. "I promise."

"How's the anxiety been?"

"About the same. It's not really worse, if that's what you're asking."

"Are you feeling depressed?"

Neena should have expected all these questions, but she hadn't thought that far ahead. "No. It's beautiful here. And I'm relieved to be working again."

"You have your meds with you? You're taking them regularly?"

"Yes." Neena glanced over at the pill bottles on her nightstand.

"Good. Since this isn't a side effect, it's important that you keep taking them." A horn blasted on Carla's end of the line. "Is there anything else I need to know?"

"No. I'll let you go. Thank you for calling me back so quickly." Neena never wanted to feel this dependent on a therapist. She never wanted to be this vulnerable. She never *had* been this vulnerable. At least, not in her adult life.

"I'm serious, Neena. Don't wait too long to get yourself help if you need it."

"I won't."

She sat there for several minutes once they'd hung up. If hallucinations weren't a regular part of panic disorder, then what did that mean about John? What did it mean about *her*? Just when she'd thought she might be getting better, her world had shifted again. She felt like she was balanced on a surfboard, bobbing and swaying to keep herself afloat.

But what she'd told Carla had been absolutely true. She was here on the island to work, and she needed to get back to it.

She headed downstairs to grab one more cup of joe from the coffee station, then she planned to walk around the inn—both inside and out—until she could find Gus. Surely, the longest-term employee there could give her behind-the-scenes anecdotes that no other publications had included in their articles. Justin may look down on fifty-year-olds, but there was something to be said for old school journalism.

Still, Neena had faith in the younger generation. Maybe not in Justin specifically, but she trusted that Rosie and her peers would persevere in an increasingly challenging world. Yes, Rosie had been difficult in recent weeks, but this was the daughter who'd sat with an unpopular girl at lunch every day her junior year of high school so the other girl wouldn't have to eat alone. Rosie and her friends had participated in the Beach Cleanup—picking up trash along the shoreline—every year since elementary school. Rosie's friend, Chandra, had already started a non-profit that raised money for children growing up in poverty. So while Justin seemed to buy into the increase-the-bottom-line-at-all-costs mentality, Neena knew there were kindhearted souls his age, just as there were in every generation.

She poured herself the cup of coffee and wandered into the gift shop across the hall while she waited for it to cool. Items for sale included logoed T-shirts, reprints of a drawing of the IvyLena, books about the island, and bags of "Evangeline's Apple Fritters" mix.

The same young woman as before was sitting at the desk in the gift shop. Perhaps she was a manager of sorts? Or maybe the inn's bookkeeper? She wasn't in the kitchen bustling to get breakfast prepared, and Neena hadn't seen her serving last night's dinner. Each of the other female employees

Neena had seen seemed to serve multiple roles—kitchen staff, waitstaff, housekeepers.

"Good morning." The young woman gave a warm smile as her gaze met Neena's.

"Good morning."

"Ms. Lee, right? The journalist?"

"That's right."

"I'm Claire. Let us know if you have any questions we can answer."

This was unfolding just as Neena would have wanted it to. "There *is* one thing you might be able to help me with. I'd like to interview your longest-term employee. I think his name is Gus?"

"Ahhhhh. Yes." Claire's smile returned. "An interesting man."

This piqued Neena's interest. Maybe it wasn't just her who felt the man's mysterious presence each time he entered the room. "Oh? How so?"

"Anyone who lives to be his age would have some stories to tell." Claire gave a mischievous look over the rim of her own cup of coffee as she took a sip.

"So nothing in particular that makes him 'interesting'?" Neena used her free hand to make air quotes.

Claire gave a good-natured laugh. "I'm sure you'll discover a lot of unique facts on your own about him. It's what you journalists do, right?"

"So you're okay if I interview him?"

"Of course, assuming he's willing. I can't imagine he wouldn't be. He's gone to the mainland to help bring over some supplies, but he'll be back soon. I'll ask him to meet you in the library at, say, eleven o'clock? Does that work for you?"

Neena smiled. "It does. Thank you."

Claire glanced at her computer monitor, which faced away from Neena.

"I'll let you get back to work," Neena said. "Thank you for arranging the interview."

She finished her cup of coffee, happy to have accomplished such an important goal. She would meet this enigmatic Gus and listen to the stories he could tell about life at the IvyLena. The management had made it clear to Justin that they wouldn't violate the privacy of any of their guests, but there had to be morsels of life on the island that would interest the readers of *Coastal South Travel*. How had the place remained so quaint and exclusive at the same time? What had changed since Gus had started working there in the 1960s? She'd work hard to mine the depths of his memory. This article had to be spot-on. It had to make that little twerp Justin look good for the editorial board. It had to save her career.

And only after she'd gotten what she needed for the story would she ask Gus about last night. What he'd meant when he'd indicated the church and then nodded yes to her. Did he…see people, too? But maybe that was silly. Did employees of the inn even visit the church, which was miles away on the other end of the island? Especially on an island that had a limited number of vehicles on it?

But she'd have to figure out a way to conduct the interview somewhere other than the library. No way could she ask him her personal questions in a place where other guests could overhear.

She gathered her notebook from her room and made her way to one of the sturdy wooden tables on the lawn behind the mansion. The sprawling canopy of moss-draped live oaks created a shady spot for her to make a list of questions she would ask Gus later in the day. She wrote down a couple of questions, then paused, thinking. Gulls cried in the distance.

"Hey, you need to come with me." The male voice came from her right, though there was no one in that direction.

Ugh. Was John going to bother her during her entire stay on the island?

"Near the banana plant," he said.

She turned her head in an unhurried fashion, as if her body knew not to let the couple out on the lawn know that she might be engaging with someone who wasn't really there.

He materialized a few feet away and walked toward her. He leaned against the huge live oak, a stance she'd seen him in many times in magazines throughout the late eighties and early nineties. *She* had definitely aged since those days, but he had not. She took a deep breath, wondering what would come next.

"I need you to take a walk with me." The same urgency as yesterday filled his voice.

His presence no longer alarmed her the way it initially had. Maybe she was getting used to it? Or maybe she was just finally accepting her particular brand of crazy? She glanced down at the questions in her notebook, trying to figure out how to make him go away.

"I need your help with something," he said. "It's important."

But she needed to plan for her meeting with Gus. She needed to keep her focus on the reason for her being on Cumberland Island to begin with. She could deal with whatever was going on inside her mind once she got back to Jacksonville. Hopefully Carla could help. Or maybe Neena needed an entire team of therapists.

"You help me now, and then we'll figure out a way I can help you with your article."

Her head snapped up. *Could* he help her? Could he tell her things that had gone on the weekend of his wedding? Well, duh, obviously he could—if he were real and not some figment of her imagination.

But maybe—just maybe—he wasn't just inside her mind. If that was the case, she'd have to corroborate anything he told her with someone else. It had been a while since she'd studied up on journalist ethics, but even so, she knew a hallucination—or even a ghost—couldn't serve as a primary source for an article.

Still, it was tempting. Anything that might help her write a kick-ass article to restart her career was at least worth exploring.

Slowly she closed the cover on her notebook. She turned to John, nodded, and rose.

Maybe he was a hallucination. He might even be a ghost. But either way, she had just agreed to follow him.

Chapter Six

Neena looked to John for instructions on what she should do next. How, exactly, was she supposed to interact with him when there were other guests nearby?

"They can't see me," he said as if he could read her mind.

Could he read her mind? But wasn't that a redundant question, especially if—as she suspected—he existed only *in* her mind?

"They can't hear me, either," he continued. "We're going to be walking a bit, so you might want to go change your shoes."

She glanced down at the dressy sandals she was wearing. They'd been a splurge about three months ago. It seemed like a different lifetime then—before Kevin's death, before her panic attacks had started, before her income had become a pair of big fat zeroes. The shoes now seemed like such a frivolous purchase. If she still had the cash, she could use that ninety dollars to pay the overdue portion of her electric bill.

She turned to John and nodded, unwilling to appear to the other guests like she was talking to herself.

He pointed toward the end of the long dirt driveway that led toward Main Road. "Start walking that way when you come back outside. I'll meet you out there."

She berated herself as she went to her room. She needed to focus on her article, so why had she agreed to this ill-advised outing with him? And what could she possibly do to help him?

The autumn day would still get hot and humid enough that she changed into shorts and a T-shirt, in addition to her tennis shoes. She stuffed her small backpack with the two bottles of water she'd brought to the island in her purse. She had no idea what this little jaunt would entail, but best to be prepared.

Ten minutes later, she approached the end of the long drive, nervous that she had yet to see him. What would the other guests on the lawn think if she got to the end of the drive and just turned around and returned to the inn? She was still contemplating that question when John appeared by her side.

She ducked behind one of the stone columns that marked the entrance to the inn so other guests wouldn't think she was talking to herself. "I was about to give up on you."

"I told you I'd be here." He flashed her that smile that had graced so many glossy magazine pages.

But his charm wasn't going to work on her. "So dead people have demanding schedules, do they?"

His eyes showed a mix of compassion and patience. He held her gaze, as if he was deciding how to respond to her snark. Then he pointed to the private path on the other side of Main Road. "You haven't been to the beach since you've been here, so this is going to kill two birds with one stone."

"And if I help you, you'll help me with my article?"

"We'll get to that later. But either way, this might address what you've been struggling with since your brother died."

"How much do you know about me?" She fell in step with him as they headed toward the path on the other side of Main Road. The branches of the trees were more twisted there, a result of the constant breeze from the Atlantic.

"I know your bucket list includes a trip to the Galapagos Islands."

Neena sucked in an involuntary breath. She hadn't told anyone on earth about that.

He continued. "I know you were going to ask Kevin to help you paint your living room kind of a sunflower yellow, but his death derailed that project, at least for the time being. I know you and Rosie aren't getting along great these days."

So he *could* read her mind. But didn't that just prove he was a hallucination—something created within her own head? Maybe it was the connection between her family and his—that's why she was hallucinating him here, in the place where he'd gotten married. "Rosie's named after your grandmother, you know."

He turned to look at her as he placed a hand over his heart. "I'm honored. Thank you."

She stubbed her toe on the root of a live oak, which reminded her to look over at his feet. Did he levitate along the path or was he, too, at risk of tripping over one of the ever-present roots? He wore scuffed hiking boots that trod along the path in the same way she did. As a matter of fact, he looked completely real. His footfalls even made the same quiet scratch on the well-worn path that hers did. His feet left indentions in the sandy soil. The only indication she had that he wasn't a living, breathing person was that he'd been dead for more than twenty years.

The path curved and seemed to come to an end up ahead, where the thick blanket of trees gave way to a corridor of bright sunshine. The sound of waves confirmed they were near the ocean, though she couldn't see it yet.

"So how exactly am I supposed to help you?" she asked as they trudged forward. The trail had given way to much softer sand, which made walking more difficult. She wiped a trickle of sweat from behind her ear.

"There's been a huge blowup at the campground here on the island. A big family argument," he said.

"And?"

"Carolyn hates conflict. She would do anything to avoid it. We once had to leave a restaurant that had a three-month waiting list to get in because the couple at the table next to us was having a tiff."

He really expected her to believe this nonsense?

He ignored her I'm-not-falling-for-this look and continued talking. "That's part of the reason she despised the paparazzi so much. She hated having to do battle with them every time she left the house."

"This has absolutely nothing to do with me."

He held out his arms in a beseeching gesture. "Don't you get it? I've waited for years for someone who could hear me, and you're finally here. It's a good sign, like maybe things are about to change for me. Like she could show up at any minute, but if there's this tension hovering over the island"—he held his hands high, palms down, like clouds overhead—"it could scare her away."

"Because of something going on at the campground?" Neena didn't try to hide the skepticism in her voice.

"She's very sensitive. Very attuned to what's going on around her." A tender look crossed his face. "It's one of the things I love most about her."

They'd reached the end of the path. The beach lay before them, sloping downward toward the shoreline. Seagulls ran along the sand, darting from the incoming waves. A man and woman walked slowly along the water's edge, their heads down as they searched for shells or shark's teeth.

John's voice pulled her gaze from the peaceful scene before her. "There's this kid, Ethan. A sophomore in high school. He had a big fight with his parents, but really he just needs someone to talk to. He doesn't have any friends, but he needs to vent about his parents, like every kid does."

She'd had enough of this BS. "I'm out of here," she said as she turned to head back toward the path that had led them here.

John rushed to catch up with her. "You don't have to believe it. You just have to try. And remember, I'm going to help you with your article."

She stopped and glared at him, considering his last sentence. "Why would some teenager talk to me—a stranger—on the beach?"

"You look a lot like his science teacher, who's the only person he trusts these days. I think that will help."

This was getting more nonsensical by the minute. How had Neena gotten herself into this?

She opened her mouth to object, but John motioned with his chin toward something behind her. "Here he is."

She turned. They both watched a tall thin man-sized person come from behind the dunes and walk in their direction. As he got closer, Neena could see he was actually a teenager. His curly black hair and the neckline of his oversized T-shirt were soaked in sweat. His dirty board shorts were a faded green.

John pointed in the direction of the shoreline. "That canopy over there belongs to you." Two bright orange beach chairs sat beneath a bright yellow awning.

She turned to ask him how she—a fifty-six-year-old woman—was supposed to get a teenager to talk to her. But John's body twisted and rose, circling in the air like smoke from a campfire. Within seconds, he'd been carried away by the sea breeze.

She watched as the boy trudged closer to the water, then flopped onto the sand, his long thin legs stretched in front of him. His back curved forward in a look of exhaustion.

She observed him a few minutes longer, then dug into her backpack as she approached.

"You look like you could use this." She held out a bottle of water.

He shielded his eyes from the sun as he looked up at her, a look of suspicion on his face.

She moved it closer to him. "Go on. It's an extra. It's pretty hot out here."

He took it from her, unscrewed the top, and took a big swig.

"That's my canopy over there, if you want to get out of the sun." She knew she shouldn't push too hard. Kids his age needed to think they were making all their own decisions. She'd learned that much during Rosie's teenage years. She walked to the awning and sat in one of the chairs.

They sat for several minutes, maybe twenty yards from each other—him on the wet sand closer to the shoreline, with her behind him. Finally, he drained his water bottle and stood. He made his way back to the awning and plopped into the chair next to her. His flip-flopped feet, covered in sand, reminded her of a puppy who would one day grow into his large paws.

"Is this the beach for that fancy hotel?" he asked.

"I think so." She hadn't paid that much attention to the few signs she and John had passed on the way here. "Is that where you're staying?"

His eyes darkened. "I *used* to be staying at the campground, but not anymore." Anger tinged his voice.

She grunted. "Must be a story there."

He remained silent, looking out toward the waves. She took the second bottle of water from her backpack and handed it to him.

She, too, watched the ocean as she pondered what had brought her to this point. John had said she was supposed to help this kid, but how?

Finally, the boy spoke. "This trip was my birthday present from my mom and dad." He rolled his eyes. "We're supposed to be here studying the sea life."

"Sounds like a pretty good gift." Good for his parents for giving him an experience rather than *things*. She made a mental note to arrange for more experiences with Rosie. They'd have to be inexpensive ones—like hiking through the woods or going to the farmers market—but there wasn't much time before Rosie built her own adult life, which would mean even more separation from Neena than there already was.

The boy's stony silence returned. He dug a canal in the sand with his big toe. Two or three minutes passed. Something told Neena that she needed to not rush him.

Finally, he spoke. "All they ever talk about is getting into college. They think I'm obsessed with becoming a marine biologist. All because Mrs. Wilkerson—my science teacher—asked me to be on the turtle team."

"The turtle team?" Neena asked, grateful he was at least talking now.

"We locate the nests where sea turtles have laid their eggs, then mark them with caution tape so people won't bother them. We put a screen over them to keep out the raccoons or coyotes or other predators. And if a nest is likely to get flooded at high tide, then we move it to safer ground."

She nodded, impressed. "Seems like a worthwhile activity."

"I'm just a beach walker now—we go out early in the mornings to find the tracks the mother turtles have left on the beach—but I'm hoping in a year or two I'll get to be one of the people who relocates the nests."

"It must have been an honor that Mrs. Wilkerson asked you to join the team."

He gave a quick smile. "Yeah, she's my coolest teacher. And sea turtles are cool, too, but it may not be what I want to do for the rest of my life."

"How old are you?" she asked.

He ran a hand through his unruly head of black curls. "Fifteen."

"You seem pretty 'with it' for a fifteen-year-old." She let out a half-hearted laugh. "I was a mess when I was that age."

He studied her out of the corner of his eye but didn't say anything. At least he looked curious.

Her intuition told her to continue. "My dad had taken off years earlier. My mom wouldn't come out of her bedroom for days at a time." Neena had been too embarrassed to invite any friends over because the house was such a disaster, despite her efforts to keep it clean. Just when she got things put away, Kevin would come through and mess everything up again.

Ethan stared forward as if he hadn't heard her.

She decided to add the coup de grâce. The part of the story she'd never told anyone. "I rode my bike to a gift shop about a mile from home and got caught stealing a bracelet. I needed it to take as a gift to a birthday party I'd been invited to, but I knew Mom wouldn't take me to get one."

He turned to look at her but didn't say anything.

"Like I said, I was kind of a mess."

He grunted. "That's nothing like it is now."

She fought the urge to tell him the store owner had called the police and she'd had to go to juvenile court, but this wasn't about her. It wasn't a competition between how difficult her life had been and whatever he had going on. This was about getting him to talk. It was about getting him to reconcile with his parents. "How are things different today?"

He returned his gaze to the ocean. She had the distinct feeling he was avoiding eye contact with her. Silence sat between them as thick as the coastal humidity.

"Let's just say I can understand why your mom hid in the bedroom all the time," he said.

Neena gripped the arms on her beach chair. Was he telling her that he had major bouts of depression, too? Was he suicidal, like Mama had eventually become? The conversation now felt more serious. More urgent. "Do your parents know you feel that way?"

His chin quivered. She looked away, giving him some privacy. Finally, he spoke. "All they care about is logging back in to work after dinner to check their emails."

Neena recognized his loneliness. She'd felt the same thing when she was his age and her only parent had been distant and unavailable. "What about Mrs. Wilkerson? Could you maybe talk to her?"

His hands moved to the arms of his chair as he sat forward. He planted his feet on the ground more firmly. "I've got to go."

Neena feared she'd pushed too hard. That she'd scared him away before she could encourage him to talk things over with his parents. Before she could somehow lower the aura of tension that hovered over the island. Did she even believe in such woo-woo things? Apparently she did, since she'd hallucinated entire conversations with someone who'd died twenty-five years ago.

The boy's cell phone pinged, and he pulled it from his pocket. He fumbled it and it fell face down in the sand. The neon green skull on the scuffed case stared back at her, mocking her failure to help the boy.

He picked up the phone and turned it over. A jagged crack splintered one corner of the screen, but she could clearly see the incoming meme. A close-up of male genitalia with the word "FAGGOT" written in all caps below it. He quickly locked his phone and stuffed it back in his pocket, undoubtedly hoping she hadn't seen it. He didn't look in her direction or acknowledge what had just happened.

She sat, shocked by the vulgarity of it. Of course, she'd heard of "dick pics," but had never actually seen a picture like that. She knew kids could be mean, but she'd never witnessed such cruelty.

"Thanks for the water," he said, though his voice held no sense of gratitude. He stood and trudged away from her without looking back.

Her mind continued to whirl. Was he being bullied because he was gay? Is that what the text meant? That wasn't something a teen should have to deal with on his own, but she had no assurances that he'd talk to his parents or Mrs. Wilkerson about it.

No, Neena had failed to help him. She'd failed on the assignment John had given her. Just like with Mom and Kevin, she'd failed when someone needed her help.

The boy was a couple of car-lengths away when a gruff male voice blared from behind her. "Ethan Montgomery?"

She turned to see a National Park Service employee with a megaphone running toward the boy.

The man stopped when he was even with her. His chest heaved from the exertion of running through loose sand. A wet ring rimmed the bill of his ranger cap. He raised the bullhorn to his mouth again. "Are you Ethan Montgomery?" His voice carried over the sound of the waves.

The boy turned but didn't initially say anything. He looked as if he was deciding what to do. Finally, he walked toward the man, which brought him closer to Neena. "I'm Ethan Montgomery." He pulled himself to his full height, towering over the shorter, stockier man.

So John had been right. The kid's name really was Ethan.

"Your parents have been looking for you for several hours, son," the park ranger said.

"Okay." There was no apology in Ethan's tone. No remorse. Just a hard-edged indifference.

Another park ranger—this one on a four-wheeler—arrived via the same path Neena and John had hiked to get there.

"We're going to take you back to the campground," the first man said as he motioned toward the vehicle. "To your parents."

Ethan's shoulders sagged as the man took him by the arm and guided him toward the ATV. After a brief discussion that Neena couldn't hear, Ethan straddled the long seat behind the driver and the two drove off down the beach.

Neena's mind cycled through the events of the afternoon as she watched the pair get farther and farther away. His name *had* been Ethan, and his science teacher *was* someone he seemed to trust. So John could not only read *her* mind, but he knew what was going on with other people, too. Did that mean he wasn't only in her head?

But if he wasn't a hallucination, did that mean he was…a ghost?

She didn't even believe in ghosts. But how else could John know what was going on inside her *and* inside other people?

If he *was* a ghost, maybe she should be relieved? It at least meant that her whacked-out brain hadn't created him. That she hadn't conjured him up from the depths of her still-recovering psyche.

She wasn't sure what she thought of all this.

She let out a long breath and turned to retrieve her backpack before heading back to the inn. But she jumped at the man sitting right beside her, in the chair that had once held Ethan. Her palm flew to her chest, and she let out a squeak before she realized it was John. "Oh, my God. Would you please not sneak up on me like that?"

"I'm not sure we eased the tension on the island." He looked glum as he flung a seashell across the sand like he was skipping a rock across the surface of a pond. "We may have made it worse."

She leaned down to lift her backpack. "Yeah? Well, I did what you asked me to do. Now how are you going to help me with my article?"

He looked out over the waves. "I'm still figuring that part out."

Of course he was. She'd been such a sucker to agree to this deal to begin with.

She pulled her cell phone from the side pocket of the backpack to check the time. Eleven thirty-two in the morning.

Damn it.

Her interview with Gus was to have started more than a half an hour ago.

CHAPTER SEVEN

Neena rushed up the front steps of the inn, now forty-seven minutes late for her scheduled interview with Gus. It wasn't at all professional, but she'd conduct the meeting in the shorts and T-shirt she'd worn to the beach. Taking time to change would make her even later than she already was. She'd been scared to death that the rush back to the IvyLena would cause a panic attack, but so far so good. Her nerves were frayed, but she still seemed in command of her body and mind.

She ran up the wide, sweeping stairs to the library. No one was there, so she raced down to the gift shop, which doubled as Claire's office.

The younger woman looked up at Neena as she entered. She glanced down at the corner of her computer screen, then frowned. "Aren't you supposed to be meeting with Gus right now?" The puzzled look on her face was all that saved Neena from feeling reprimanded.

She swiped her forehead with her fingertips, hoping Claire didn't realize how sweaty she was. Late, sweaty, and underdressed. "I am, but I got held up at the beach. There was a teenager who'd been missing from the campground and I..." God. She had to stop babbling. "Luckily they found him."

"Well, that's good." Claire's gaze took in Neena's attire, from her sandy shoes to her hair, which had to be windblown from the ever-present breeze along the shoreline.

"I was just in the library and Gus wasn't there. He probably thinks I blew him off."

"Do you want to wait here while I see if I can find him?"

"Yes. Please. I'm so sorry for my tardiness."

Claire's lips pressed into a tight line as she nodded, a look Neena wasn't sure how to interpret.

"I'll be back," Claire said as she strode out of the gift shop, across the entry hall, and down the stairs that led to the kitchen.

Neena paced as her mind served up a heavy dollop of worry. Would word get back to her new boss that she had been so unprofessional as to show up to her meeting late? A meeting that had been personally arranged for her? That would be a huge strike against her, especially with Justin's track record of getting rid of anyone older than his generation.

A young couple—newlyweds?—came into the gift shop. The woman giggled as the man lovingly wrapped his arm around her shoulders, pulled her close, and whispered something into her ear.

Neena felt like she didn't belong. This place was the perfect destination for fairytale weddings and honeymoons and milestone anniversaries—none of which she'd ever experienced. She was generally quite happy with her solo existence, but sometimes pangs of regret hit her much stronger than she cared to admit.

She stepped out of the gift shop and into the entry hall, reminding herself that she wasn't here for some special life event or even a vacation. She was here for work.

And that damn John had made her take her eye off the prize.

No, she couldn't blame someone else. This was her fault. She knew better than to let him insert a distraction in her life, even if it was a teenager who desperately needed help.

From now on, her only focus would be to get this article finished and ready to send to Justin's inbox the second she got back to the mainland.

Once that was complete, she'd work on drumming up more writing assignments. No way was she going to lose her house because some dead guy wanted her to help "cleanse the aura of the island." She could write her article without his help, especially if it meant not having to put up with his bullshit.

There were eight rooms at the IvyLena, so maybe twelve to sixteen guests at any given time for him to hassle. It didn't need to be her. She was done with ghosts, regardless of how famous the guy had once been.

She turned at the sound of one of the massive front doors opening behind her. Perhaps it was Gus, looking for her.

But it was Dwight, the friendlier of the two brothers she'd first met waiting for the ferry. He lowered a worn backpack off his shoulders. Like her, he was a bit sweaty and his hair was windblown. On him, it looked rugged. Outdoorsy. She was sure she didn't exude the same beachy vibe.

He dipped his head in greeting. "Good morning."

She remembered now how much she'd loved his Southern accent. She pushed a wayward strand of hair from her face, hoping to tidy her disheveled look. "Good morning."

"Neena, right?"

She smiled and nodded, flattered that he remembered her name. "And you're Dwight?"

"That's right. Did you go on any of the tours this morning?"

She shook her head. "I went to the beach, but now I'm waiting to interview one of the employees. I'm a journalist writing a story about the island."

"Interesting," he said. "Who do you work for?"

The bleakness of her situation sliced through her mind. Justin had barely wanted to give her this assignment and she had exactly zero other engagements in the works. "I'm freelance, actually. This one is for *Coastal South Travel*."

He smiled. "Ahhhh. I know it well. I read it a lot when I was trying to figure out where to move after I sold my business in Greenville."

So she'd been right. His accent *was* from upstate South Carolina. "And what did you decide?"

He jabbed a thumb behind him, toward the north. "I'm just up the coast on Hilton Head. What about you? Where do you live?"

"Jacksonville."

He nodded. "Nice."

A brief silence fell between them. She nervously fiddled with the strap of her backpack.

"I'd love it if you joined me for dinner tonight," he said.

She looked up. Her face heated as she realized that the newlyweds inside the gift shop could likely hear them. "But what about your brother?"

He waved a dismissive hand. "He's been spending all his time on a work project that was supposed to be over by now. He's actually got a conference call at seven tonight, so he's asked the staff to save him a plate for later." He inclined in a sort of brief bow. "Which frees me up to have dinner with you."

"Ummmm. Sure...?" She felt flustered. She hated the way her voice rose at the end of her response, but she hadn't been asked out on a date in months. Maybe even years. So much for not letting anything distract her from her article.

He smiled. "Great. Are you okay if I ask the staff to move your seat at dinner to the smaller table?"

The voices of the newlyweds floated from inside the gift shop. Thank God they weren't listening in on this conversation. "That's fine." Neena would welcome the opportunity to get to know him privately, without the other guests at the communal table intervening in their conversation.

He smiled again as he returned the pack to his back. "I look forward to it. See you then."

She watched as he made his way toward the back staircase that led to the kitchen. His lean legs and muscular calves told her he was likely a runner. Or maybe an avid hiker?

She may have screwed up her interview time with Gus today, but she wasn't at all sorry about her dinner plans with the *other* interesting man at the inn that week.

***

Neena entered the dining room that evening determined to push aside the guilt over her failed interview with Gus. Claire had let her know that Gus had gone on to other duties out in the garden once it had become apparent that Neena wasn't going to make their scheduled appointment.

Claire would try to connect Neena with Gus tomorrow, but there wasn't any guarantee since he hadn't initially been scheduled to work that day.

Damn. Damn. Damn. Neena hoped she hadn't screwed up her best chance to show Justin the kind of in-depth story a seasoned travel writer could produce.

She'd spent the rest of the day looking through old photos taken at the inn over the years, doing her best to capture in words the feel and elegance of each passing era.

For now, though, she'd push work from her mind and concentrate on only one thing: her dinner with Dwight. She was nervous, so she'd spent the last fifteen minutes sitting on the bed in her guest room doing breathing exercises the inpatient therapist had taught her at the hospital. She never knew when a panic attack would occur, and it would be hugely embarrassing if she had one when she was with Dwight.

He stood and pulled out her chair as she entered the dining room. His dark hair stood out against his mint-colored shirt. His brown sport coat looked perfectly tailored.

"Are you sure I'm not putting your brother out by joining you for dinner?" she asked as soon as they were both seated. The scent of garlic wafted up the stairs from the kitchen below.

"He's going to sleep as soon as the current call is over. He has to wake up at 2 a.m. for another one with Dubai."

Ugh. "Does he do that in the carriage house where y'all are staying? While you're trying to sleep?"

Dwight chuckled and nodded. "Luckily, we've got the entire second floor. It's a pretty big suite, and his bedroom is on the opposite end from mine."

"Seems a shame to come to a beautiful place like this and not enjoy it."

"Yeah. I'm beginning to understand why his wife divorced him. This was supposed to be my 'condolences' trip for him. A chance for us to reconnect after all these years. But now I'm seeing how much truth there is to him being married to his job."

Why did he need to "reconnect" with his brother? A broken family relationship might signal that Dwight was trouble. "Have you two been estranged?"

He rolled his water glass between his palms as he spoke. He seemed to study the ice cubes inside. "Nah. Just not as close as we used to be. He's a year older than I am, so we were constant buds when we were kids and teenagers. We were even roommates in college. But he's lived on the West Coast for a couple of decades now, and I've stayed in South Carolina."

The server approached to take their drink orders.

"I'll have a seltzer with a lime," she said.

He raised his eyebrows. "You okay if I have an adult beverage?" he asked.

She waved a dismissive hand. "Of course. I'm just...not in the mood right now." The truth was, she wasn't supposed to drink with her newly prescribed meds, and besides, alcohol was the only thing not included with the nightly room rate. She didn't know if they'd add her drink to Dwight's bill or hers. Best to avoid any awkwardness.

Once the server had left, Dwight reached out with his forefinger and gently touched where her wedding ring would have gone. "I've assumed you aren't married, but if I'm wrong, now's probably the time to say so."

She liked his up-front communication style. "Never have been. You?"

A shadow of grief passed through his eyes. "Divorced. For seventeen years."

Wow. He'd had a strong reaction for someone whose relationship had ended such a long time ago. "No one since then?"

He shrugged. "No one serious."

Whoa. Red flag number two. But, wait. She'd had only a couple semi-serious boyfriends in that length of time, too. Maybe she should cut him some slack. "I do have a child, though. Rosie. She's twenty-three and finishing her master's degree."

"Impressive." His expressive face brightened, then got more serious. "But being a single mom is hard. You must be one tough lady."

She reveled in the look of admiration on his face. "And believe it or not, I did it on purpose. In vitro fertilization when I was in my mid-thirties and had no man in sight."

His eyebrows rose. "Doubly impressive. And brave."

Her mind flashed to Rosie's angry words during their last few phone calls. "Well, she's certainly testing me these days. Can someone have a college degree *and* the terrible twos at the same time?"

His rich laugh drew the attention of the older couple at the near end of the communal table. Dwight mouthed an apology to them for his loudness, then turned back to her. "I guess nobody's family is perfect. We just have to work with what we're given."

She nodded. Sadly, between Mama's mental illness and Kevin's addiction, she'd been dealing with what life had doled out for years. Surely the recent difficulties with Rosie would have a better outcome than she'd had with Mama and Kevin.

A fortyish-looking woman entered the room and made her way to one of the private tables at the other end of the narrow room. Her auburn hair was swept into an updo that looked both elegant and effortless. Her body-hugging dress flattered her shapely figure. The asymmetrical neckline and bold blocks of color were chic, but still fit into the old-world charm of the inn. Neena had never felt as put-together as this woman looked.

A ten- or twelve-year-old girl—undoubtedly the woman's daughter since she had the same thick mane of auburn hair—joined her at the table set for two. Neena would love to take Rosie on a girls' weekend at a place like this, but there was no way it would ever fit into her budget.

"Makes you miss Rosie, doesn't it?" Dwight nodded toward the woman and her daughter.

"It does. Especially that age. When there was a least some innocence left." Neena returned her attention to him. "And what about you? Any children?"

Again, a dark, almost brooding look passed through his eyes. He quickly diverted his gaze to the silverware he fiddled with in front of him. "I...ummm...don't have any."

His statement sat in the middle of their table, as solid a presence as the breadbasket.

She rushed to ease his pain. "How long are you staying on the island?"

"The entire week." His demeanor perked up as he joked about his predicament. "Seven straight nights of calls with Dubai."

She laughed. "So you stalked the only solo traveler here and forced her to have dinner with you?"

He held his pointer finger in the air. "First of all, I only stalked you a little. And secondly." Another finger came up. "I would have wanted to have dinner with you, regardless of what my brother was doing."

Her face heated. It had been a long time since a man had flattered her in this way. It was nice to enjoy his company. To forget—for just a bit—about the fights with Rosie, and the precariousness of her career, and the panic attacks that snuck up when she least expected them.

She welcomed the distraction when the server arrived to deliver their drinks.

Once the young woman had left their table, Dwight raised his tumbler of amber-colored liquid. "To new friends."

Neena clinked her glass against his. "To new friends."

***

By the time dinner was over, Neena felt the most content she had in years. Their dinner had been delicious—flaky sea bass covered with sauteed, island-grown bell peppers in a delicious lemony sauce. Tender new potatoes. Warm rolls made in-house. Southern buttermilk pie for dessert. The conversation with Dwight had been fast-paced and engaging. The evening had been a delight.

He stood as she excused herself to go to the ladies' room.

"Be right back," she said.

The dining room was mostly empty by then. Some of the other guests must have returned to their rooms, but she could also hear low voices coming from the adjacent sunporch.

She was looking toward the small gathering of guests as she headed toward the tiny bathroom tucked under the staircase—the only powder room on the main floor. Her head whipped around the second she ran into someone. Her first response was to startle and step back, but then she realized the other person was elderly and she'd knocked him off-balance.

Gus.

She grabbed one of his arms with each of her hands and held him there until she was sure he'd regained his equilibrium. "I am so sorry," she said.

His mysterious eyes locked on hers. He didn't acknowledge their collision or her apology. He simply looked inside her heart and soul.

She stood there, mesmerized.

After several seconds, he finally spoke—his voice, low and gruff. "I see him, too."

Her heart thudded. "You see who?"

"The boy. I see the president's son."

CHAPTER EIGHT

Neena stood in the hallway of the inn, unable to move as her mind tried to catalog all the ramifications of what Gus had just said.

I see him, too.

I see the president's son.

He swayed a bit to the left, though her hands were still on each of his arms. This close, he looked even older than she'd thought he was earlier.

"Do you need to sit down?" she asked. "Can we find a place to talk? Privately?"

"You missed our appointment today," he acknowledged.

"I know. I'm sorry. But it seems like we are...meant to talk." There was no way she could let today's slipup get in the way of learning more about this man. He was important to her both for the article and for the mysterious connection that pulsed between them.

He nodded slowly and jabbed a thumb toward the back staircase, which led down to the kitchen. "Outside. Go through the kitchen and out the back door."

She'd never been past the front part of the kitchen, where guests picked up their picnic lunches from big glass-front refrigerators or filled sports bottles from the silver urns of cold beverages. The bulk of the cooking took place on the other side of a single-door-sized opening that made it difficult for guests to see much. Still, she would figure out where she needed to go. She had to talk with this man, but she'd left Dwight in the dining room.

She'd meant to go only to the ladies' room and be right back to their table. But she couldn't leave Gus hanging for the second time in one day. There was too much at stake.

She motioned toward the dining room. "I've got a dinner companion. I need to tell him I'm not coming back, then I'll meet you down there. Will I be able to find you if I go through the kitchen?"

She couldn't interpret the look that crossed Gus's face. Disappointment? Skepticism? Mistrust? Something else? "I promise, I won't stand you up this time," she said.

Finally, he seemed convinced. "Go through the green door on the far side of the kitchen. There's a door to the outside beyond that. I'll be sitting behind the shed that's right out back. No one will hear us talking out there."

She lightly squeezed his arms and then let them go, a sign of camaraderie. "Okay. Give me five minutes."

He nodded, then turned and made his way toward the back staircase.

She'd have to figure out later what she'd tell Justin if word got back to him that she was snooping around behind one of the inn's sheds after dark. So many things could go wrong here, but there were too many unanswered questions. She had to know she wasn't going crazy each time she saw John's ghost. Maybe Gus had answers for her.

She went to the ladies' room as quickly as she could and made her way back to the table with Dwight. He smiled and stood as she approached.

"Listen," she said as she perched on the edge of her chair, not settling in like she had before. "I have to go talk to one of the employees."

His brow crinkled. "Right now?" He looked at his watch.

It had to be after eight o'clock. The sun had already gone down, and the dining room had mostly emptied. "I know it seems odd, but I accidentally stood him up earlier today and he wants to talk to me now. Outside." She immediately cringed, wishing she could take that last word back.

He frowned. "Is that safe? Maybe I should come with you."

Her heart warmed at his protectiveness. No one had treated her like that in years. She'd been on her own for decades, protecting both Rosie and herself from the world. She reached out and touched Dwight's hand. "He's about eighty years old. I'll be okay."

"I really don't mind. We could bring our drinks and—"

"No." Her voice was too loud. Too sharp.

He sat back a bit, surprised by her vehemence.

She quickly tried to soften her response. "I mean..." *Think, Neena, think.* "It's been a bit of a chore to get him to talk to begin with. I'm afraid if I show up with someone he's not expecting, especially after I missed our appointment earlier today, that maybe he'll clam up. Not talk to me at all. I really need him for my article." Unless Dwight saw ghosts, he wasn't invited to their soiree.

"I was really enjoying our evening together." There were possibilities in his gaze—promises of even more connection between them.

"Me, too." She hoped her smile conveyed how much she meant it. And how disappointed she was to have to bring their evening to a close. "But I've got to make this a killer article so I can get more assignments from this tough new editor." He didn't need to know how strapped for cash she was. How getting her income flowing again was so important. She rose. She couldn't keep Gus waiting. "Thank you. It was a lovely evening."

He gave a slight nod as he rose. "Good night, Neena."

She couldn't tell if he was angry or just resigned to the fact that she'd cut their time together short. Either way, she couldn't worry about that now.

As she made her way out of the dining room and toward the back staircase that would lead to the kitchen, a female employee came up the stairs, an armload of neatly folded linens, likely getting ready for breakfast tomorrow morning. Neena immediately cut her gait short and pretended to admire a painting on the wall. It would be odd for a guest to be entering the kitchen at this time of night, and she didn't want to raise any suspicions.

When the woman had passed, Neena rushed down the back staircase and through the kitchen. Thankfully, the only employees in the room had their backs to her, washing pots and pans in an oversized sink. She located the green door Gus had described and quickly slipped inside. It was some kind of mechanical room with pipes and furnaces and other equipment she didn't recognize. A single overhead bulb was all that lit the crowded, storeroom-type space. It looked to be about the size of a two-car garage, though with all the apparatus, she wasn't sure she could see the whole thing. She stood still, getting her bearings, then stepped around a metal shelving unit filled with tools. In a far corner of the room, another door was cracked open. In the thin opening, the bright moon shone through a curtain of Spanish moss. *Outside.* Was this Gus's signal to let her know the path to their meeting spot?

She looked around for other exits, but there didn't seem to be any, so she crept toward the open door and slowly pushed it open. The moonlight illuminated a gray wooden shed. A stooped, lone figure leaned against it.

Owls hooted overhead as Neena made her way the short distance to the shed, wondering what the gravel beneath her feet was doing to the only pair of black heels she owned. She couldn't afford new ones, so hopefully they weren't being torn up too badly.

By the time she'd made it to the building, Gus had moved to the other side, out of view from the inn. Two cut-up logs were arranged on end, making a stool for each of them.

He motioned for her to sit. "I figured we needed some privacy. To talk about the boy."

"The president's son?" she asked. She might as well use the phrase he'd used to describe John Jr., though she'd come to think of him as just "John."

"You're the only other person I've met who can see him."

"How do you know?" She wished she had her notebook. A good journalist should *always* have her notebook. But she hadn't known this meeting was going to take place. When she'd left her room, she'd thought she was having dinner with Dwight.

"I can't really explain it." He looked up into a nearby tree where an owl had just hooted. "I just know."

"Does he talk to you, too?"

"No." He still hadn't looked at her. It was like they were old friends, sitting beside a campfire with no need to gauge each other's expressions.

"He wants me to help him find his wife," she said.

Gus only nodded. It was as if he knew this already.

Then an idea struck her. "But I need to be working on my article, not out 'easing my soul burden' or whatever nonsense he thinks he's helping me with in exchange for finding her. That's why I was late for our meeting today. He had me out on some field trip. Do you think maybe you can help him find Carolyn?"

Gus scoffed. "No, ma'am."

"Why not?"

"I ain't seen her since the week they were married."

Her gaze snapped to his profile as her eyebrows rose. Her hunch had been right about interviewing him. Even if he protected the privacy of the island's most famous guests, his input on what had happened behind the scenes could make her article killer. She would show that little twerp Justin the quality of work a seasoned professional could produce.

Yes, her interview with Gus could be the centerpiece of her article, but that would be when they sat down for the official interview. When she had her notebook and her questions on hand. For now, they were talking about Carolyn. "But the wedding was more than two decades ago. So why is John looking for her here? Why not in New York, where they lived? Or off Martha's Vineyard where they..." She couldn't bring herself to say the word. *Where they died.*

Gus slowly turned to face Neena. The moon glinted in his eyes. "I'm pretty sure he's been waiting for you."

CHAPTER NINE

"**J**ohn has been waiting for *me*?" Neena repeated Gus's words back to him. Why the hell would the son of a slain president take such an interest in *her*? This was all so crazy. So inconceivable. She didn't even believe in ghosts.

"I hadn't seen him since last winter." The old man turned to her, his light blue eyes almost iridescent in the moonlight. "But he was in your room when I dropped off your luggage on your arrival day. Just sitting in one of the armchairs, waiting for you to get there."

"Did you talk to him?"

The old man shook his head. "I can't hear him. I only see him. And besides, I knew why he was there."

The Spanish moss hanging from the trees swayed as a breeze blew in from Cumberland Sound.

"So you think I should help him find Carolyn?" she asked.

He raised his hand to his chest. "I know how much it hurts to miss my own wife. And I think a person should help anyone who's in that much pain."

She thought about her own pain. How the deaths of Mama and Kevin had shaped her. How she'd never again be completely at peace.

An owl hooted nearby. Another one answered, giving her a chance to think about what all this might mean to her. To her ability to finish her article on time. She didn't need this distraction in her life, especially when her work was sure to be so closely scrutinized.

"She sure was a special lady," he said. He let out a short chuckle. "She loved Evangeline's apple fritters."

"I saw that y'all sell the mix in the gift shop."

"It was Evangeline's secret recipe." Pride brimmed in his voice, though Neena wasn't sure why. "Carolyn had one every day she was on the island. The kitchen staff mixed up the dry ingredients for her before she left. A sort of wedding gift from them. That gave them the idea to start selling bags of it in the gift shop."

Yes. This was exactly the kind of detail that would make Neena's story stand out. She'd read many other articles on the wedding, and none had included these kinds of specifics. This kind of charm. This simple man had seen so much over the years. "What else do you remember about her?"

"She was a beautiful bride. Graceful and poised, like a ballerina. And that boy was so smitten with her. He couldn't take his eyes off her whenever they were together."

"I can't believe the entire island kept their wedding a secret."

A dreamy, faraway look filled his eyes as he gazed out toward the river. "We all felt like we were part of something special. And I guess we were."

"I'm sorry I missed our meeting earlier. But I'd really like to set a new time—"

Footsteps crunched on the gravel behind them. They immediately quieted. An older couple, each with a glass of wine, chattered as they strolled in the moonlight.

"You should go," Gus said.

And then he disappeared around the corner of the shed without another word.

***

Neena opened her eyes to sunlight streaming around the edges of the blinds in her guest room. Ugh. Morning already.

She'd lain awake most of the night, thoughts of John and Gus and Dwight tumbling through her head like the balls in a bingo cage. Though John was a huge distraction, she had to admit that Gus was right. If she could ease his pain by helping him find Carolyn, then that's what she wanted to do, but only *after* her article was complete and ready to send to Justin the second she reached the mainland.

Only Gus had to do with her immediate goal: to write the best damn article she could and prove to Justin that she was worth keeping on board as a writer for the magazine.

Even so, she couldn't stop thinking about Dwight. He'd looked so disappointed last night when she'd had to leave dinner abruptly. Yes, he was an "extracurricular activity" amidst this important work assignment, but she met so few interesting men these days. Scratch that. She met so few interesting men *ever*. Granted, she was generally happy with her solitary life, but she wanted to find out more about him. To spend more time getting to know him. She'd learned last night that he'd moved to Hilton Head after he'd sold his company in Greenville. That meant he lived only three or four hours from Jacksonville, which opened up some...definite possibilities.

She pushed the luxurious duvet from her legs and slid off the high bed until her feet met the tapestry rug below it. She crossed the room to her messenger bag and pulled out her notebook and a pen.

Since an early age, she'd prided herself on taking charge of things. And since there would likely be other people around when she saw him at breakfast, she needed to be prepared.

Dwight –
Walking around the grounds this morning. Join me?
I'll leave from the front steps at 10 a.m.

Neena

She worked to justify this jaunt in her mind. She needed to walk around the grounds for her article anyway, right? And inviting Dwight along would perhaps make up for her abrupt departure last night. She owed him that much.

She took a quick shower, tucked the handwritten note in the pocket of her casual pants, and made her way to the coffee service and continental breakfast setup on the main floor. Though she'd wait a few more minutes until the hot breakfast was served, she peeked under the red-and-white-checkered napkin covering the basket of baked goods on the coffee stand. The homemade blueberry scones and banana bread looked delicious, but they weren't what she'd hoped to find: the apple fritters Gus had mentioned the night before. *Carolyn's favorites.* Just the first of many details she hoped to learn from Gus as she crafted an article that would blow Justin—and the magazine's readers—away.

She stepped aside as two couples entered the small room and prepared themselves cups of coffee and hot tea. They exchanged morning pleasantries and encouraged her to join them at the communal table, which was around the corner in the next room.

"I'm...ummmm...waiting for someone," she said and immediately felt foolish. The server had told her yesterday there were only about fifteen guests at the inn, so it would be completely obvious that she was hanging around the coffee station hoping to connect with Dwight.

"You're sure, honey?" the women asked, a look of pity in her eyes. "He can join us at the main table when he comes to breakfast." She lowered her voice to a whisper. "Sometimes you need to play hard to get."

Busted.

Neena's face heated. She forced herself not to become defensive. Instead, she pasted on a smile. "I'd love to join you. Thank you."

They'd finished the starter—small glasses of a creamy mango smoothie—and were diving into delicious fluffy buttermilk pancakes and bacon when Dwight and his brother entered the dining room. Though Neena had been sure to position herself near a couple of empty chairs at the communal table, the brothers made their way to the private table where Neena and Dwight had dined together the night before. There'd been no promise between them of more time spent together, but it still felt like a rejection. She concentrated on adding butter and syrup to her pancakes as she tried to hide her disappointment from the other diners at her table.

The woman who'd invited Neena to join them patted her arm—a small show of support that only made Neena feel more exposed. Luckily, Neena's back was to Dwight, so she didn't have to pretend she wasn't watching him throughout the meal. She tried to participate in the discussion at the table as much as she could, but her nervousness made it hard to follow the conversation.

When she and the others at her table had finished their breakfast, she rose and went to the coffee station for another cup of coffee. As she returned to her seat, her gaze met Dwight's. They exchanged a smile, but she couldn't read anything into it. He might have given that same friendly-but-generic smile to any of the other guests.

She sat at her table and semi-listened as her fellow diners discussed which inn-sponsored tours they'd be joining that day. The morning tour would take them to Dungeness, the ruins of Lucy Carnegie's mansion that had been ravaged by fire in 1959. The afternoon tour would take them to The Settlement and the church where she'd first seen John.

"I remember when the pictures from the Kennedy wedding were published." The woman's voice had a dreamy quality. "I can't believe they kept it a secret."

"I heard there's a guy who lives right off of Main Road who thinks everyone going to that end of the island is really there to spy on him," the man next to her said.

A sixty-something woman rolled her eyes. "Like he's more interesting than John F. Kennedy Jr."

The others laughed.

"I read an article on the internet about that guy. Said he was crazy smart," another man said.

The woman scoffed. "Crazy being the operative word in that sentence."

The first man spoke up again. "Invented some computer hardware that made him millions."

Neena listened to their conversation until her phone pinged with a text. Justin: *Call me right away.*

That sounded ominous. She instinctively glanced at the others around the table, as if their conversation might be related to whatever he wanted to talk to her about. But that was her natural reaction—taking in her surroundings when a threat presented itself. Of course they had nothing to do with Justin or the office politics going on back in Jacksonville.

As soon as there was a slight break in the conversation, she jumped in. "I need to run, but it was nice having breakfast with y'all." She smiled, happy to have joined them. They exchanged pleasantries as she rose.

But she still had the note in her pocket. She was only there for a few days, which meant limited time to connect with Dwight.

She took one step toward the exit to the dining room, then stopped—unwilling to allow herself to chicken out. She turned and walked straight to his table in the back corner of the room.

His face brightened as she approached. "Neena." He smiled.

"Dwight." She gave him a nervous smile and nodded a greeting to his brother. She held up her phone. "I've got to call my boss right away, but here." She pulled the note from her pocket, tucked it under the silverware at his place setting, and turned, exiting the room before he had a chance to read it.

CHAPTER TEN

Neena stepped onto the veranda of the IvyLena, closing the massive front door behind her. She made her way to one end of the long porch, hoping for some privacy in case any other guests came out there after finishing breakfast.

What could Justin want that was so urgent? If her financial situation wasn't so desperate, his pushy text message would have annoyed her. One of the benefits of being a freelancer was that she could complete her projects independently, without having to be at the beck and call of a boss who might need her at any moment. She loathed that she was now at the mercy of this kid.

She pushed the button to dial his number.

"Neena." His tone sounded urgent. "I've been waiting for your call."

"I called you as quickly as I could. What's up?" She hated that her voice shook. She missed the confident Neena from her past. From before Kevin had died. From before her first panic attack. From before Nancy and Lori and Jeff had been fired.

"One of the sales reps told me about your hospital stay." His tone was accusatory. Aggressive.

She sucked in a breath. This was not a conversation she'd planned to have with him. Ever. Her hospital stay was none of his damn business. Besides, it could give him another reason to get rid of her. "And?"

"I had no idea about it. I mean, I knew your brother had died. But you having a nervous breakdown is an entirely different matter."

"That's not what it was. And besides, I'm fine now. Working hard to write a great story." She added pep to her voice. A way to convince him that what she said was true.

"Mackenzie can be there before nightfall if you need someone to take over."

One of the recent college grads who'd interned at the magazine during the spring semester. "Why would I need that?"

He scoffed. "Because you had to be Baker Acted after your brother died?" he said, referring to Florida's Baker Act, which allowed for temporary, involuntary detention in a mental health facility if family members or others feared a person might harm themselves or someone else. "Because you couldn't handle it on your own?"

"I was in the hospital voluntarily. I called the ambulance myself. I thought I was having a heart attack."

Justin snorted on the other end of the line.

Shouldn't someone so young be a little more understanding about mental health issues? He'd grown up in an era when they were talked about more openly than during her generation. "I don't need anyone to take over for me."

"You'd better not let me down, Neena." His voice held a warning tone. "The editorial board pressured me into having someone write this story—the cover story, no less—and they've asked about it a couple of times. It's like the one topic they know anything about, so they're extra-invested in it." *The old coots*, she could almost hear him say under his breath.

She smiled and nodded as the newlyweds walked out the front door and down the wide steps to the front lawn. She didn't want them to hear her arguing. "You've made your point," she said into the phone in a gentle, conversational tone. "Is there anything else I can help you with?"

"You give some more thought to Mackenzie taking over for you. I will *not* look bad because of you." He hung up the phone before either could say goodbye.

She held her phone to her chest and closed her eyes as she tried to regain her composure. She felt flighty. Unmoored, whereas she liked to be grounded. In control. To always have a plan for whatever came next. She took in several deep breaths and did the visualization exercise that Carla had taught her. *A meadow. Butterflies. Songbirds.*

She could go sit in one of the Adirondack chairs that faced the river, but she hated that Justin's ire had polluted her morning with such negative thoughts. This beautiful place should remain quiet and tranquil and undisturbed by the outside world. It should certainly not be filled with worry over the ageism that awaited her back in Jacksonville.

She decided to go lie on her bed while she centered herself some more. Besides, she'd need to brush her teeth and put on more lipstick in case Dwight met her for the walk she'd invited him on around the grounds—another reason to be anything but calm.

Forty-five minutes later, she slipped out the front door again. The woman with the auburn hair stood on the veranda at the top of the wide staircase, looking as radiant and put-together as she had the night before. She wore bike shorts and a green V-neck, body-hugging tee that made the brilliant color of her hair stand out even more. A single thick braid cascaded past her collarbone.

"Good morning," the woman said with a dazzling smile.

Neena returned the greeting.

"It's that way to the garden, right?" The woman pointed toward the left. "We're doing the tour at ten."

"I think it's not too far that way. Just follow the road." Neena moved to the closest rocking chair, positioning herself to see Dwight at the bottom of the big staircase if he chose to show up.

The large screen door opened, and the woman's auburn-haired daughter stepped onto the porch. Her legs had that long, gangly look of a girl who had not yet begun to fill out. She handed her mother a floppy sun hat, and the pair made their way down the wide staircase. Neena wondered what a different person she might have been had her family had the wealth to vacation in places like this. How might Rosie be different if she'd grown up accustomed to this lifestyle? No wonder rich people felt entitled. Their breadth of experiences—of moving through life with such ease—must give a comfort and confidence that the rest of the world wasn't privy to.

Neena watched as the pair got farther away from her. A pang of jealousy radiated through her chest when the girl slipped her hand into her mother's. Their faint, laughter-filled voices floated through the air like the tinkling of a faraway wind chime.

It had been years since Rosie had held Neena's hand. Years since they'd shared the easy camaraderie these two seemed to effortlessly radiate. How had Neena let such distance grow between them? How could she recapture the closeness they'd once had? How could she help Rosie see that her current boyfriend didn't treat her the way she deserved to be treated?

A head of dark hair came into view at ground level. Dwight made his way to the bottom of the staircase in front of her, a small pack strapped to his back. She stilled. Though her nerves thrummed, she didn't want to look overeager about his arrival. Maybe he wasn't even here to go with her on her walking tour of the grounds. Maybe he would tell her he wasn't interested in going. Or wasn't interested, period.

"Neena." He raised a hand and bounded up the stairs toward her.

She breathed a sigh of relief at his enthusiasm, then stood and smiled. "Hello again."

"I haven't been passed a note from a cute girl since third grade," he teased.

She suddenly felt embarrassed by her action. "What did your brother say about all that?" The overly serious Carl probably thought she'd been childish. Or too desperate. Or both.

Dwight waved a dismissive hand. "I think he's happy I've found someone to hang out with so I'll leave him alone."

"So you're going with me this morning?"

He gave a quick frown, like there was never any doubt about it. "Of course. But let's start at the dock. I've got something to show you."

***

Neena was already sweating as the dirt road curved its way toward the dock. The walk was only the equivalent of three or four city blocks, but the October air was hot and steamy.

Dwight stopped and placed a hand on her arm before she took her first step onto the wood planks of the dock. "Step quietly."

She gave him a quizzical look.

"You'll see in a second," he said as he crept gingerly out over the water. When they reached the railing at the end, he brought his forefinger to his lips—the quiet sign—and then pointed downward.

Below them, two manatees lay nearly motionless in the water. The bigger one munched soundlessly on seagrass.

"I saw them here yesterday at about this time," Dwight whispered. "I think they're a mama and her baby."

"That's one big baby," Neena said. The smaller one was the size and shape of a tall Oompa Loompa.

"Okay. Maybe he's a teenager."

The mother had large slashes of scar tissue on her back.

"I hate that they get hit by propellers so often," Neena said.

Dwight nodded. "It's my first time seeing one in the wild in years. Carl and I used to see them all the time when we were kids. My grandparents had a place on a spring down near Tampa."

She turned to look at him, pleased to be getting to know a bit more about him. "Do they still live down there?"

He looked at her, too. "Nah. They passed away years ago. We held on to their place for a long time but ended up having to sell it."

"Too much to take care of all the way from South Carolina?"

He quickly moved his gaze to the horizon. "There were...extenuating circumstances."

Neena lowered her head to watch the manatees, not wanting to stare at him. She remained silent, though, hoping he'd fill in some details.

"Let's start our tour of the grounds," he said eventually and headed from the dock back toward land.

He turned to wait for her near the line of trees that rimmed the island. "Which way, boss?" he said when she'd reached him. Clearly their previous conversation was over.

She pointed to the opposite end of the large round oval that made up the grounds of the inn. On the other side, the dirt road disappeared into a canopy of trees. "I thought we'd see where that road goes, if you're up for that."

"Are you going to protect me from all the forest animals?" he joked.

She laughed. "I guess, if you need protection."

They took off walking in the direction she'd pointed, veering away from each other every so often when a pile of horse manure lay in the middle of the dirt road.

"I didn't see you on any of the tours yesterday," he said. "They were pretty interesting."

"I had a daylong tour from a local historian earlier. Something my office had arranged before I got here. I guess they didn't want me to miss anything."

"So you saw Dungeness and Plum Orchard and all that?"

She nodded. "And the Stafford House and The Settlement."

"I could almost see JFK Jr. getting married in that church," he said.

She sucked in a breath. Had Dwight seen John when he'd visited the church, too? "Do you think he's still there?"

Dwight cocked his head, his brow furrowed. "Do I think he's still at the church?"

She shrugged, trying to look casual. "Still there or maybe he visits every now and then?"

He gave a good-natured chuckle. "Maybe you should write fantasy novels instead of travel articles."

"What? You don't believe in ghosts?" She was still testing him. Had he seen something inside that church?

His voice got quieter. More serious. "I believe the people who are a part of us are always with us, even after they're gone, like my grandparents. But I'd call them spirits rather than ghosts." He placed his palm over his heart as he spoke, then slowly lowered it. "But that doesn't include any Kennedys—dead or alive. At least for me, anyway," he said with a teasing smile.

The ground crunched underneath their feet as they walked in silence. So Dwight hadn't seen John. Maybe John had appeared to her because her family had always had such close ties to his? Because her mother and father had once worked on his father's presidential campaign? Granted, none of the existing Kennedys would even know who her family was, but that didn't mean her family hadn't followed them closely over the years.

Dwight broke the silence. "What about you? Do you believe in ghosts or spirits or whatever?"

"I agree that our loved ones stay with us. Like some part of them is alive inside us." At least the original Kevin was still with her. The little boy who used to make her cook him grilled cheese sandwiches and who broke his arm the first time he'd ever tried to skateboard. Not the strung-out Kevin who would show up on her doorstep from time to time as an adult. That wasn't the real Kevin. That was someone who'd been lost. Unable to find his way back to who he really was. It had broken her heart.

She was about to ask him what other spirits were still with him when he placed his fingertips on her forearm, gently encouraging her to stop walking. He pointed to a stand of trees not far to their left. A white horse and a brown horse stood watching them, their ears perked on high alert.

"They're beautiful," she whispered.

"Those two were at the inn yesterday. Right out front, by the stairs. Someone said they're brothers."

"They look pretty healthy for wild horses, but I also feel kind of sorry for them out here having to make it on their own."

"Hey, they're living on this beautiful island and we're not." His playful gaze flitted briefly to hers, then returned to the horses.

She studied his features as he watched the animals—his strong, freshly shaven jaw; the narrow nose; the little sunbursts on the outside of each eye, more tan lines than crow's feet.

The horses went back to grazing, no longer disturbed by the presence of people.

"Should we keep walking?" Dwight whispered.

She nodded and they took off down the dirt road.

The farther they got from the inn, the more magical the forest became. Small fields of palmettos filled the spaces between stately live oaks. Spanish moss seemed to drip from every available limb, making the place feel like they'd landed in a fairy tale or maybe Middle Earth. The trees and foliage were so dense that in many places not much sun reached the shadowy forest floor. There were no buildings or other people in sight. The quietness was a reminder of how remote they were.

Their conversation veered in several directions as they got to know each other—where they'd gone to college, what they did in their spare time, whether or not each was a good cook. When they talked about their most embarrassing moments, he'd good-naturedly admitted that he'd been beaten up by a girl in the middle school cafeteria. His deep laughter rolled across the lush undergrowth as she told him about the time she'd accidentally wet her pants while laughing too hard on a first date.

He reached out to hold her hand but released it when he pointed to a bright red fungus growing up the side of a tree. He had an eye for the minute details of nature. Honed, he said, by a love of photography—a hobby he wished he'd taken more time to develop over the years. Several times, he veered off the dirt road to get close to a tree or a fern or a fungus, studying the texture and architecture of each plant before rejoining her on their walk.

They finally decided to turn around when they reached a sign that read Private Property—No Trespassing. Presumably one of the few private residences on the island was on down the road, probably overlooking the river. What would it be like to have a home in such an enchanted place?

Neena hated to head back toward the inn. This had been the first time in years that she had felt like her old self. Like a carefree woman rather than a mom or a sole breadwinner or the responsible older sister. Somehow, their carefree afternoon together had allowed her to just be Neena, without the burden of responsibilities and unpaid bills and a new mental illness to grapple with. She wanted to feel like that forever.

Maybe John was right. Maybe she did have a soul burden. Maybe the burdens of life had been with her for so long she hadn't even realized the weight she'd been carrying.

But she didn't want to think about any of that. She wanted to enjoy her time with the handsome man beside her.

Dwight stopped. "Look at that." He pointed to an old tree whose lower branches grew perpendicular to the ground, snaking along a couple of feet above it. But the part he pointed to was a lush, gorgeous fern that grew partway up its trunk.

"What's the white stuff up high?" she asked.

"I don't know," he said. "Let's go look."

She tromped with him about twenty feet through the forest, trying not to think about what kinds of creatures might be lurking beneath the undergrowth. When they reached the tree, she could see that the fern gave way to stairsteps of white mushroom shelves that reached thirty or forty feet up the trunk. The beauty and wonder of nature. She wished she was as adaptable and resilient as these organisms that found a way to thrive in such a hot and shadow-filled environment.

Dwight stood behind her as they studied this newfound specimen. His closeness was both comforting and exhilarating. His warm breath tickled the back of her neck. He didn't quite touch her, but she wished he would.

She turned to face him, looking up into his dark brown eyes. "I'm glad you came with me today," she said.

He glanced down at her lips and drew in a deep breath. His hand rose and cupped her elbow. He took a step closer and lowered his face to hers. "I'm glad you invited me."

Chapter Eleven

Neena's eyes drifted closed as Dwight's lips brushed hers.

"Is this okay?" he asked in a whisper. His breath was minty.

"Yes," she said without opening her eyes. She didn't want to make any movement that might cause her warm exhilaration to end.

His hand glided from her elbow up her arm as his lips settled on hers. She felt like a character from a fairy tale, kissing a prince in the middle of this enchanted forest. These feelings—his touch, this place, this magic—were all that mattered in the moment.

He took a tiny step forward and deepened the kiss. A low moan escaped from her throat. It had been years since she'd felt this desirable. She'd always known she didn't need a man to complete her, but this feeling was so damn *good*.

He slowly pulled away and gave a sly half-grin. "This spot is my favorite on the island so far."

An intoxicating daze muddled her mind, and she was pretty certain she had a goofy smile on her face. "Mine, too."

"So what is it—maybe three hours from Hilton Head to Jacksonville?"

She liked that he was already thinking about how they could spend time together after they left Cumberland Island. "Something like that."

"Maybe I can drive down and take you to dinner sometime."

"I'd like that." But three hours was a long way to come just for dinner. Would he expect to spend the night with her? Or maybe he would get a hotel room? She wouldn't sleep with him so early in their relationship, so would it be awkward to set him up in Rosie's bedroom? She had no idea how all that was supposed to work. But she'd worry about it later. For now, she simply wanted to enjoy spending time with him.

"We can figure out a date when we're back at the inn," he said. "But for now, we have a forest to explore." The mischievous look on his face made him look much younger than his—what?—fifty or sixty years? She'd need to ask how old he was.

He took her hand and gently led her back toward the dirt road. Once they got there, he didn't release it but kept his fingers intertwined with hers as they talked about the technology company he'd built and sold, her years at Florida State University, and the woodworking shop he'd set up for himself in an outbuilding on his current property.

Her heart sank as they reached the edge of the forest. The vast back lawn of the inn lay before them. Her time with Dwight today would soon be over.

As they approached the mansion, he pulled his phone from his pocket and looked at the time. "The picnic lunches should be ready by now. You want to go grab ours from the fridge and sit under that big tree out front to eat them?"

She laughed. Breakfast had been just two hours ago. This place had fabulous food. "I'm still full of buttermilk pancakes. And besides, I've got to get to work." No way would she provide Justin a reason to stop giving her assignments for *Coastal South Travel.*

"Yeah. Carl's probably worried you kidnapped me or something," he teased.

"And you should at least try to have lunch with him, since you *did* come to the island together."

He glanced away, like he was unwilling to let her see his eyes at that moment. He seemed more hurt by his brother's constant working than he admitted out loud. "I'm glad you invited me this morning," he said when he'd looked back in her direction.

Her face heated a bit as she recalled her boldness in passing him the note in the dining room, but she was glad she'd taken the risk. Glad she'd slipped it under his silverware before she'd rushed outside to call Justin.

Justin.

Her dreamlike morning snapped to an end. She was no longer part of a fairy tale set inside a magical forest. She was the regular old Neena again, with her near-zero bank account and the twenty-seven-year-old boss who likely wanted to fire her. "Thanks for joining me." She nodded, then pointed toward the inn. "I've got to go check in with the manager on something."

"Then I'm headed back to the carriage house. I'll see you later?"

"Sure," Neena said, then watched him walk away before heading inside the inn.

She was glad to find Claire, the inn's bookkeeper/manager, sitting at her desk in the gift shop.

"Ah. Ms. Lee," the woman said when Neena entered. "I've got good news for you."

Thank God. Neena needed all the help she could get to write the best damn article possible. "Oh? What is it?"

Claire smiled. "Gus is coming over to meet with you later this afternoon. He'll be on the ferry that should arrive around 3 p.m."

***

Neena and Gus seemed to have an unspoken pact as Claire introduced them to each other that afternoon: to act as if they hadn't met before.

Because there was no way they could explain the connection they had. That they both saw the dead son of an assassinated president.

"I thought we'd go out to the table under the big oak out back." Neena pointed toward the sprawling lawn behind the inn. Claire had suggested they meet in the library, but if they did that, someone standing in the entry hall at the foot of the stairs would be able to overhear their conversation. Out on the lawn, they'd at least be able to see other guests approaching. Gus was valuable to her for the article she was writing, but she also wanted to ask him some more about seeing John.

Gus shrugged. "Fine by me, ma'am. Wherever you'd like to sit."

"Well, I'll be here at my desk," Claire said. "You two let me know if you need anything,"

Neena wasn't certain if she should help Gus down the wide front stairs that led from the veranda to the lawn. He was certainly old and stooped, but she'd also seen him hauling firewood, luggage, and a wheelbarrow full of plants out in the garden. No, best to let him walk on his own, though she remained close beside him in case he stumbled.

When they'd gotten settled at the sturdy wooden table under the Spanish moss, she took a deep breath. Everything about this article was important. "I'd like to focus the bulk of our conversation on your experiences at the inn. I've got a really important article to write, and I think you can help me with details that haven't been covered in other publications."

He nodded. "I'm fine with that."

"I mean, we need to talk about how we both see...a ghost...but I can't include that in my article." Not with a boss who already thought she was unstable.

Again, Gus nodded. "I don't suspect John would want you to."

"Have you ever been interviewed by a reporter before?"

He chuckled. "No, ma'am."

Score. She may have hit gold with Gus. An angle not covered by the *New York Times, Southern Living, Garden and Gun,* and all the other publications that had covered the island and/or the wedding. But the problem was that he didn't seem to be someone who offered a lot of information. She'd need to get him talking if this was going to be a fruitful interview. "Okay, well, I'd like to ask you questions about your time at the inn, but if you think of something interesting that I don't ask about, tell me about it anyway, okay?"

"Yes, ma'am."

She opened her notebook to the first page of questions she'd written in advance, each with room to write his answer below it. "Tell me why you've stayed working at the inn for as long as you have."

He shrugged. "I'm not sure what else I'd do. It's what I know. These people are like family."

"Claire said you started working here when it first became an inn in the early sixties." Claire had also told her that he'd grown up in St. Marys, Georgia, which was just across the river on the mainland. "That would have made you pretty young at the time."

"Twenty-two years old."

"Had you been to college or in the military or anything like that?" The Navy's Kings Bay Submarine Base, across the sound from Cumberland Island, was visible from the dock, but it hadn't been built until the late 1970s.

He got a faraway look in his eyes. "I always wanted to be a Marine, but my daddy died when I was nine. Mama did everything she could for us, but I stopped going to school after eighth grade so I could make money to help buy food for my brothers and sisters. There were six of us kids, and I was the oldest."

So he'd been forced to become the man of the house when he wasn't even ten years old? What a shame to be limited by those circumstances. As beautiful a place as this was, becoming a Marine would have opened the world for him. Instead, he'd spent his entire life in the same little corner of coastal Georgia. "That's a tough blow." To see his career gone before it ever got started.

He shrugged. "It is what it is." He had a peace about him, like someone who was content with what life had dealt him.

"Do your siblings still live around here, too?"

"I got one sister still alive. She's in a nursing home in Valdosta."

"Did you ever marry?" Or maybe he still had a wife?

A slight grin crossed his face, then disappeared. "My sweet Evangeline. We were married forty-seven years. She passed in 2010."

"Evangeline? As in 'Evangeline's Apple Fritters'?"

His smile broadened. "The one and only."

"She worked at the inn?" Maybe that's how the two of them had met?

He shook his head. "Nah, but she was the best baker in Camden County. *Everyone* wanted some of her pastries, but the IvyLena was the only place that ever convinced her to bake for them. They had kind of an in with her because of me." He winked at Neena. "She'd get up before dawn and make a batch every day, then I'd bring them to the inn when I came over on the ferry. Wrapped all up in a towel to keep them warm." He chuckled. "It was hard not to eat them on the ride over."

"Tell me about her."

He looked out into the trees before him. "She was the most beautiful woman I'd ever seen. Well, she wasn't a woman when we first met. We were in third grade at the time. But later, she was the first and only girl I ever asked out on a date. Her daddy didn't want her to go out with me since I didn't have any money, but she was strong-willed." He chuckled. "If Evangeline set her mind to something, it was going to happen."

How did a man who was so clearly in love with his wife deal with that loss? Maybe if Neena knew the secret, she could learn to cope with Kevin being gone. Hell, for that matter, she wasn't even certain she had ever learned to cope with Mama's death.

He scrubbed his hand down his face. "She died of ovarian cancer. That's one of the reasons I've stayed working at the IvyLena for so long. They were good to me during all those months I was by her side. It was like she held on because she was worried about me. But I finally told her to let go. That I'd be okay without her."

Neena let the silence sit between them for a few seconds, allowing him to treasure his wife's memory.

He took out a handkerchief and wiped his nose.

"Did y'all have any children?" she asked.

"Two girls and a boy."

"And where are they now?"

He fidgeted in his seat. "The girls both live near Atlanta. Moved there right after college. My boy, he—" Gus's voice cracked. "He was in the navy. His helicopter crashed during a training mission out in California in the mid-nineties."

"Wow. I'm so sorry. You've been through a lot." Yet Gus kept going. He'd faced these hardships throughout his life and he just kept chugging along. His calm demeanor conveyed peace and acceptance. Perhaps there was a lesson there for her to learn. Perhaps that's what this week was about—putting her nose back into her work and moving forward, just as Gus had done.

"I thought we were going to talk about the inn," he said.

She smiled. "Oh, we are. But a little background information is always helpful." Details like how the employees at the inn had become his family would make her article richer. On the other hand, she didn't want to make him uncomfortable. He had, after all, returned to the island on his day off to talk to her.

"I don't mind you knowing about me and my family," he said. "I just don't think anyone wants to read about me."

"Fair enough," she said. "Tell me how the inn differs today than what it was in, say, the 1960s or 70s."

He chuckled. "Our goal is to keep it the same—the service, the food, the antiques. We want people to feel like they've stepped back in time."

"I read an article from the *New York Times* that said the IvyLena was 'overflowing with nature, good food, and old-world charm.'"

He nodded. "That's the idea."

The place didn't even have Wi-Fi—just one way they preserved their separation from the hubbub of everyday life. "What memories stand out most about life at the inn?"

"I can't talk about the guests who've been here. We protect their privacy."

She'd overheard one of the older couples saying that Tom Hanks had stayed there over the last several months. "Understood. But what memories do you have that aren't specific to any one guest? For example, has a hurricane ever blown through? Has anyone had to make an emergency trip to the mainland for dinner ingredients the chef realized she desperately needed? How long does it take a plumber to get here? How do you bring it all together so seamlessly? Things like that."

He smiled and settled back in his chair. "Now those things, I can talk about."

They spent the next couple of hours with him telling her about life at the inn. How he knew which job applicants over the years were cut out for work on this remote island and which were best to move on to another opening somewhere else. How there was never any question about some of the core tenets of each stay: communal dinner, a set menu, dinner jackets for the men, honor bar on the main floor, fresh produce and flowers from the garden at each meal. The inn had been farm-to-table decades before it had become a trend.

He told stories of lavish weddings, uncharacteristic cold snaps, close calls with hurricanes, and—rarely—guests who'd stepped too close to one of the wild horses and gotten kicked. Most of the other staff members performed multiple functions—meal prep, housekeeping, serving meals—but he had his own list of chores. He liked being alone. Being outside. Chopping firewood. Helping the gardener. Every employee had their assignments that kept the back-of-the-house at the inn running smoothly.

One of his assignments had always been to make sure that the seating areas under the large live oaks remained ready for guests. Sometimes that included wiping off rainwater from the chairs so guests could sit. Sometimes it meant putting the tables and chairs back in order after a larger group had pulled them together.

"That's how I first met him. Back when he was alive. A few of his family members stayed here the couple of days leading up to his wedding. I went out there one night at about dusk," he said. "Wanted to make sure everything was in order for the next morning. And there he sat, all by himself."

"He?" Neena asked.

"The boy. The president's son."

It was Gus's first mention of the week she was here to write about. Her skin tingled in anticipation of what he might share. "Did you talk to him?"

"He jumped up and apologized, like he was in the way or something. Such a nice kid."

John would have been in his thirties at the time, but perhaps to Gus, he *had* been a kid. "And what did you say?"

"I told him to sit back down and asked if there was anything I could do for him. I think he just needed some alone time, you know? Most of the wedding party was down at the Greyfield, and it may have all been a bit…" Gus studied the front of the inn, as if searching for the right word. "Overwhelming."

She wondered if John's standard for "overwhelming" was different from the average person's. He'd met heads of state, been followed by paparazzi since he was a child, mingled with the rich and famous. Yet making a lifetime commitment to another person would be a huge deal for anyone.

Gus continued. "He asked if I was married."

Her journalist's radar went up. This was the kind of anecdote that would be perfect for her story. "Go on."

"I said I was, so he asked me my top three tips for a happy marriage. Can you imagine? Me, a plain old guy from coastal Georgia giving marriage tips to an American royal?"

"What were your tips?"

"Let me see if I can remember." Gus looked up at the Spanish moss above their heads as he thought. "I probably said something about always making your wife feel special. Always making time for her. Always helping out around the house. Never boozing or chasing other women. That sort of thing. We chatted for a bit, but then one of his cousins came around the corner and dragged him back down to the Greyfield."

"So much for his alone time," she said.

Gus nodded as he picked at a spot of tree sap on the tabletop. "So much for his alone time."

"What else do you remember about that week?"

Gus seemed to think a minute, then looked up. "This isn't that week, but you'll probably find it interesting: Camden County law requires that a person be present to get a marriage license. So one day about a month before the wedding, this buddy of mine who works as a clerk at the Camden County courthouse told his supervisor he needed to take a longer-than-normal lunch hour because he had a dentist appointment, but the supervisor denied the request. My buddy asks again because he doesn't want to no-show on the dentist, ya know? But the supervisor just keeps saying no, even though that's the kind of request she normally wouldn't think twice about. My buddy's madder than a hornet but calls ole Doc Carson to cancel the appointment. Then a couple of hours later, in walks John F. Kennedy Jr. there to get his marriage certificate. The supervisor just turns to my buddy and winks. She'd *known* they were about to have a celebrity in the office and didn't want my buddy to miss it."

A server approached from the inn with a tray in her hand. Gus gave Neena a slight shake of his head. A sign that she was not to let on that he'd told her these things?

"Claire wanted me to bring you some refreshments," the young woman said.

"Thank you," Neena said. She pulled back the red-and-white-checkered napkin that covered the basket. She waited for the young woman to get far enough away from their table before she spoke again. "Are these the apple fritters you were telling me about the other day?"

He leaned forward and peered inside, then nodded. "Evangeline's recipe. The ones Carolyn liked so much."

Neena broke off a corner of one of the pastries and placed it in her mouth. The delicious crunch of the outside gave way to a fluffy, sweet inside filled with apples and cinnamon. No wonder they were Carolyn's favorites.

Neena had a lot of material for her article, so this was as good a time as any to talk about the other topic they needed to discuss. "When did you first see John? I mean, after he died?"

"New Year's Eve, 1999." The memory seemed to subdue Gus, rather than excite him.

"You know the exact date?"

"It's a pretty big deal when you see your first ghost."

Indeed, it was. She knew that all too well. "That's almost six months after he died. Was he looking for Carolyn then, too?"

Gus opened his mouth, then closed it. She stayed silent, waiting for him to speak. Journalists learn early on that people often rush to fill awkward silences. She needed Gus to tell her what he knew.

"I can't hear him talk. I'm pretty sure that's why he's been waiting for you." He inclined his head in her direction.

"Did he come that night because of Y2K?" The upcoming change to a new century had been a big deal back then. Programmers had worked for months to get computers and software to accept a date that didn't start with a 19. Some people had even claimed the world would end that night.

Gus shook his head.

"Then what did he do?" she asked. "Why do you think he made himself visible to you on that particular night?"

"You know what? You're right. I think he was looking for his wife." Gus's gaze darted away.

He was purposefully avoiding her. He was *lying*. Neena *knew* it. She'd long ago learned to tell when a source was withholding information. "And how do you know that, especially if you can't hear him talk?"

Gus looked at his watch, then rose. "The ferry leaves in a few minutes. It's the last one leaving the island today. Best I get on down to the dock."

She placed a hand on his arm. "You're not telling me the entire story. About the night you first saw his ghost."

"I've got to go, Ms. Lee." He shook her hand loose and scuttled off down the dirt road toward the river.

Chapter Twelve

Neena sat on the back lawn of the inn, still trying to make sense of Gus's quick departure from their meeting. Her old interviewing skills had kicked in, increasing her confidence that maybe the old Neena was back, but then he'd stood and rushed away. The hastiness of it all had made her nerves stand on edge.

After sharing so much about the inn and the week of the Kennedy-Bessette wedding, Gus was clearly hiding something about the night he'd first seen John's ghost. He'd been too evasive. Too fidgety when she'd tried to find out the rest of the story.

But she couldn't concentrate on that now. The most important thing was that he'd shared a lot of good, behind-the-scenes information for her to include in her story. The outline of an article was forming in her head. It would be less about the beauty of Cumberland Island—a topic that had been widely covered before—and more about what it takes to pull off the genteel charm of the IvyLena Inn. A behind-the-scenes look that hadn't been covered in any of the other articles she'd read in preparation for her visit here.

She remained on the lawn, filling in her notes while her memory of the interview was still fresh in her mind. She thanked the server when the young woman came back to retrieve the tray of refreshments.

Neena returned to her room a half hour later, hoping to get about an hour's worth of work done before dinner. She hadn't been this eager to write an article in ages. It was good to have the excitement zinging through her body again, especially after all those weeks feeling unmoored after Kevin's death.

But when she went to the dresser to retrieve her laptop, she stilled. The bottom drawer—the drawer that had been stuck when she had unpacked her suitcase—was ajar.

She quickly stood and looked behind her, toward the door to her room. Had someone been in here while she was out on the front lawn with Gus? The guest room doors, after all, had no exterior locks on them—just antique doorknobs that were likely original to the mansion. She'd had total trust in this place and its inhabitants, but still, there was no denying what she saw in front of her.

Panic zipped through her body. She closed her eyes and took three long breaths, just as her therapist had taught her to. But she had to see what—if anything—was missing. The most valuable item in the room was her laptop. She pulled it out from under the clothes in the middle drawer. *Still there.*

A thief might also go for jewelry. She opened the top drawer and pulled out the little case that held her earrings. None of them were valuable, but they were all still there.

She crept to the bathroom and pulled aside the curtain on the old clawfoot tub. *No one.* She returned to the bedroom and checked under the bed. In the closet. Behind the drapery. *No one.*

She walked slowly back toward the dresser and peered inside the bottom drawer. There was something in there. A dark rectangular thing. She pulled at the handles. The drawer slid open with ease.

Her hand flew to her mouth. She let out an involuntary gasp at what she saw inside the drawer: the phone belonging to Ethan, the teenager she'd met on the beach. The case with the neon green skull she'd seen when he'd dropped the phone in the sand. She reached in and carefully grasped it with only her thumb and forefinger, as if she didn't want to taint the evidence at a crime scene. Slowly, she rotated her arm so she could see the front. Cracks fanned out from a break in the upper right corner, just like Ethan's had been.

How had it gotten there? Instinctively, she turned and looked around the room again—her body's natural reaction to potential predators. *No one.*

She lowered herself into the upholstered chair near the dresser. Her legs shook. Maybe this was the universe telling her that her discussions with Ethan weren't over? That she needed to engage with him again? Her mind whirred, trying to figure it all out.

Then it hit her. This had nothing to do with the universe in general.

This had everything to do with John.

John had been in her room.

John wanted her to return the phone to Ethan.

Her last conversation with the boy had been a bust, but now even her own intuition seemed to agree. Ethan still needed help. And she was apparently the person who was supposed to make that happen.

***

By late morning the next day, Neena had typed out the article's outline, as well as a few bullet points about each section. She'd roughed out a tentative opening paragraph but now needed to get up to move a bit. It seemed as good a time as any to embrace John's little errand of returning Ethan's phone to him. She went down to the kitchen to get the picnic lunch the staff had prepared for her. She got a knapsack off the hook near the refrigerator—the staff here had thought of everything—and put the lunch inside, then filled a sports bottle with water.

"You finding everything you need?" asked one of the staff members who was slicing vegetables at the long center island.

"I am. Thank you." She loved the intimacy of this place. How she felt like she was a guest in someone's home.

Once she had her lunch all set, she walked the short distance to the inn's open-air barn, ready to select a bike and head to the campground. She tapped the right front pocket of her shorts, making sure Ethan's phone was still there. John—*the big chicken shit*—hadn't shown up again since she'd discovered it in her dresser drawer. Even so, it was obvious what he wanted her to do.

The bikes were all similar—beach cruisers with the wide tires necessary for riding on the beach or in the sandy soil near the coast—but she tested a couple out for height. She hadn't ridden a bike in decades, but she looked forward to the challenge. She knew in her gut that whatever was going to heal her mind and her body lay outside her comfort zone. And riding a bike was definitely out of her norm.

She'd chosen the bike she would use when she heard voices approaching. Within seconds, the woman with the auburn hair and her daughter rounded the corner and entered the open side of the barn.

"Oh." The woman stopped and let out a little yelp of surprise.

"Sorry. I didn't mean to scare you," Neena said.

The woman raised her sunglasses and perched them on top of her head. "No worries. I just didn't expect anyone to be in here."

"I'm Neena. I saw y'all at dinner last night."

"I'm Jewel." She laid a hand on her chest and then pointed to her daughter. "And this is Emma."

Though Jewel's outfit was as put-together as before, there was something a bit...off...about her demeanor that Neena couldn't pinpoint. Perhaps it was the sort of slack-jawed look on her otherwise perfect face?

"I heard you're a journalist." The girl's eyes danced with excitement.

Neena smiled, flattered. "I am."

"Are you on TV?" the girl asked.

"I'm not that kind of journalist. I write articles for magazines. The people on TV are called broadcast journalists. I'm what's known as a print journalist."

The explanation didn't dampen the girl's enthusiasm. "Have you ever interviewed BTS?"

Neena tried not to laugh. She didn't want to offend Emma. "No. I'm not that important. I don't think they'd agree to an interview with me. And besides, I write mainly about the southern United States."

"Do you *want* to interview them?"

Not really. "I guess I would if I had the opportunity." She glanced toward Jewel, who seemed lost in her own thoughts as she rocked back and forth on her feet. Neena pointed to the fluffy white towels Jewel carried. "Y'all are headed to the beach?"

The woman's attention snapped back to their conversation. "Have you been?" she asked.

"I went yesterday." It was the whole reason she was standing there now. Had she not met Ethan then, she wouldn't be returning his phone now. *Damn John.* "Well, I'll get out of your way." Neena wheeled her bike toward the large opening that served as the doorway.

Jewel stumbled a bit as she stepped aside to let Neena by. Maybe the dirt floor of the barn wasn't as flat as it looked?

"Y'all have fun," Neena said. They had their picnic lunch with them, too. She wished she was having lunch at the beach with Rosie today.

"You, too." Jewel waggled her fingers at Neena.

Neena stopped when she got even with Emma. She bent down and spoke in a mock whisper. "I haven't ridden a bike in about thirty years, so don't make fun of me, okay?"

"Can I shoot a video?" The girl reached into her pocket and withdrew a phone. "If you have a really good crash, it could go viral on TikTok."

"No!" Neena was horrified at the thought.

Emma sighed loudly and stuck the phone back in her pocket. "My mom won't ever let me video her, either."

"Smart woman," Neena said as she slung her leg over the bike and hoped to God this afternoon didn't require a medical intervention of any kind. She wobbled at first, but balancing was easier as she picked up speed. She giggled to herself. She was doing this. She was actually doing it!

Sweat ran from her scalp by the time she'd pedaled her way to the campground. Her T-shirt clung to her back. Still, she was glad she'd made the trek up Main Road. If nothing else, she'd proven to herself that she was regaining strength. That she wasn't afraid of a challenge. She felt invigorated. Sweaty, but invigorated.

She'd passed one other couple on bikes but had otherwise had the road to herself. She sped past Boone Calhoun's little gatehouse of a cabin, glad when she'd made it by without any sign of him.

The remainder of the ride reminded her how good it felt to exercise her body. The lush foliage shaded her from much of the sun, but there was no escaping the ever-present humidity this time of year in the coastal south.

As she approached the campground, her plan—or lack thereof—troubled her. How was she to find Ethan? How was she to know which of the tents belonged to his family? Hopefully, the process of elimination would work.

The first campsite she saw had a young couple—twenty-somethings—setting up a tent. Another campsite had small toys out front. It wouldn't be impossible for Ethan's parents to have a toddler, too, but it seemed unlikely.

Her anger at John grew as she walked her bike around the campground. Why was she even out here, doing his bidding, when she had an article to write? An article that could make or break her future employment?

Logically, she knew she should be mad at herself. She'd read recently that when we're mad at another person, it's often because we haven't set or enforced our own boundaries. Why didn't she just ignore him? Hand in the phone to lost and found at the inn or to the park rangers or whatever, then be done with it?

But she'd come this far, so she'd see this through.

Finally, she saw a tall woman outside a nearby tent. She had the same slender build and curly black hair as Ethan.

"Excuse me," she said.

The woman turned.

"Are you Ethan's mom?"

The woman frowned. A mix of suspicion and worry crossed her face. "Is everything okay?"

"I'm Neena Lee. I chatted with Ethan a little bit on the beach the other day and then I found this phone on the path leading back to Main Road." So it was a lie, but how else could she explain why she had it? She pulled it from her pocket. "It looks like it might be his."

The woman's shoulders sagged with relief. "Oh, thank God. His father was about to kill him. He's lost two of them already." She tucked the phone in her pocket. "He and his father just left for a hike, but I'll tell him you brought it back. What was your name again?"

"Neena." She stuck out her hand.

The woman shook it. "Shelley."

Neena wanted to leave. She *should* leave. But she'd heard enough news stories to know that LGBTQ teens killed themselves at a much higher rate than other teens. If Ethan was being bullied because he was gay, she wanted to help. She didn't want any family to go through what she'd been through when Mama had died by suicide. "Listen, Shelley." She spoke haltingly, not sure how to proceed. "I know this is none of my business, but Ethan got a...disturbing text when I was talking to him yesterday."

Shelley's eyes narrowed.

Neena rushed to answer the questions that were likely going through Shelley's mind. "He was hot. I offered him a bottle of water. He sat under my awning for a bit to get out of the sun."

The other woman still didn't seem convinced.

Neena decided to go right for the punch line. "I think someone's harassing him. Maybe by calling him gay?"

A look Neena couldn't interpret made its way across Shelley's face. Denial? Worry? Something else?

Shelley scoffed. "I don't know what you're talking about. And besides, he's not gay." There was a hint of defensiveness in her voice.

"I saw a text come in on his phone. A picture of...male genitalia...with the word 'faggot' written across it."

Shelley waved a dismissive hand. "It was probably just his friends giving him trouble. You know how boys can be."

"Not based on his reaction when he got it. He seemed pretty upset." He'd looked stricken and ashamed.

Shelley pulled the phone from her pocket and typed in a passcode.

"He may have deleted it," Neena said.

Shelley scrolled through the phone.

Neena couldn't see what was on the screen. "Look," she said. "If someone was bullying my daughter, I'd want to know. So I could help protect her. Help her navigate through it."

Shelley looked up, the look of suspicion still in her eyes. "Is your daughter gay?"

Neena shook her head. "No." At least if Rosie was gay, she wouldn't be involved with the likes of Caleb.

Shelley's gaze returned to the phone as she continued to scroll. Neena stood, silently watching. Wondering what she should say next.

After a couple of minutes, Shelley pulled the phone closer to her face. She read something, scrolled down, then scrolled back up and read it again. The color drained from her face. She squeezed her eyes closed and was silent for several seconds. "His father will be devastated," she finally choked out.

"If Ethan is gay?" Neena's voice was quiet. She was trying to understand, not defend or pass judgment.

Shelley held the phone to her chest. "He's...one of those big macho men. He's all the time calling gay people names and talking about how disgusting they are."

"So if Ethan *is* gay, he might not tell y'all?"

"With the way his father behaves? I doubt it."

So Ethan might be living in silence—and perhaps even shame—over who he was? Growing up in a household where he couldn't talk to his parents about something that was as much a part of him as his slender build and dark, curly hair?

But then Neena had seen a family in central Florida last year—a mom, dad, and two sons who looked to be in about kindergarten and first grade. The dad had yelled homophobic slurs at a couple of guys who held hands as they walked by the outdoor seating area where the family had been having lunch. If Ethan's dad had that kind of behavior—if he'd spoken out that vehemently against gays for all of Ethan's life—then no wonder Ethan hid it.

Just like Kevin had hidden his drug use for all those years. Just like he'd hidden it a couple of months ago, even when he was living under her roof. Sure, Kevin had been hiding something destructive, whereas Ethan was simply embracing who he was. One of many who epitomized that love is love. But still, they both hid a secret they wouldn't discuss with their loved ones.

Mama had held all kinds of secrets inside her, too. Thoughts and feelings that Neena had never been privy to. Of course, Neena had known for years that Mama had internal demons, but she'd never really understood what those demons were. There had been plenty of outside evidence—the inability to cope with life in general—but Neena had never really known or understood what made Mama's life so unbearable.

So maybe Neena shouldn't judge Shelley too harshly. It was possible, after all, to not know a lot about a person, even when we love and live with them.

"He's really going to need your support," Neena said. "He *does* really need your support, especially if he's being bullied by other kids."

Shelley still cradled the phone to her chest. "You should go," she whispered.

Neena placed her hand on Shelley's arm, ignoring the desperation in the other woman's voice. "I wish the best for your family. Ethan's a great kid." He'd actually been an obnoxious, surly teen to her, but all kids were great kids, no? At least until they were taught how to be homophobes by people like his father. She turned to retrieve her bike and go.

"Neena?" Shelley called after her.

She turned.

"Thank you for letting me know. About the text, I mean." Shelley's face was a mix of emotions—anxiety and resignation and worry. She held up the phone. "And for returning this."

"It's not going to be easy." Those family dynamics were going to be a huge challenge. "But as the parent of a grown child, I can tell you it's going to be worth it."

Shelley nodded and smiled. Neena was pretty sure she was crying, but at least she looked hopeful.

Neena turned and continued toward the bike. *It's going to be worth it.* Maybe she should listen to her own advice. Maybe she should stop being so mad at Rosie and double down on the fact that *their* relationship was worth the struggle, too.

Chapter Thirteen

As Neena wheeled her bike into the barn at the IvyLena Inn, she tried her best to get Ethan and Shelley and their family out her mind. She had an article to write and—thankfully—the Ethan-related tangent of her life seemed to be over.

She parked the bike and started the walk to the inn, which was about a football field away from the barn, closer to the Cumberland River. Humidity hung in the air like an invisible blanket, but it felt good to have worked her body. It was something she needed to do more often. Her therapist had told her that exercise would help with her anxiety problems, too.

As she approached the mansion, Jewel's daughter, Emma, came down the wide front steps.

"How was the beach?" Neena asked.

"Good. We even found a shark's tooth." She motioned back toward the inn. "It's up in our room."

"You headed somewhere without your mom?" Neena couldn't help it. A mother was always a mother, even when it came down to looking out for other people's children.

"She's taking a nap."

"And she's okay with you going out on your own?" This island was probably the safest place either of them had ever been, but still, the girl was only about eleven years old.

A look of worry crossed the girl's face. "I tried to tell her, but she wouldn't wake up."

Their earlier encounter crossed through Neena's mind—Jewel's slack-jawed look, her inattentive demeanor, the way she'd nearly tripped on even ground.

It reminded her of the early days of Kevin's drug use, when she was just beginning to understand how bad the problem was. It was their first Thanksgiving after Mama's death and Neena had tried her best to make a holiday meal. The house was on the market, so it was likely to be the last Thanksgiving in the place they'd grown up. But when she'd gone to roust Kevin from his childhood bedroom, it had been like he was in a coma. She'd tried everything to awaken him but had ended up eating the dry turkey breast and mushy stuffing by herself at the dining room table, all the while mourning the loss of her family.

"Well, stay away from the river," Neena said to the girl. "There are alligators down there. And stay away from the ocean."

"I know. Rip currents," Emma seemed to be trying out an impatient-teenager tone. She strolled toward the large oak that graced the front lawn.

Neena ascended the front steps, passed through the library, and entered her room, unable to shake the reminder of Kevin's drug use. Could Jewel be using, too, despite her glossy exterior? Or maybe she had some kind of medical condition. She looked healthy, but pain was invisible, so perhaps she was on some kind of medication. She could even have some sort of chronic illness. It wasn't like most people went around chatting up strangers about their health issues. A glint of admiration sparked in Neena at how poised and glamourous Jewel looked, even with the difficulties she might be facing.

Neena needed to get to work, but the heat and humidity during her bike ride had made her sweat through her clothes. Thank God she'd thought to bring a couple of extra outfits on the trip. She took a quick shower, then grabbed her laptop and picnic basket and headed to the front veranda. Luckily, one of the large porch swings on either end was available. The shade and the ceiling fans kept it cool enough to make a great work and lunch space.

She'd type a bit, then take a bite of the salad—turkey, radishes, carrots, and spicy chickpeas on a bed of arugula—then type a bit more. Her article was shaping up nicely. Gus's input added a depth she hadn't seen in any of the other articles about the place.

As she packed the empty cardboard lunch box back inside the basket, Dwight came bounding up the stairs.

"I've been looking for you," he said.

"I've been right here, working away." She ran her tongue over her front teeth, checking for any rogue bits of lettuce that might have lodged there.

He pulled his phone from his pocket. "Mind if I have your phone number so I don't have to roam the island every time I want to find you? I'm going to need it when I get back to Hilton Head anyway."

Her face heated. It had been years since a man had asked for her number. "904-555-6562."

He typed it into his phone as she read off each number.

"N-E-E-N-A," she said when it was time for him to type in her name.

He looked up and frowned. "How else would you spell it?"

She hit "Save" on the document she'd been working on. "Most people spell it N-I-N-A."

"Wouldn't that rhyme with China?"

She laughed. "That's what my mom thought, too, but most people spell it that way."

He spoke the name of each letter as he typed it into his phone. "Your last name is L-E-E, as in Robert E.?"

"Yes, but no relation."

The sternness in her voice caused him to look up. "You're not fan of Confederate generals?"

"I did a genealogy project in middle school specifically to prove we weren't related."

He laughed. "Well, don't worry. I have no Confederate bumper stickers on my truck."

"Or flags in your yard?"

"Or flags in my yard."

"Or tattoos?" She'd like to see him naked. To check that one out for herself. She imagined his long, strong body lounging in her bed back in Jacksonville.

"No tattoos whatsoever. Do I pass the test?"

She laughed. "You pass the test. At least the first part."

He leaned toward her to whisper. "I thought the first part was in the woods yesterday."

Her face heated again. She looked away, but wished she'd had the nerve to keep eye contact with him. "You passed that part, too."

He rose and clapped his hands together. "Hot damn."

She grinned but glanced nervously at the guests on the other end of the porch. "Will you stop it? You're going to have everyone staring at us."

"Then go for a walk with me. Come on, you need to stretch your legs after lunch anyway."

"Have you eaten your lunch already?"

He motioned toward the river. "Carl and I ate down there a little while ago. But now he's back at work, and I'm getting ready to take a pretty lady out for a stroll." He gave a bow like the men might have done when this mansion was first built.

"You're awfully sure of yourself."

"Thirty minutes. That's all I'm asking."

She thought back to how Rosie had said Neena never had any fun. Well, here was *fun* standing right in front of her. Maybe she should take him up on it. "Thirty minutes. That's all. Then I've got to get back to work." She gathered her laptop and notebook in her arms.

A wide grin spread across his face as he picked up the picnic basket. "I'll return this back downstairs to the kitchen while you take your computer up to your room."

"Meet you back here in about five minutes?" That would give her time to brush her teeth, put on some lipstick, and grab her sunglasses.

He stepped aside to let her go in front of him. "It will be the highlight of my day," he said softly in her ear as his fingertips grazed the small of her back.

Her step stuttered at the intimacy of it, but she quickly recovered and made her way to the large front door. Spending time with Dwight Leggett would definitely be the highlight of her day, too.

CHAPTER FOURTEEN

Dwight stood at the edge of the veranda, his face tipped up to the sun as he waited for Neena to freshen up in her room. She studied him for a moment before opening the front door to join him. She'd grown fond of those lines on his face, etched by a lifetime of experiences she had yet to learn about. She wanted to know more about that life. More about the man who made her breath catch every time she looked at him.

"I got us something to drink while I was in the kitchen." He held up two of the sports bottles that were stored under the beverage urns downstairs. "One water, one hibiscus lemonade. Your pick."

"You're fine with either?"

He nodded, so she took the one containing water from his hand.

"Where are we headed?" she asked as they descended the wide stairs at the front of the mansion.

"I don't know. Maybe down along the river. See what's out beyond the garden?" He gave her a teasing grin. "It's close enough that I won't keep you out beyond your thirty-minute curfew."

He fell in step with her as they reached the ground and walked in the direction they'd indicated.

"You know, not all of us sold a company and are now living a life of leisure," she said. "Some of us have to work for a living."

"A buddy of mine has been bugging me to consult on his start-up, so I may be back in the workforce before long, but it would be on *my* terms."

"Oh? And what would those terms be?" What kind of boundaries did a person set if they had the luxury of not needing the money to live on? She presumed that was Dwight's situation but didn't know for sure.

They turned to the left, toward the garden.

"I don't want to work more than about ten hours a week," he said.

She snorted. "Must be nice."

"And I want to work from wherever I happen to be at the time."

So maybe he could work while visiting her in Jacksonville?

"Mainly, I don't want to get back in the rat race. I enjoy my time just piddling around my house."

"You must be a big golfer, living on Hilton Head."

He shrugged. "Every now and then, but not as much as you'd think. Normally I putter around my garage or go for a hike or sit on the deck and read."

"Oh? What do you read?"

"Mostly fiction. Some non-fiction as long as it's not too 'here's how you build a company' or 'here's how to become a great leader.' I read enough of those when I was younger. It's like, I'm past that point in my life, you know?"

"I'd give anything to just sit on a deck and read all day."

He laughed. "I didn't say I did it all day. But I have read about 150 books so far this year."

"So you've just proven my point." Though she said it in a teasing manner, she couldn't think of anything sexier than a handsome man who read. Hilton Head's winters would get chilly enough to light a fire in the fireplace. She imagined the two of them, each with their own book, curled up under the same blanket, maybe a hot toddy or a glass of wine within reach.

The Cumberland River lay before them, stretching as far to the left and the right as they could see. Without speaking, they made their way to the shade of a huge live oak. The drape of Spanish moss framed their view of the water, like a lacy border made specifically for this moment.

Dwight leaned his back against the tree. "So what do you do for relaxation?"

"Go to bed." She said it with a laugh, but the truth was, these last few weeks, the panic attacks had left her so drained she could do little else.

"No. Seriously." He inserted his finger in her beltloop and gently pulled her toward him.

"I read a lot, too. Mainly audiobooks." Her therapist had told her that exercise was important, so she'd been trying to walk every morning—sometimes in her neighborhood and sometimes at the beach at sunrise. But as much as she loved listening to a good story, there had been a lot of times recently when she wanted to just sit quietly, doing nothing. Letting her body and mind process everything she'd been through. She knew she'd get back to her old, voracious reading habits, but for now, she needed that time to heal.

His hand moved to her back, rubbing it through her shirt, despite the fact that she'd gotten a bit sweaty on their walk to the river.

"Why do I feel like a teenager who's snuck out of the house and is hiding from her parents?" she asked.

He nuzzled her ear and trailed kisses down her neck, his breath warm against her skin. "Because we've got to get away from the inn to get a little privacy?"

She leaned her head away from him, giving him more access to that sensitive part of her body. While he shared a suite in the carriage house with his brother, she had a room all to herself. Maybe she should invite him there? But no, she didn't want to imply that she'd sleep with him. And, besides, what if John showed up? Or was already there, watching them? That would be creepy. She shuddered, just thinking about it.

"Are you okay?" Dwight said.

"I'm fine." She placed her fingertips on his face and guided his mouth to hers.

As they kissed, he pulled her closer to him until they were body to body, with him still leaning against the tree. His hands roamed her back, her hips, her shoulders. Her fingers twined through his dark hair. Maybe she *should* invite him to her room. But, no, she needed to keep her wits about her.

"How much time left before my curfew?" she joked when their lips finally parted.

He gently tugged her into an embrace, her head against his chest. She could hear his heartbeat through his soft cotton T-shirt. "What curfew?" he asked.

She pulled away and looked up at his face. She expected to see a playful grin, but his eyes held nothing but desire.

"I wish you didn't have an article to write," he said.

"I wish you weren't so handsome." *And such a good kisser.* "It makes me want to skip out on work." She wound her fingers through his and gently pulled. "But I've got to get back."

He let out a guttural sound of good-natured frustration. "I'm definitely coming to Jacksonville."

She cast him a sideways smile. "And I'll definitely enjoy that."

He reached out and grasped her hand. They walked that way in silence most of the way back to the inn. She liked a man who didn't need to fill the quiet with unnecessary words. Who could simply enjoy her company.

"Have dinner with me tonight?" he asked as they approached the mansion.

"Will Carl be sleeping?"

"You could join us even if he does come to dinner. It could be the three of us."

She hated to horn in on their brotherly outing together but didn't want to miss out on another meal with Dwight if he would otherwise be alone.

"You talk to Carl and let me know what he's going to do. We can make a game-time decision in the dining room right before it starts."

They'd reached the wide front steps of the inn.

"Will do," he said as he bent to kiss her cheek. "Thanks for hanging out with me for a bit. I had a great time."

"Me, too."

She watched him walk across the front lawn, toward the carriage house he shared with his brother. Maybe he was the silver lining in all this mess. Maybe Kevin's death and Justin's reluctance to assign her a story had all been meant to lead her to this. To him.

Maybe, just maybe, there would be some happiness after all.

***

Neena had been back at work on the porch for about an hour when her phone rang for the third time that day. *Rosie.* She bit back a tinge of guilt. She'd ignored two of her daughter's calls before her walk with Dwight, not wanting whatever drama Rosie brought on to interfere with her work. There'd been no voicemails left, so she assumed everything was okay. But still, she needed to be there if her daughter needed her.

"Hey, honey," she said as she answered the call, hoping for a pleasant conversation this time around.

"I'm going to call you every hour on the hour until you send me the money from Grandma."

Neena took a deep breath, reminding herself of the conversation with Shelley. Ethan and Rosie and every other kid was worth the struggle. "I'm here on a work assignment. And through the connections of one of our editorial board members." *So it would be nice if you didn't cause a scene.* She kept her voice low, embarrassed that the other guests relaxing in the nearby rocking chairs might overhear. "We can talk more about this when I'm home." *And once this article is handed in to that kid who isn't much older than you are.*

"This is such bullshit, Mom. You're hanging out at some fancy hotel that someone else is paying for, but you can't let me use *my own money* for someplace I want to go?"

"Is there some other topic you'd like to discuss?" She tried to keep her voice cheery. The older woman in the rocking chair closest to her had already turned around once to look at her in a judgmental way.

"Every hour on the hour, Mom. I'm calling until you say yes," Rosie said before she hung up.

"Goodbye, honey," Neena said for the benefit of the other guests nearby, though the line was already dead. She reminded herself—again—that there would always be rough patches between parents and children. And for now—as unpleasant as it was—it was Neena's job to teach Rosie that she didn't always get what she wanted right away. That planning for her future home was more important than running off to Europe with Caleb.

Neena immediately texted Rosie:

I won't be answering my phone when you call. Please text me if there's an emergency.

She tried to get back into her work, but her anger at Rosie kept swirling through her mind. Maybe she should take a walk to clear her head.

She gathered her belongings and headed back to her room to drop off her computer.

As she tossed her laptop onto the bed, the dresser caught her eye. The third drawer down—the one Ethan's phone had been in—was open about three inches. A shudder ran across the width of her shoulders.

No.

"Damn you, John," she said aloud, though there was no one in the room to hear her. She didn't need this distraction. And she certainly didn't need anymore "assignments" from him.

She took a deep breath and rolled her neck around on her shoulders, trying to ease the tension building at the base of her skull. She crossed the room and slid the drawer open. A brochure of some kind rested at the bottom of it.

She pulled it out. The Grand Hotel on Mackinac Island. Phrases like "Experience the Tradition" and "America's Summer Place" lured travelers to the historic inn on an island in one of the Great Lakes. She'd read about this place in a couple of the articles that had also featured Cumberland Island. The places listed in those "Great Inns of America" type articles all appeared to be pricey—definitely places that only wealthy people could afford.

She turned and looked around the room, but there was no John here to tell her what this brochure was supposed to mean. Surely he didn't think she needed to visit there. Her bread and butter over the years had been writing travel articles about southern destinations. Her primary source of income had been *Coastal South Travel*, at least until her newly minted anxiety disorder had sidelined her for a month and they'd put *that kid* in charge when they ousted her old boss.

But maybe this was John's way of telling her she needed to expand her area of focus? Take her career to the next level? She sure as hell didn't have the funds to travel to Michigan on her own. So what could this mean?

Again, she looked around the room for potential clues.

Nothing.

CHAPTER FIFTEEN

Neena poured herself a glass of wine at the Honest John Bar that evening and made a mental note to talk to Claire, the inn's manager, in the morning. Neena's stay was free, but since alcohol was not included in the room rate, she probably needed to pay for it. She'd give Claire her credit card number in the morning. Thank God her most recent payment—the minimum due—had already been applied to her account. Otherwise, even this minimal charge might not have gone through.

Despite the extra expense, she *really* needed the glass of wine. Thanks to Rosie, her nerves were frazzled. As promised, her daughter had called once an hour, to the point where Neena had silenced her phone. Instead of answering, she'd texted Rosie back.

Don't forget: Please text me if there's an emergency.

She hoped to God that putting her phone on silent didn't make her miss Justin, should he try to reach her for another obnoxious call to see if Mackenzie needed to take her place. He would likely assume the worst—that she'd shirked her responsibilities to the magazine—if she didn't answer. Anger burned in her chest. She'd been meeting journalistic responsibilities since before those two had even been born.

She picked up her glass and made her way down the hall to the living room, where light hors d'oeuvres were served each night before dinner. Walking into a roomful of strangers was always nerve-racking, but tonight she was downright anxious, still unsure if she'd eat at the communal table or join Dwight and Carl for dinner.

Her shoulders relaxed a bit as she saw young Emma perched on one of the side chairs along the perimeter of the wall. She'd made it back to the inn without being eaten by an alligator or carried away in the undertow of a rip current. Jewel chatted nearby with an older couple—new arrivals Neena hadn't seen before.

But there was no sign of Dwight or his brother. She'd waited until fifteen minutes prior to dinner to arrive in the living room, not wanting to appear overeager. So where was Dwight? They'd agreed that her joining him or not would be a game-time decision. And game time was—she looked at her watch—twelve and a half minutes away.

"I heard you're a journalist," a female voice said from behind her.

She turned to see a Black woman in a fuchsia-colored sheath. She appeared to be perhaps in her mid-thirties. A gorgeous oversized silver necklace rested on the rich fabric of her dress. Dangling silver earrings accentuated her slender neck.

Neena smiled. "I am."

"I saw you interviewing that older gentleman out on the lawn."

Neena nodded. "He's their longest-term employee."

"Such a beautiful place to work. Though I'd rather visit as a guest." She winked and laughed softly at her own joke.

"It is definitely a nice place."

The woman motioned to a man across the room—the only other Black person in the room. "Michael and I came here for our honeymoon, so when we finally got a weekend without the kids, I wanted to come back."

Neena wondered how a relatively young couple who was raising a family could afford a place like this. She was so far out of her league in this crowd.

The woman continued. "He wanted to go back to the Rockies, but I wanted to at least be within driving distance in case something happened to one of the kids."

Neena tried to appear like she was listening to the woman while at the same time surreptitiously watching the arched entryway for Dwight. Still no sign of him.

"Do you have any children?" the woman asked.

"A daughter. Rosie. She's finishing up grad school."

"Mine are twelve, ten, and six. Two boys and a girl."

Neena stiffened as Dwight entered the room, his brother behind him. Her nerves hummed, like a high school girl hoping the cute guy talks to her in the cafeteria. Dwight's gaze searched the room and quickly landed on her. She wished she could remember what the woman beside her had just said. "So where are y'all from?" Neena asked.

"Atlanta. Well, Decatur, actually. Do you know it?"

"I've been there a couple of times." The town was completely surrounded by Metro Atlanta, though Neena still had trouble believing that such a quiet charming little village could be right in the middle of such a bustling urban area. "I've covered the Decatur Book Festival for the magazine I work for." *Or at least the one I used to work for.* Justin's smug countenance floated through her brain unbidden.

The woman's face brightened. "Ooooh. The kids and I love the Book Festival. They bring so many good authors to town."

Neena looked over the woman's shoulder. She'd lost track of Dwight. Just then, a hand cupped her elbow. She turned.

"Good evening." He gave a polite smile to the woman in fuchsia. "May I please borrow Neena for a moment?"

The woman smiled at Dwight, then raised an eyebrow in a conspiratorial glance she shared with Neena. "Of course."

Neena placed a hand on the woman's arm. "It was nice chatting with you. Have fun on your 'no kids' weekend." She followed Dwight to the other side of the oversized living room. His brother was nowhere in sight.

"Carl is joining me for dinner, but I'd like for you to join us, too," he said.

"I don't want to get in the middle of your visit."

"It's fine. I mean, how much time can two people spend together without getting tired of each other?"

"But you haven't really spent that much time togeth—"

Dwight's gaze rose to someone behind her. She turned.

"You remember Carl, don't you?" he said. "Carl, this is Neena."

Carl smiled as he handed Dwight a highball glass filled with an amber-colored liquid. He had one for himself, too. "I hope you'll be joining us for dinner tonight," Carl said.

She searched his face, trying to determine if he actually meant it or if he was just being polite. She couldn't tell which was the case. "You're sure you don't mind?"

"Any time Dwight can get a date, he needs to take it," Carl teased. "He doesn't get that opportunity very often."

Dwight grunted, then took a swig of his drink. Neena was certain he had no trouble getting women to go out with him.

The bell chimed from down the hall, calling the guests to dinner. It was one of the traditions that made the IvyLena Inn seem like a throwback to a simpler time.

Dwight held his hand out. "After you."

They joined the other guests as they walked through the wide entry hall to the dining room in the back of the inn, then let the servers know that Neena would be moving from the communal table to dine with the two men. Dwight pulled out her chair as they settled into a four-top in the quiet corner near the fireplace. Once again, she wished she could come back during a colder month when the multiple fireplaces throughout the mansion would be lit.

The printed menu at each place setting announced the dinner for the evening: baked tarpon in a cream sauce, soufflé made from island-grown sweet potatoes, and a salad made with roasted beets and goat cheese.

The server immediately delivered a starter to each of them—the hugest chilled crab claw Neena had ever seen. Each claw had already been cracked open, the labor of reaching the succulent meat already performed by some unseen worker behind the scenes. She'd never had such a delicacy. She waited until the brothers dug in to make sure she was eating it correctly. The mustard sauce swirled artfully on each plate made a tangy accompaniment to the tender appetizer.

"Thank you for letting me join you for dinner," Neena said.

"Thank you for occupying my brother's time so I can get some work done." Carl tossed them both a teasing smile. "He's kind of a pest."

Dwight rolled his eyes.

"I'm here working, too," she said, hoping to build some camaraderie with Carl. "I'm writing an article about the island and the inn."

"So, a travel writer?"

She nodded. "Freelance. I write for a number of publications." Maybe if she said it out loud, the universe would respond to make it true. She couldn't afford to have *Coastal South Travel* remain her primary source of income, especially with Justin's track record of firing older workers. "And what about you? What do you do?" Had Dwight told her what Carl did for a living? What kind of business he'd had in Dubai? She couldn't remember.

"I'm a marketing consultant. I specialize in the logistics industry."

She nodded, though she didn't really understand what that might entail. "Dwight says you've been in Los Angeles for a long time."

"Almost thirty years." Carl took a drink from the glass of water in front of him.

So he'd gone out west shortly after college. That must have been a big change for Dwight, after having been so close with his brother throughout their childhood and college. Just thinking about it made her miss Kevin. How close they'd once been. If anyone should have been able to save him, it was her.

"And now that his daughters have established their own lives out west, I don't think we're ever going to get him back to the South," Dwight said.

She hoped to God that Rosie would come back to Jacksonville after graduation, or at least somewhere nearby. Caleb's family was in West Palm Beach—too far away for Neena's liking—but hopefully he would be out of the picture soon. "So all girls?" she asked Carl.

"Three, including a set of twins."

"That must have kept life interesting." She glanced toward Dwight as she remembered the dark look he'd gotten yesterday when he'd said he and his wife never had any children.

Carl chuckled. "It still does, even though they're young adults now."

"Oh, I know. I've got one daughter. She's twenty-three." Neena loved talking about Rosie, but she wanted to steer the conversation to a topic that could include Dwight. "So do you two go on these guy trips often?"

"This is the first time in, what?" Dwight looked to Carl. "Maybe ten or twelve years?"

"Last time was the dude ranch in Colorado," Carl said.

Dwight smiled. "That was a fun trip."

She wished she had memories of vacations spent with Kevin as an adult. They wouldn't have been able to afford expensive getaways like Dwight and Carl, but she'd love to just sit in a diner with her brother, eating burgers and greasy fries while they had a heart-to-heart discussion.

"What do you mean, 'a fun trip'?" Carl leaned toward his brother, both hands on the table, palms down. "I was *hospitalized*."

Neena glanced from one brother to the other and back again. She was pretty sure Carl was just giving Dwight trouble, but maybe not?

Dwight also leaned forward, the seated version of getting in his brother's face. "Only because you're a wimp."

But Carl didn't back down. "I was having trouble *breathing* and we were *forty-nine miles* from the nearest hospital."

"I didn't want to miss the whitewater rafting."

Carl rolled his eyes and sat back in his chair. He turned his head to look at Neena. "I might have been dying and he was more concerned about his afternoon activity."

Dwight gave a good-natured scoff. "I'm pretty sure people don't die from altitude sickness. At least not that many."

Carl placed his forefinger inside the fingertips of his other hand, mimicking a pulse oximeter. "Our oxygen levels are supposed to be above 95. Mine was in the high *sixties* by the time he got me to the hospital in Gunnison."

"And you were fine by about eight hours later."

"No thanks to you."

"I drove you to the hospital, didn't I?"

Neena enjoyed their good-natured sparring. "But did Dwight go whitewater rafting?"

Dwight slapped the table, then pointed at her. "Now *that's* the important question."

Carl grunted. "He was late picking me up from the hospital the next day because he got rescheduled onto that morning's trip."

Dwight chuckled. "So you're not dead and I got to go whitewater rafting. Everyone's happy."

Carl leaned toward Neena in a fake whisper. "And now you know why we haven't been on another guys' trip in such a long time."

She laughed. "Well, I'm pretty sure no one's going to get altitude sickness here."

"No, but I'm thinking of feeding him to a gator." Carl sat back as the server arrived with their meals. "That'll teach him."

Neena moved her wine glass, making room for her dinner plate. Everything she'd eaten here had been delicious—somehow both fancy and down-home at the same time.

The discussion at the table flowed freely as they enjoyed their fish and its accompaniments. They talked about how the world had changed since their younger days, how politics had seeped into every crevice of society, and how each of them had been terrified by *Jaws* when they were younger.

Dwight caught and held her gaze a couple of times, making the dinner feel more intimate than it might have otherwise. And Carl continued to be more engaging than she'd expected him to be, which eased her worries about her joining them for that night's meal.

They had just been served their dessert—a warm pear and pistachio crisp—when Carl circled back to earlier in the conversation. "So tell me some of your favorite places you've written about as part of your job."

"Well, I cover the southeastern United States, so a lot of places in Florida—Sanibel Island, the Keys. But also places like Savannah and Charleston and Asheville."

"So nothing, say, north of Virginia?" Carl asked.

She nodded. "We pretty much cover any place that *Southern Living* considers to be the South." She felt like a fake. Her future with *Coastal South Travel* was so uncertain, but here she was acting like she was involved in editorial decisions. Damn Justin for sapping away the confidence in her career that she'd once had.

"Did you ever consider trying to branch out?" Dwight seemed genuinely interested. "I mean you, personally, so that you could see other parts of the country? Maybe new territory like New England or the Rockies or the Great Lakes?"

"You know, I never have, but maybe I should." A moment passed in silence as she searched for a way to keep the conversation flowing. Her mind flashed back to the brochure she'd found in her room earlier. "In fact, there's a historic inn in Michigan that I saw in a lot of the same articles that featured the IvyLena Inn. The Grand Hotel on Mackinac Island. Have you heard of it?" She thought she was pronouncing it correctly—the last syllable rhyming with "paw" rather than "sack."

Carl immediately lowered the fork that was just about to reach his mouth. He cast a hard look in his brother's direction.

"Don't look at me," Dwight said. "I didn't tell her anything."

The mood at the table had shifted, like a menacing storm cloud suddenly hovered above them.

"Tell me what?" she asked, wishing she knew what this seismic mood shift was all about.

Carl's glare moved from her to Dwight and back again. Then he lowered his head and stabbed at slivers of pear like he was trying to murder them.

Dwight gave her an apologetic look but said nothing.

"I found a brochure in my dresser," she said to the top of Carl's head. "For that hotel. It must have been left by the previous guest who stayed in that room. Or maybe the IvyLena Inn and the Grand Hotel belong to one of those hotel collectives, like they cross-advertise because they have the same type of clientele." Okay, so both statements were a lie, but there was no way she was going to tell them that John F. Kennedy Jr. kept leaving trinkets for her to find.

"I didn't tell her anything." This time Dwight leaned toward his brother and said it in a demanding whisper.

The people at the communal table rose, momentarily shifting the trio's attention to that side of the room. The woman in the fuchsia dress came toward them and placed one hand on the back of the extra chair, leaning forward. "I know it's a thousand degrees, but some of us want to make s'mores. The staff is going to build a fire in the firepit on that end of the building, in case y'all want to join us."

Neena smiled up at her, thankful for the welcome distraction. "Thank you. That's nice. We might do that." She actually had no idea what the brothers would do. She had no idea what was even going on between them right now. She just wanted to get back to whatever conversation was going on at their table so she could figure out what the hell had made them behave like this.

The woman waggled her wine glass. "Don't forget to bring your adult beverages." She turned and followed the others out of the dining room and down the entry hall toward the front door.

Carl stood. His face was grim. "Thank you for joining us tonight, Neena. It's been...enlightening." His voice was gruff. Distant. He strode briskly toward the exit to the dining room without acknowledging his brother.

Neena watched him leave, then turned her attention back to Dwight.

His face was white. His eyes, round and questioning.

She swallowed and pushed her dessert away. It was delicious, but her emotions had highjacked her entire body. Her stomach would rebel if she ate any more.

She nailed Dwight with a steady gaze, determined to get some answers. "What was that all about?"

Chapter Sixteen

"Please tell me what just happened here," Neena said as Dwight stood and pushed his chair under the dining table.

"We should get out of the way so the employees can get their work done," he said.

It was true that the couple seated at another private table were the only ones still in the dining room, but Neena wanted to know what had made Carl so angry when she'd mentioned the hotel on Mackinac Island. Was this Dwight's way of evading her questions? How had she managed to bungle something so badly when she had no idea what was even going on?

She picked up her wine glass and followed Dwight through the entry hall and out the front door. When they'd gone down the wide front steps, instead of turning right toward the fire pit where the other guests were gathered, he turned left. They started walking, side by side, down the road in front of the mansion. It was dark out, but lights from the expansive veranda cast a faint glow along the ground in front of the building. Moonlight glimmered on the surface of the river. The temperature was still warm, the air thick with humidity.

Dwight took a deep breath, then spoke. "When it started becoming clear that Carl's wife was finished with their marriage, he got into a relationship with someone else. Someone significantly younger than he is."

"And?" She still didn't understand how any of this related to her bringing up the Grand Hotel at dinner.

"He told Susie he was going to a work conference, but instead he took the new girlfriend to Mackinac Island."

A cold shudder cascaded through Neena's body, despite the heat and humidity. She'd randomly raised a topic in their dinner conversation that directly related to Carl's life. No wonder he suspected Dwight of telling her his secrets.

Damn John. This had all been a setup.

"The Grand Hotel was somewhere Susie had always wanted to go, but he took his mistress there instead." Dwight's tone was bitter.

Neena wished she could see his face, but they'd gotten far enough away from the inn that it was darker than it had been. "But if she was the one leaving him, did his wife care that much about the other woman?"

"It added infidelity to all his other faults when Susie filed for divorce. The way she sees it, he never had time for her and their daughters, but he had time to run off to Michigan with a thirty-year-old."

"I had no idea when I brought up that hotel—"

"I know you didn't, but how am I going to convince him of that? I mean, what are the chances that of all the places in the United States, you'd bring up that one?"

But it wasn't a coincidence. John had planted that brochure in her room. But why?

Dwight stopped walking. They were now engulfed in near-darkness. "This other woman—this *younger* woman—has two toddlers, each with a different father, but neither dad is in the picture. And I get the impression that she sees Carl as her meal ticket."

"He's still seeing her?"

He scuffed his foot on the worn path beneath their feet. "Sadly, yes. It's like she needs someone to support them all, and he was dumb enough to get into this rebound relationship once he knew that Susie was leaving him."

"Can you not talk any sense into him?"

Dwight grunted. "That's what this trip is all about. I mean, he thinks it's a 'sorry your wife left you' trip, but it's also about trying to get him to see what a huge mistake he's making jumping into another relationship so quickly, especially with a woman who…seems to be at a very different point in her life."

Neena wondered how much money Carl really had if he was in the midst of an expensive divorce, especially when he'd been unfaithful. Didn't that generally mean that the one who'd cheated had to pay out more money to the aggrieved spouse? But she really had no idea how divorces work. And Carl's finances were none of her business.

They started walking back toward the inn.

Her brain searched for some way to comfort Dwight. "Well, if there's one thing I've learned having a twenty-three-year-old, it's that we can't control what other people do." If she could, Caleb would have been out of Rosie's life long ago.

He gave a short chuckle. "Your daughter's…making different decisions than you would make?"

"I don't even want to talk about it. And—believe me—you don't want to hear me whine about her latest boyfriend."

"So what about the rest of your family? Any brothers and sisters?"

They took a few of steps in silence as she contemplated what to say. She'd only had to tell a couple of people about Kevin's passing, and she still wasn't sure she could say it out loud. She also hated that she was embarrassed by his manner of death, but on the slight chance that she and Dwight might date, she wanted all her dirty laundry out on the line. She was too old to play games with men. "I had one brother. He died of a drug overdose just over a month ago."

Dwight stopped walking. He touched her arm. "That's like…that just happened."

She stopped, too, and nodded, then realized he might not be able to see her through the darkness. "This is my first writing assignment since he passed away."

"Are you okay?" He started walking again. "I mean, that's a lot to deal with."

Again, she had an important decision about how much to reveal. No way would she tell Dwight about the ghost she'd been hallucinating, but should she tell him about her hospitalization? About the panic attacks she'd had since she'd gotten out? She believed in honesty, but was it too soon to tell him? She didn't want to scare him away. "I've...had some trouble coping."

"Well, it does kind of make Carl's marital escapades seem like small potatoes."

"But both wreck families," she said, then realized what a downer she was being. She wanted this man to feel good in her presence. Carefree. Enchanted, even. This was not the conversation to make that happen. Still, she had a niggling desire to come clean to him. To tell him how her body had reacted in the wake of Kevin's death. To start their relationship with honesty.

As they approached the inn, a faint glow from the firepit shone from the far end of the mansion.

Dwight jiggled the remnants of ice in his highball glass. "I could use another drink. You want one?"

She shook her head. "No more for me, but you go ahead and have one." She didn't want the extra cost of another glass of wine added to her bill. And besides, she shouldn't drink too much, given her new meds. She also didn't want alcohol to disrupt her sleep. The older she got, the more likely that was to happen. And good sleep was a valuable commodity. She'd had far too many restless nights recently. Many times, she'd awoken to a memory of Kevin's lifeless body on the twin bed in her guest room.

"You'll sit with me if I have another?" he asked.

She smiled. "I'll find us a spot on the porch while you go inside to get it."

"Deal," he said as they started up the wide front steps.

She settled into the porch swing at the end farthest from the group at the firepit. Her guest room was right above it, so she and Dwight would have a little privacy, with no one near to overhear their conversation.

A few minutes later, he came back out the wide front door, another highball in his hand. He settled onto the swing next to her, close enough to feel intimate, but not so close as to make them even hotter in the still-humid air.

"I really am sorry about what happened with Carl. At dinner, I mean," she said.

He placed one of his hands over hers on the seat between them. "I'm really sorry about your brother."

She appreciated his empathy. Maybe she should relax and tell him the full story. If this was going to turn into a real relationship, she wanted him to know everything. "I...um...wasn't totally honest with you earlier."

He turned to look at her face. "Oh? How so?"

"I had to be hospitalized after my brother died. I thought it was a heart attack." She laid a hand on her chest. "I mean, I had chest pains and trouble breathing and all kinds of things going on in my body. But it turned out to be a panic attack. I now know that kind of thing can happen after a trauma." Again, the vision of Kevin's body in her guest room flashed in her mind.

"So it's...better now? I mean, was it, like a onetime deal?"

She appreciated Dwight's soft-spoken, caring demeanor. "Panic disorder is a form of anxiety, so I guess it can always be there, lurking below the surface. At least that's what it feels like. It could go away, or it could be with me for the rest of my life. They don't really know. I'm learning how to manage it."

He raised his chin in acknowledgment but didn't say anything. It was as if he was waiting for her to finish what she had to say.

"It's just that..." How did she explain what had happened? "My brother had come back to me. He'd moved from Charlotte to live with me. I was supposed to be the safe space. The place where he'd get a new start. He seemed to really want to get clean this time."

"But then he started using again?"

A couple of tears ran down her cheeks. She hadn't thought she had any more tears after all the crying she'd done over the last few weeks. "I hadn't known that he had. I mean, he had started staying out late sometimes, but he was a fifty-one-year-old man. He could do what he wanted."

"Whatever happened to 'we can't control what other people do'?"

"But you don't understand. He'd come to me to help save him. Just like with Mama—" She stopped. She'd planned to be honest with Dwight about recent events in her life, not drag the dirty laundry out of all the closets in the entire house.

"Your mom died of an overdose, too?" He tried to hide it, but Neena saw the look of surprise on his face. Or was it distaste?

"No!" she said, then forced herself to slow down. To take herself out of reaction mode. She took a deep breath. "My mother died more than twenty years ago," she said quietly. "Suicide. But all those...feelings of helplessness...bubbled up again once Kevin died."

"I can understand."

"I feel like...I failed them both. Like I should have been able to help them. To save them."

"You've felt this way about your mother for two decades?" His words came out haltingly. Warily. There was also a strong undertone of sympathy and concern. But still, he pulled his hand away from hers, as if distancing himself.

She felt abandoned by the gesture but caught herself before the pity set in. If he couldn't handle that part of her life, then she didn't need to get involved with him.

"I'm...getting stronger every day. More resilient." That didn't answer his question, but she was proud of the progress she'd made. Proud she was back at work. Proud of how she was learning to manage this new component of who she was.

"And you've felt this way about your mother for two decades?" he repeated.

Why was he focusing so much on the time frame?

He continued. "Like you should have saved her?"

She nodded. "I was away at college when it happened, but I realize now that she'd had depression for most of my teenage years. Kevin and I had to face that together, you know? And—"

"Two *decades?*"

"A little more than that, actually. But why does that matter?"

He switched his glass from one hand to the other, then back again.

Her heart pounded in her chest. He was stalling.

He stared down into the melting ice cubes. "I...don't want to say anything I'll regret tomorrow."

She sat up straighter, her body now on high alert. "What does that mean?"

His gaze rose to hers. "I have some experience with grief. How it can change people."

She searched his face for more information but found none. "Did you have someone close to you die by suicide?"

He stood and faced her. "No."

Then what could it be?

"Good night, Neena. I appreciate you being so open with me."

She stood, too. The swing swayed backwards, then came forward and smacked her in the side of the knee. Perhaps the universe's way of reiterating that she shouldn't have told him everything, at least not so soon. "Will I see you tomorrow?"

He bent stiffly and kissed her cheek. "Thank you for having dinner with us."

Chapter Seventeen

A slight drizzle had led several of the other guests to plant themselves on the front veranda immediately after the next morning's breakfast as they waited for the rain to stop. But that was okay with Neena. After the sleepless night she'd had, she needed to be near the caffeine, anyway, not on the front porch. She set up a workstation at one of the tables on the glassed-in sunporch, just steps away from the coffee station.

Dwight and Carl had come to breakfast together. Dwight had made a point of coming over to say "good morning" to her but had given no indication that he was ready to finish their discussion from last night.

So, she tried to block him out of her mind as she powered up her laptop and got to work on her article. She made a list of follow-up questions she wanted to ask both Gus and Hiram, the local historian who'd taken her around the island on her first day. Perhaps she could invite Hiram inside the inn for coffee. Was that allowed here? Could she invite a non-guest in for a beverage? The signs at the end of the drive definitely said Private Property and Guests of the IvyLena Inn Only. Once again, she was reminded of how grateful she was for the opportunity to experience such a special place. A place that was out of reach for most people—both financially and logistically.

She'd worked about thirty minutes when Claire came out of the gift shop and approached her.

"Good morning," Neena said as she looked up.

"Do you know someone named Rosie?"

A cold chill slid down Neena's back. *Oh, God. What had happened?* "She's my daughter. Is everything okay?"

"She's called our reservations office in St. Marys a couple of times wanting to speak with you, but the person there explained that the office wasn't in the same location you were."

Neena pulled her phone from the outside pocket of her computer bag. "But everything seems okay with Rosie? Is she hurt?" She glanced down at the screen. There were no texts from Rosie or anyone else.

"She's fine, I think. But she seems worried about you. She said you weren't answering your phone and that she was going to call your boss at the magazine to make sure you were okay."

Neena felt her eyes widen. *Oh, God. Rosie was going to call Justin?* But Neena didn't want to give Claire the impression that anything was wrong, so she schooled her features to hide her apprehension. She smiled, while at the same time trying to stop the buzz of activity rushing through her nervous system. She could *not* have a panic attack. At least not until she knew what was going on. "I'll call her right away."

"Is your cell phone getting service? They usually work fine here for most carriers."

Again, Neena gave her best calm-and-collected smile. "I had it on silent while I worked." No way was she going to drag her family drama into her work. "I'm sorry she bothered y'all."

"No worries. I'm just glad everything is all right."

Neena stood while Claire headed back to her desk in the gift shop. Neena would definitely make this call outside, where no one—especially a member of the inn's management team—could hear her. Best to release her seething anger at Rosie in private. And she *absolutely* wanted to get to Rosie before she called Justin.

Luckily, the morning drizzle seemed to have stopped. She walked out the front door of the inn, down the wide front steps, and onto the lawn facing the river.

"Hello?" Rosie's voice sounded innocent, though caller ID would have told her who was calling.

Neena wasn't falling for that act for one second. "You called the inn?" Her tone was angry. Accusatory. But she didn't care.

"I was worried about you. You weren't answering your phone." Fake concern dripped from Rosie's words.

"I told you I wasn't going to answer any more of your calls. And to text me if there was an emergency." Her back stiffened at the realization. Maybe something *was* wrong. "Is everything okay?"

"I'm just proving that I can be as stubborn as you are."

"You could be endangering my *job*." Justin was already worried about Neena's ability to complete this assignment. If word got back to him that her daughter had caused an issue at the inn, that would be another strike against her.

"Oh, Mom. Stop being such a drama queen."

"My stay here is a result of a favor to a member of their editorial board. I—*you*—don't need to do anything to cause a scene while I'm here." Neena's voice was stern, but she tried to keep it low in case it carried farther than she thought it would. There were almost assuredly still guests on the front veranda, though her back was to it.

"Then tell me I can use Grandma's money to go to Europe with Caleb."

Neena could not give in. This was bratty behavior on Rosie's part and Neena would not reward it by letting her daughter have her way. But Neena also couldn't let the same bratty behavior make her look bad to the management staff of the inn. "No more calls to the inn or their reservations office. Do you hear me? If I don't get any more assignments from *Coastal South Travel*, then *I'll* have to use Grandma's money to pay my own bills."

"But that's *my* money." Now Rosie was yelling. "You can't use it."

"Well, that's certainly not my plan. I haven't used it all these years I've had access to it." The late-morning sun now beat down on the lawn, so Neena made her way to the shade of a live oak draped in Spanish moss. A couple of Adirondack chairs sat beneath it, but she couldn't sit. Not with so much anger thrumming through her body. "But you don't seem to understand how important this assignment is. I'm barely able to pay my bills now, after being out of work for a month." She'd never been this honest with Rosie about her finances, but perhaps it was time her daughter understood.

Rosie remained silent for several moments before she spoke. "I'd never really thought about..." Her voice trailed off.

"About how we *all* struggle to pay our bills?"

"And about how you haven't been making any money since you've...been...you know...not feeling well."

Rosie had driven over from school twice during the week Neena had been in the behavioral health unit. Neena hated that her daughter had seen her in such a vulnerable state. She'd always tried to model strength and independence.

And now, here she was showing how vulnerable she was from an economic standpoint, too. "I'm working hard to get back on my feet. And I'm really optimistic about how this article is going to turn out."

"I have no doubt you can pull it off." A kindness not there before had snuck into Rosie's voice.

Neena smiled. Maybe her daughter was growing up after all. "Thank you."

"I mean, you've pulled off some pretty amazing stuff over the years, starting with raising a kid on your own. I still have no idea why you'd do that on purpose."

"But aren't you glad I did?"

"Ask me that question again after my stats final."

Neena laughed.

"Listen," Rosie said. "I'm giving you a break for now, but we're not done talking about Grandma's money." A car door pinged in the background.

"Where are you headed?" Neena asked, grateful for a less contentious topic.

"Nowhere." The car motor came to life.

"You won't even tell me where you're going?" What had happened to the grown-up Rosie who'd been on the phone just moments ago. The one who had shown a modicum of empathy and politeness.

"God, Mom. Give it a rest. I'm just going out to pick up a breakfast sandwich."

Neena could sense their conversation was coming to an end. Just as well, since the angry Rosie was back. "Please don't call the inn again. And text me if there's an emergency."

"Yes, Mother," Rosie said in a sarcastic tone before they each said good-bye.

Neena lowered the phone to her chest and closed her eyes for a few seconds, trying to ground herself. She couldn't let John or Rosie or Dwight's unexplained behavior last night interfere with her work or—God forbid—set off another panic attack. She had just a couple more days to finish her article.

She jumped as a voice came from behind her.

"This doesn't seem like a good time," John said. "But we really do need to talk."

Chapter Eighteen

Neena spun to see John sitting in one of the wooden Adirondack chairs, one leg crossed over the other. His casual posture was aggravating. She wanted to be that relaxed, too, but the phone call with Rosie had made every nerve in her body stand on end. She glanced up at the porch to see if there were other guests who might witness her talking to him.

Convinced they were alone, she placed her hands on her hips. "We most definitely do *not* need to talk."

"You haven't even started looking for Carolyn. That was our deal."

"We do not have a *deal*."

"Then why were you talking to Ethan's mom? Why were you asking Carl about Mackinac Island?"

She took a step toward him, wagging her finger like an angry parent. "You really need to stop leaving those things in my dresser. And going in my room when I'm not there? That's...an invasion of privacy." Had he always been this pushy? Or had the Kennedy name and those good looks opened so many doors for him that he was used to always getting his way?

"I need to find my wife." His soulful eyes showed a conviction she'd rarely seen in others. "I can't really be at peace until I do."

"And how am I supposed to help with that?"

His gaze shifted to the river, which was a couple hundred yards away from them. "I haven't figured that out yet. I just know we're supposed to work on your soul burden first."

She raised both hands in the air in frustration. "I do *not* have a soul burden. I don't even know what that is."

"But you now realize that Ethan's family could be that close to him and not even know he's gay."

"And what the hell does that have to do with my supposed 'soul burden'?" Was she allowed to curse at a Kennedy?

"We can be close to someone and not even know what's going on inside them."

Her shoulders tensed. She really needed to get back to work. "I'm never even going to see those people again." She waved one arm wildly in the direction of the campground.

"We can be close to someone and not even know what's going on inside them," he repeated slowly. Methodically. Like he wanted it to sink in with her.

Intellectually, she knew what John was saying was true. Ethan's mom had missed what was going on with him, the way Neena had missed what had been going on with her mother and her brother. The demons that had chased each of her family members. The demons that had ultimately killed both of them. But if Neena had been more observant, more empathetic, maybe she could have seen those things more clearly. Maybe she would have known what to do. Maybe she could have saved Mama and Kevin, or at least made them feel less alone.

She sank into the chair beside John.

But what about the brochure for Mackinac Island? What did Carl's affair and divorce have to do with her?

We can't control what other people do. She'd said that sentence to Dwight about Carl, but did she really believe it? If so, then why did it not apply to her and Kevin and Mama? Why did she feel so responsible for their deaths? If we can't control what other people do, was it really her responsibility to save them?

She sensed a crack in the thick wall of certainty that had been such a solid presence in her life.

She turned to look at John, who had an understanding look on his face. His eyes were filled with sympathy. "Show yourself a little grace, Neena. You did your best."

Tears brimmed in her eyes. "But my best wasn't good enough." If it had been, Mama and Kevin would both still be alive.

He rose and came to her, squatting in front of her so that he was on her level. He held her hands in his. Though she hadn't been able to feel his wrist when she'd first seen him at the church, his touch now felt real, his skin soft and warm against hers. "You can't hold yourself responsible for what other people do. What other people *did*."

"And you think that's my soul burden?" A couple of tears ran down her cheeks.

"I know it is." His solemn eyes seemed to focus only on her, like nothing else in the world mattered. No wonder people had loved this man.

"And we need to find your wife?" Her voice was weak, like she was surrendering to the idea.

He nodded once. "We do."

"I don't know how—"

"Neena." Dwight's voice called to her from off to her right.

She turned. He was coming up the road from the dock. Undoubtedly checking on the manatees again.

The warmth of John's hands slid away. She wanted to reach out and grab them, but she knew he was gone.

"Do you have a minute?" Dwight asked as he got closer.

"A few." Her mind was still spinning from her conversation with John.

Dwight frowned at her. "Are you okay?"

She swiped at the tears on her cheeks. "Yes." She held up her phone. "A sad conversation with a friend." It wasn't really a lie. Maybe John *was* becoming her friend.

"Can we talk about last night?" he asked.

"*Please.*"

He pulled over one of the sturdy wooden chairs to face the one she sat in. He lowered himself into it and took a deep breath, as if he didn't know where to start.

She sat silently, though what she really wanted to do was tell him to hurry up and talk. She wasn't sure how much of this anticipation she could take.

Finally, he spoke. "So here's the thing." He flattened his lips together and avoided making eye contact with her.

This couldn't be good. "Yes?" She wanted to get whatever unpleasantness was about to follow out of the way.

"My wife and I tried for a really long time to have kids." His voice cracked on the word "really." "We tried everything. Went to specialists. Monitored her ovulation. Had fertility massages. Had in vitro fertilization a few times."

She knew from her own experience that these procedures weren't cheap, either. Luckily, she'd gotten pregnant with Rosie on the one and only time she'd been able to afford IVF—and that was after scrimping and saving for a couple of years. Dwight clearly had money now, but she wondered if he and his wife had been young and struggling financially when they were trying to have a baby.

He continued. "It's part of why we sold my grandparents' property down near Tampa—to help pay for the treatments. The emotional toll of the whole process was devastating. She did get pregnant. Three times, actually." His eyes misted. "Two miscarriages and a stillborn baby girl."

"Oh, Dwight." She covered his hands with hers, just as John had done to her. She wanted him to feel as heard and seen as she had.

He nodded. An acknowledgment of her sympathy. "It was a really, really rough few years."

"I'm sure it was."

He stood and paced in front of her. "We eventually had to resign ourselves to the fact that our family was just going to be the two of us."

She wanted to ask if they'd considered adoption, but she didn't want to interrupt him.

"It took a toll on our marriage, too." He was still pacing. "We both went into a funk. It took a couple of years, but I eventually came out of it. But my wife—Brenda—never did. I tried to find ways for us to reconnect. To build a different life than the one we'd imagined—one without kids. To find new things that would make us happy. But she never could get past the grief. It was all-consuming for her, and it ate up everything else in its path." He stopped and faced her.

"Including your marriage?"

He nodded and ran his fingers through his hair. "Including our marriage. So in the end, I'd lost the dream of having kids *and* I'd lost my wife."

She didn't know what to say. She didn't want to say anything that would sound hollow or misguided. "That must have been difficult." But she still didn't know what all this had to do with last night.

"It was the hardest thing I've ever been through." His voice was quiet and constrained.

"Thank you for telling me." She could see how difficult it had been for him. But it was also encouraging. If he was sharing something this close to his heart, perhaps he, too, saw the potential of their relationship.

The squawking of two gulls drew her gaze to the river.

"And that's why I can't continue seeing you," he said.

What? Her eyes snapped back to him.

He ran his palms nervously down the front of his shorts. "I know we talked about me driving down to Jacksonville and all that, but that's not going to work for me anymore."

"Why not?" She was still confused about what all this had to do with her.

"You and I have had a really good connection. I've enjoyed spending time with you. But I...I can't be with another woman who can't get past her grief. When you told me about your mom and your brother last night, that time with Brenda all came crashing back." He swept his hand in front of his face. "All the pain and the helplessness and the constant sorrow. I can't go through that again."

"My brother died *a month ago*. Of course I still have grief."

"But your mom died twenty years ago, and you said how affected you still were by that and...I just can't...be in another relationship where grief is like this...presence that never goes away." He held his hand out, palm up, like he was holding a heavy rock in front of him.

She swallowed and looked away. The drooping of the Spanish moss matched what was going on inside her.

She wasn't going to argue with him. She wasn't going to beg a man to be with her if he didn't want to be. She'd thought their relationship had a lot of potential, but this was apparently the end. "I'm sorry you feel that way."

"I'm so sorry. Relationships are difficult," he said.

Yes, but why did *she* have to pay the price for the fact that his marriage had imploded? She stood. "Thank you for at least having the guts to tell me to my face. You could have just ghosted me once we got back to our respective cities."

"I'm not the kind of guy who would just disappear with no explanation."

"I didn't think you were. And that's what makes this even sadder. You seem like one of the good guys." She reached out to touch his arm. "I enjoyed our time together."

For the second time this morning, a handsome man's soulful eyes bore into hers. "I did, too." His mouth curved into a sad, slight smile. He leaned down and kissed her cheek. "Goodbye, Neena."

She couldn't speak, so she nodded instead. She hoped he understood.

She turned to watch as he walked away. When he'd rounded the corner of the mansion, she sat back down facing the river. This was a magical place where people came to rekindle relationships. To celebrate important moments in their lives. Yet her relationship with Dwight had ended here before it had ever really gotten started.

She wondered if John had seen what had just happened. Maybe he'd give her a break because of it and stop badgering her to help him find Carolyn. Neena most definitely was *not* in the mood to think about fairytale weddings or love that spans eternity.

She pulled her phone from her pocket and set an alarm. She would allow herself fifteen minutes to sulk, then she'd get back to work on her article. She couldn't afford any more downtime. As interesting as it might be to see what finding Carolyn might entail, there was only one man Neena needed to please now.

She scoffed at the thought. Justin was about five years older than Rosie. Barely a man, which made it even more aggravating that he played such a key role in whether she would be able to pay her mortgage. To keep the house she'd worked so hard to get. She'd lost so many things recently. She would *not* lose that, too.

***

Neena knew the fifteen minutes she'd allowed herself to grieve after the breakup with Dwight would not be enough. She assumed he'd continue to float through her mind at unexpected times, even months in the future, like whenever she saw a handsome, dark-haired man. Or maybe when she'd spy a mushroom growing in someone's yard during her morning walk.

But she was determined to have her completed article ready to send to Justin the second she got home. She would prove to him that she was not damaged goods, either because of her age or her mental state or whatever other thing he had set in that barely-out-of-the-teen-years mind of his.

She was proud that she'd gotten to work when the alarm on her phone had chimed and that she'd worked a solid two hours, making good progress on the article. Someone in a fragile mental state would not have been able to do that after the "setback with Dwight," as her therapist would have called it.

She closed her laptop and made her way to the inn's kitchen. She generally enjoyed her solitude, but a wave of loneliness swept through her as she retrieved her picnic basket from the refrigerator. She could be having lunch with Dwight, but instead she'd need to figure out where to go—alone—to eat.

"Ms. Lee?" Claire said from her desk as soon as Neena had returned to the main floor of the inn and passed by the gift shop.

"Yes?"

"Did your interview with Gus go okay?"

"It was great." Better than great, actually. The more Neena worked on her story, the more convinced she became that Gus's anecdotes would be what made it a success. "Thank you again for arranging it." Neena's phone pinged in her pocket. She pulled it out as they were talking.

A text from Rosie: *The safe in your closet.*

That's all it said, but there were three little dots—evidence of Rosie typing more.

Broken into.

Neena's body went cold. The picnic basket was suddenly too heavy to carry. She set it on a display table filled with books about the island.

Claire was talking about some new half-day tour the inn was developing, but Neena couldn't listen to her. Someone had broken into her house?

"I'm sorry. This text is an emergency. I've got to go," she said.

She needed to get upstairs, to the privacy of her own room, before she burst into tears. Or stopped breathing. Or collapsed. Any of those things were possible with a panic attack. Most of all, she needed to talk to Rosie to see what had happened. She felt so violated. She'd been barely holding her life together and now this. It was all too much to bear. This felt like the final Jenga piece being pulled from the stack—the one that would cause all the others to come crashing down.

Were the police already there? Were there enough fingerprints that they'd be able to track down the person who'd done this to her? There wasn't anything hugely valuable in the safe, but still, someone had rifled through her most intimate and important paperwork—Rosie's birth certificate, Mama's and Kevin's death certificates, her favorite pictures of each of them, Mama's will.

Then something new occurred to Neena as she bounded up the wide, sweeping staircase toward her room.

What was Rosie doing in Jacksonville when she was supposed to be two hours away, at school in Gainesville?

Chapter Nineteen

Neena rushed to her room, still perplexed by the fact that Rosie was in Jacksonville. Had she been at their house when someone had broken into the safe? Had they taken anything? Was there a door or window that had been smashed in and would need to be secured? Did she know a handyman who could do that for her?

She pulled her phone from her pocket again. No missed calls, so it wasn't like the police—or anyone else—had tried to call her before they'd reached out to Rosie.

She flung her laptop and picnic basket onto the bed, then dialed Rosie's number.

"Are you okay?" she asked the second her daughter picked up.

"I'm fine." Rosie sounded terse, but then this was a stressful situation for both of them.

"Were you there when it happened?"

"When what happened?"

Why was Rosie acting so calm? "When someone broke into the safe?"

"*I* broke into the safe."

"You?" None of this was making sense.

"I used the key you keep under the flour canister."

Neena's body sagged onto the bed. She'd shown Rosie where she'd hidden the key in case anything ever happened to her. "Why?"

"I wanted to see exactly what Grandma's will said about the money she left me."

"You left school and drove two hours because you didn't *believe* me?" That must have been where Rosie was headed at the end of their call earlier this morning. Neena had heard her car pinging at the end of their conversation. It was almost noon now. Rosie would have had just enough time to make it to Jacksonville. Anger percolated inside Neena—because Rosie had lied, because she'd made her mother worry so much about a potential break-in. "You told me you were going to get a breakfast sandwich, but you were headed to the house? In *Jacksonville?* Why would you not tell me the truth?"

"Why would you not tell me the truth about Grandma's will?"

"What are you talking about?"

Papers rustled in the background on Rosie's end of the conversation. "Here's what it says: 'Five thousand dollars, payable to each grandchild on their twenty-third birthday.' My birthday was in *May*, Mom. *Four months ago.*"

"What's the rest of it say?"

"The next paragraph talks about Grandpa's woodworking tools going to some guy named William Osborn. There's nothing more about the money she left to *me*."

"It doesn't say it's for a down payment on your first house?"

Rosie huffed. "Woodworking tools, Mom. The next paragraph is about *woodworking tools.*"

Neena's mind reeled. She specifically remembered a conversation in Mama's kitchen. Mama had talked about how a small inheritance from a spinster aunt had helped Neena's parents buy their first home and how Mama wanted to do that same thing for her grandchildren. Neena had been in college at the time. She didn't yet understand real-world finances and she certainly hadn't been contemplating any children in the near future.

But that conversation still haunted her. Two months after it, Mama had killed herself. Neena had always wondered if Mama had already been preparing then. Already planning her suicide. There had likely been other clues that Neena hadn't picked up on. Clues that might have allowed her to save Mama's life. Why had she been so self-centered and immature? "Grandma specifically told me—"

"It doesn't matter what she *told* you, Mom. It matters what's in the will in black and white."

"I'm going to have to read it for myself. Do *not* take that will with you when you go back to Gainesville. Put it back in the safe, just like you found it. And I'm not at all happy about the fact that you drove all that way just to see what it said."

"It's a good thing I did. Otherwise, I never would have known the truth."

"I really did think it talked about a down payment in the will." She'd never want Rosie to think that she'd intentionally lied to her. But it had been years since she'd looked at the document. "I know that was her intention for the money. That's why she made it for when you were twenty-three and out of college. She thought a person would be more responsible then than when they were turning eighteen or twenty-one."

"How about twenty-three and about to get a *graduate* degree?" There was a banging noise on Rosie's end of the phone, like something falling off a shelf or countertop.

"Is someone there with you? Did Caleb put you up to this?"

"He's got a big paper due tomorrow."

"That doesn't answer my question."

Rosie let out a dramatic sigh. "I'm here by myself, and no, he didn't put me up to it. He's not the root of all evil, ya know."

But he was a condescending jackass who treated Rosie like she was disposable. "I'll take a look at the will when I get back to Jacksonville. Are you going to stay there for a couple of days?" Maybe a little face-to-face time would help their relationship.

"I'm headed back now. I have a stats class tonight."

So Rosie had made the four-hour round-trip drive because she doubted her mother? Neena took a deep breath as she tamped down her anger. There were plenty of things for them to fight about. No sense arguing about something that couldn't be changed at this point.

But if the will really said what Rosie said it did, then her doubting Neena had been justified.

"And you're sure the will doesn't say anything about a down payment on a house?" Neena asked, still unable to believe what she'd been told.

"I've answered that question already. And listen, Mom, I have to go. I'll text you to let you know when I've made it safely back to Gainesville."

"Rosie—"

Neena sat on the bed for a moment with the phone to her ear, though it was clear her daughter had already hung up. Neena had been ninety-nine percent certain the will had said that money was supposed to be used for a down payment on a house. But had she only convinced herself of that because she felt so strongly about Rosie not going to Europe with Caleb? Had Neena's mind only recalled what she'd *wanted* the will to say? Her mind had done so many odd and unpredictable things lately—maybe this was just one more.

She and Rosie had built a lifetime of trust with each other. Granted, their relationship had been strained in recent months, but they'd always been a team. Facing the world together. Always there for the other one. Neena didn't want this issue with the will to chip away at that trust. Rosie was the most important thing in her life, and trust was a difficult thing to rebuild once it had been broken.

She vowed to spend more time thinking about how to fix this. How to convince Rosie that she hadn't lied to her on purpose. That would be a good topic to contemplate during the forty-five-minute ferry ride back to the mainland. *After* her article was complete and ready to send.

She turned to her bed to retrieve her laptop and picnic basket—ready to head to the porch to get some work done—but something twinkly caught her eye. It hung out of the bottom dresser drawer. Her shoulders slumped.

No.

Not another trinket from John.

She did *not* have time for this.

She stomped across the room and yanked open the drawer. Who cared if John could see her anger from wherever he was right now? He needed to quit distracting her from her work. To let her do the job she came here to do.

She stilled. The long ribbon that lay inside the drawer was about a half-inch wide and bedazzled with all kinds of sparkly fake jewels—clear and purple and pink and orange. There seemed to be at least one in every color. A white rectangle of laminated paper was attached at one end.

The item was somehow familiar. Her brain tried to recall where she knew it from, but it was out of place and out of its correct chronological order within her life.

But still, she knew that lanyard.

She suddenly felt like everything in her body had stopped—her heart, her breathing, even the circulation of her blood.

It was decades old. How had John gotten ahold of it?

She reached out and lifted it from the drawer. She turned the name badge to face her. "Vicki Sylvester, Sandalwood High School, Jacksonville, FL." It was, indeed, the lanyard Ms. Sylvester wore at their debate tournaments when Neena had been on the team in high school. While all the other sponsors wore boring lanyards to identify their name and school, Ms. Sylvester had *bedazzled* hers, though that word hadn't existed back then. Teenaged Neena had admired her teacher's pizzazz and individuality.

The woman had been Neena's mentor throughout high school. Yes, she'd nurtured Neena's love of words and logic and current events, but she'd been more than just a debate team sponsor. At a time in her life when Neena's own mother had been unreliable and barely left her bedroom, Ms. Sylvester had been a mother figure. She'd let Neena help organize the logistics of their out-of-town debate tournaments. She'd talked to Neena for hours as they drove to the various cities where the competitions were held. She'd even picked Neena—out of all the girls in the school—to babysit her toddler on the rare nights when she and her husband went out.

A pang of regret lanced through Neena's body. Why had she not stayed in touch with one of the most important people in her life? Had she ever told the woman how much she'd meant to her?

"John?" Neena turned and spoke into the empty room. She'd never conjured him into existence before, but it was high time she took a more active role in their "relationship."

She waited in silence, looking around the room expectantly. She held the lanyard gingerly, with the reverence it deserved. But after a couple of minutes, she was still alone in the room.

Annoyance nipped at her nerves. She held the lanyard higher, in front of her—a sort of offering. "Will you please tell me what this means?" she said to John, though she had no idea if he was listening or even where he was.

Again, more silence.

Damn him.

She tucked the lanyard inside her suitcase, nestling it inside the folds of the softest shirt she'd brought. She planned to keep this item, regardless of his plans for it. She'd try to track down Ms. Sylvester when she got back to the mainland, after her article had been turned in. She did a quick calculation in her head. Ms. Sylvester had maybe been in her mid-thirties when Neena was in high school. She would be elderly now, but there was still a good chance she was alive.

For now, though, Neena needed to get to work. She picked up her laptop and picnic basket and made her way to the front porch.

She nibbled at her chicken salad sandwich as she typed. The hint of dill gave it a delicious and unexpected flavor. She should be enjoying this time—and being productive—but her mind bounced back and forth between her conversation with Rosie and the lanyard tucked inside her suitcase. Her therapist would have called this "ruminating."

The fudgy brownie for dessert soothed her soul even more than the sandwich, but even so, she couldn't set aside the guilt that she'd let Ms. Sylvester slip from her life. The woman had been so much more than a teacher. She'd made Neena feel like she could *be* someone. Like she was smart and filled with potential. Like Ms. Sylvester expected great things from Neena. Had she lived up to them? Would Ms. Sylvester be disappointed to learn that Neena wasn't an editor-in-chief somewhere? That she hadn't won a Peabody Award? Maybe, but Neena would never forget how she'd always felt around Ms. Sylvester—like a bright light shone down on her every time she was around her favorite teacher.

A shuffling sound below the porch drew Neena's attention from her thoughts. She learned over the short stucco wall that served as the porch's railing. A floor below her, Jewel leaned forward, bracing herself with one hand on the outer wall of the mansion below the veranda. Her shoulders heaved and a retching sound came from her throat, though Neena couldn't see any vomit.

Jewel's hand slid down the wall as she dropped to her knees.

Neena set her laptop and brownie wrapper aside and rushed down the front steps and around to the side of the building.

"Are you okay?" She gathered Jewel's long auburn hair into a ponytail to keep her from throwing up on it, just as she'd done with Rosie when she was little. For the first time since Neena had met this woman, her hair was disheveled. Even scraggly.

"I'm fine." The woman spat onto the ground, as if ridding her mouth of something distasteful. "Please just go."

"Do you need a doctor?" Neena asked. Maybe this was appendicitis or some other emergency. How did a person even get medical care on such a remote island?

Jewel took a few knee-steps to her left and turned, placing her back to the wall. Her eyes were squeezed shut. "Need to sit."

"Do you want me to let Emma know you're down here?"

The woman's eyes popped open at the mention of her daughter. "No."

Neena almost gasped at what she saw on Jewel's face. Yes, her skin was pasty, but it was her eyes that shook Neena the most. Her dark pupils were pinpoints amidst the blue irises. The whites were streaked with lightning bolts of angry red lines. A yellowish crust of dried saliva was smeared across one cheek.

Neena had seen this look before. She'd seen it on Kevin. When he'd been on opiates.

"Are you okay?" she asked before she realized what a stupid question that was.

"Hungover."

Neena knew it was a lie. Maybe Jewel *was* hungover, but there was far more going on here than the aftereffects of too much alcohol. "Do you want to go to your room?"

Jewel's head lolled from side to side as she shook it. Her words were slurred. "Emma can't see me like this."

Neena's mind raced for something to do to help her. A glass of water maybe? How long did it take for the high to wear off? Maybe Neena's just being there would help, like the nurse who'd stayed at her side, reassuring her, when Neena had had her second panic attack that night in the ER.

"Sit." Jewel's voice was raspy and weak.

Neena wasn't sure if Jewel was talking about herself or Neena, but she took a step to the other side of Jewel, to where there was more grass and less dirt next to the foundation of the inn. She lowered herself beside Jewel and took one of her hands. It was ice cold, despite the heat and humidity.

They sat in silence for several minutes. Thankfully, this end of the building was shaded. In the distance, the gardener entered the garden gate but was far enough away that she likely didn't see them.

Finally, Neena spoke. She didn't want to accuse Jewel of anything, but she didn't want to see another family face what had happened to Kevin. "There are people who can help, you know. In case there's more going on here than alcohol."

Jewel didn't look at her or try to deny the allegation. She stared ahead, a haggard shell of the woman Neena had admired in the dining room on the first night she'd arrived. "I have a prescription," Jewel said.

Neena nodded. "My brother did, too, at first. He'd fallen off a ladder at work. But he ended up dying of an overdose." She turned to see Jewel's reaction, but there was none. "Just over a month ago. His death just about killed me." She didn't need to say what Jewel's death would do to Emma. Jewel had almost certainly figured that out on her own.

Jewel let her head fall back to rest on the outer wall of the building. Her eyes were closed. Her skin had moved from pale to a sickly shade of gray. The pair sat in silence for several minutes, still holding hands. Neena knew that a human connection was the best thing she had to offer in this moment.

Jewel finally spoke, her voice barely a whisper. "It wasn't supposed to turn out this way. I had surgery to fix...I was thrown from a horse...years ago. My back..."

Though Jewel wasn't talking in complete sentences, Neena understood how she'd gotten to this point. It was the same downward spiral

Kevin—and thousands of others—had been on. "Is it painkillers? Oxycodone, maybe?"

Jewel nodded. "No one knows about this. No one *can* know."

"But you need to get help." She wouldn't tell Jewel that Kevin had tried rehab more than once but had always gone back to the drugs.

"I thought I could handle it. That I was different from other people. That knowing I needed to care for Emma would be enough." Jewel rested her head on her bent knees. "I mean, what kind of a mother am I that I can't even stay straight for my own daughter?"

Neena tried to think of something encouraging. "This happens to a lot of people. No one expects it to happen to them."

"I'm so embarrassed. Emma can never find out. Or my mom or my sisters."

But those were the people Jewel would need to rely on—her support system—if she was going to get the help she needed. "But those people love you. They'll be there for you while you get help. They'll be there for you and for Emma."

"And do you know what my friends would say if they knew? Their pity and gossip and...those women from my club." Jewel's shoulders shuddered. Her face was still buried in her knees. Neena wrapped an arm around her shoulders and held her, letting her cry.

"Am I the first person you've told?" Neena asked.

Jewel nodded.

"It will get easier the next time around." At least that was what Neena hoped. "And I'm not at all judging you."

"Because of your brother. You've been through this. But someone who hasn't been through it, they don't think it can happen to them."

"People who judge you aren't worth keeping as friends. Do you know how many—"

Suddenly, a chipper young voice called from above. "There you are," Emma said as she leaned over the edge of the veranda to where they sat. "I've been looking all over for you."

Neena looked up, but Jewel stayed still, her head bent.

"Your mom isn't feeling well," Neena called up to Emma. "Can you run down to the kitchen and fill one of those sports bottles with water?" If nothing else, that would buy Jewel more time to gather herself before having to see her daughter.

"Be right back," Emma said before her head disappeared from view.

Neena nudged Jewel with her elbow. "Come on. We need to get you moving before Emma gets back."

Jewel came to life—her movements surer and her expression perkier—as if the thought of Emma seeing her like this gave her renewed strength. The inner fortitude of a mother whose most basic instinct is to protect her child.

Neena stood and pulled Jewel up.

"Thank you." Jewel's voice was hoarse.

"Please get some help," Neena said. "Don't do this to Emma." Her heart ached for the little girl. Neena didn't want Emma to see her mother's demise the way Neena had witnessed what had happened to Kevin. It had devastated Neena as an adult. She couldn't imagine what it would do to a child.

Jewel nodded.

"Come on," Neena said. "We'll meet Emma at the front steps. I'll help you to your room."

***

Neena startled when she opened the door to her guest room. On the far side of the room, someone wearing faded jeans was bent over in front of the dresser. She could see his backside but didn't know who it was until he stood to face her.

John.

"What are you doing here?" she said, though the second her brain registered the entirety of the room, she knew the answer. The bottom drawer of the dresser stood ajar.

He gave her a shrug and a sheepish look. In that moment, he looked more like a ten-year-old boy than *People* magazine's Sexiest Man Alive. "You caught me."

"Where did you get the lanyard?" She glanced to where she'd left it in her suitcase, which looked undisturbed. "Is everything okay with Ms. Sylvester?"

"You've met Jewel and her daughter, Emma?"

Had he seen her conversation with Jewel a couple of hours ago on the side of the inn? And how could a man who could be so charming also be so damn annoying? "What does that have to do with Ms. Sylvester?"

"Tell me what you think about Jewel."

Neena huffed. She was tired of these stupid games of his, but the quicker she played along, the sooner she would likely find out what he had to do with Ms. Sylvester. "I think she better get her act together or she's going to ruin both her life and Emma's."

He raised his eyebrows, as if encouraging her to put two and two together.

No.

Her heartbeat quickened. She lowered herself to sit on the bed. "Ms. Sylvester is on drugs, too?"

His face took on a grim expression. He nodded. "Opiates, like Jewel."

"But how do you know?" she asked.

"I'm helping you with your soul burden, remember?"

She rolled her eyes.

He shrugged. "Some things I just...know. I don't really understand how it all works."

"Where is Ms. Sylvester now?"

"She lives in Boulder, but she's in a rehab facility in Denver. It's her third attempt to try to get clean."

"But what happened? And how did she end up in Colorado?"

"Her son took a job out there after college. She and Thomas fell in love with the mountains, so they moved there shortly after."

Thomas. Yes. That had been her husband's name. At least they were still together. Teenaged Neena had longed for a marriage like theirs, full of laughter and love and equal partnership.

John continued. "She had a bad car wreck a few years ago. It really messed up her neck. She got addicted to pain pills."

"So she's in rehab?"

He nodded. "And I'm hoping that's where Jewel goes soon."

The connection now made perfect sense to Neena—the bejeweled lanyard and Jewel. These two gems—these two otherwise beautiful, classy women—had both fallen victim to addiction.

"Ms. Sylvester would probably welcome a call from a former student." He pulled a business card from the back pocket of his jeans and handed it to her. A rehab center in Denver. "She's going through a rough time. Might be nice if you told her how much she meant to you back then."

"Of course." She held up the business card. "I'd love to talk with her. Thank you."

He gave her a mischievous grin. "It's all part of our deal."

Neena started to argue but wasn't ready to move on to thoughts of him finding his wife. She was still reeling from the news of Ms. Sylvester. "I can't believe she's in rehab. She's the last person I would have thought..."

"Would you have thought, early on, that Kevin would have gotten addicted?"

"No," she admitted. Early versions of her brother flittered through her mind. The funny, rambunctious grade schooler, the gregarious high school freshman who always traveled in a cloud of Axe body spray. The college grad who'd landed his first professional job in the prestigious management training program at one of the big public accounting firms. She never would have thought such an open, affable boy could become a secretive, manipulative junkie in such a short period of time. Could anyone predict who would fall victim to the evil of drugs? If someone like Ms. Sylvester—someone so smart and savvy, someone in a happy, supportive marriage—could fall victim, then probably anyone could.

John seemed to read her mind. "Even people like Ms. Sylvester get addicted to drugs. Whatever they do once they become addicted is not the fault of the family."

A thunking noise sounded outside. Neena rose from the bed and walked to the window, moving aside the sheer curtain. Below her, Gus put a chopped log into a wheelbarrow at the inn's woodpile. He wore a faded red shirt and well-worn jeans. He placed another log in front of him and raised his axe. This brief respite of watching him gave her time to think about what John had said.

It's not the fault of the family.

So John was telling her that Kevin's overdose wasn't her fault. Of course, she'd known that on an intellectual level. Kevin was a grown man—in his early fifties, no less. He got to make decisions on his own. He got to go places without her looking over his back at every turn, even when he'd moved in with her. But he'd seen her home as a safe haven. As a place to heal and recover, away from the life that had been destroying him. Yes, it isn't the fault of the family, but he had been right there, in her guest bedroom. Back in her life full time. She should have seen what was going on. She should have known, if by no other means than by the connection she'd had with her only sibling.

And yet, he'd died in her home. Based on what the police had found in the nightstand next to his bed, he'd been doing drugs there, too. Her little brother had been in the fight of his life. And she had failed him.

"Promise me you'll at least *think* about forgiving yourself for Kevin's death," John said from behind her.

She continued to watch Gus chopping wood below her window. *It's not the fault of the family.* But it still felt like she should have been able to save him. Gus raised the axe again. "I'll think about it," she said.

"Oh, and I left one more thing for you," John said.

Neena turned, annoyed.

He reached into the dresser drawer and pulled out a cone-shaped party hat. He held it up for her to see. Silver glitter formed letters on the royal blue cardboard. "Happy New Year."

"When is this stupid little game of yours going to end?" she asked.

But instead of answering, he smiled and transformed into the same little funnel cloud she'd first seen at the beach, then quickly evaporated into the air.

The party hat fell to the floor a couple of feet in front of her. Then she remembered. Gus had told her he'd first seen John as a ghost on New Year's Eve, 1999. The year John had died.

She turned back to the window. At the woodpile below, Gus was no longer chopping wood. The axe that had been in his hand earlier now leaned against a nearby tree.

He stood by the woodpile, as if with rapt attention, staring up at her window. His mysterious eyes met hers. That connection she'd always felt with him nearly knocked her backwards, away from the glass.

Her intuition told her what she needed to know: she needed to talk to Gus about what had happened on New Year's Eve, 1999.

Chapter Twenty

Neena picked up the New Year's Eve party hat from the floor and placed it on the bed. Now that she understood what it meant, she didn't need to have it with her.

What she needed to do was get down to the woodpile before Gus had a chance to slip away. He had, after all, avoided talking to Neena about the night he'd met John. She could still see the wary look on Gus's face when she'd probed about it that day out on the lawn. How quickly he'd stood, saying he needed to get down to the dock to catch the ferry.

She raced down the main staircase inside the inn, then down the front steps of the veranda and around the end of the building that held her bedroom. It was closest to the woodpile, and she did *not* want him to get away without answering her questions this time.

But as she rounded the corner of the building, she saw a flash of faded red fabric slip through the tall gate of the garden, about a football field away. She veered from her original destination and walked quickly in that direction.

She let herself into the garden and looked around. There were maybe two city blocks of space in the fenced-in area. Rows and rows of various plants—some with leafy green foliage, some already tilled under for the season. But no sign of Gus.

To her right, the porch of a small building held a refrigerator with a rusty door. No appliance could withstand the humidity of being outdoors on this island, but she could understand why the gardener would want a cold beverage nearby. A stack of discarded plastic nursery pots stood precariously near one corner of the porch. A variety of tools leaned against the weathered wood.

She pushed open the door to find Gus busying himself by tidying a workbench. His back was to her. The place smelled of damp earth. Sunlight shone through the lone window, casting a crisscross of shadows across his back.

"You know," she said. "We're going to need to talk about it eventually."

"I ain't never talked to nobody about it," he said, his back still to her.

"John was in my room when you were at the woodpile." She hoped to ease Gus into the idea of talking to her.

"I know." Gus picked up a trash can and brushed some loose soil from the workbench into it.

"*He* apparently thinks we need to talk about it."

Gus busied himself now by gathering some handheld gardening tools and placing them in a bucket. He didn't say anything.

"What happened on New Year's Eve, 1999?" she asked.

"I told you, I ain't going to talk about it."

Outside the window, John appeared. He made a "get on with it" motion to Neena.

She shook her head. She did not want to make this sweet old man talk about something that was clearly painful to him. She wasn't on this island to inflict harm on anyone.

"He needs to talk about it." John's voice sounded muffled through the window. "For his sake."

She looked to Gus, who continued to move tools around on the workbench. He had apparently not heard anything.

A few seconds passed, and Gus finally turned to her. "I can be just as stubborn as you can, ya know." But then his gaze snapped to the window. His eyes widened.

"You see him, don't you?" Neena whispered.

Gus just stood there, staring at the window.

"I know you can't hear him," she said. "But he wants us to talk about it."

Gus scrubbed his hand down his face, as if thinking about what he was going to do. He looked to the window again, then to Neena. He turned back to the bench and again started rearranging tools.

She needed to get him talking while he seemed to be at least indecisive about it. She glanced at the window, but John was gone. She was now on her own.

"Was Evangeline with you?" she asked Gus in a low, soothing voice. His wife hadn't died until years later. "On New Year's Eve, 1999?"

Gus's hands stilled. His back was still to her. He lowered his head. "Evangeline and the girls were at the house with me. But Otis wasn't." His voice cracked.

"Otis?"

"My boy."

Her mind raced to remember what he'd told her about his son. He'd been killed in a helicopter crash on a Navy training mission in California.

She reached out to touch Gus's arm. His skin was burning hot. She gently turned him to face her. "Was that the day Otis died? On New Year's Eve?"

Gus shook his head. His gaze was cast downward.

"When did Otis die?"

"October twenty-eighth."

"Of that same year? 1999?" she asked.

Gus didn't say anything, but Neena already knew the answer. "So what happened on New Year's Eve?"

Gus raised his head. Those silvery-blue eyes bore into hers. "That was the day I'd planned to kill myself."

CHAPTER TWENTY-ONE

Gus reached out to support himself on the workbench in the garden shed. He looked the weakest Neena had ever seen him.

She glanced around for a chair but found only a tall, overturned plastic bucket. She quickly slid it to him. "Sit."

He lowered himself to the bucket and rested his elbows on his knees. His hands covered his face.

She stood silently, waiting for him to speak. Now that John wasn't rushing her, she could let the old man take his time.

"Nobody ever knew that before," Gus said. "Nobody ever knew I had planned to kill myself."

She swallowed, unsure what to say. She'd never talked about suicide to anyone since Mama had died. At least not in this way. Not so intimately.

Gus raised his head. "I...I just couldn't go on living. My boy had died. And for two whole months, that was all I could think about."

She knew exactly how he felt. It's how she'd felt in the days after Kevin had died. It's how she'd felt—decades ago—after Mama had killed herself.

She tipped over another plastic bucket and set it in front of him so that she could sit facing him. She reached out and cupped his hands in hers. "I've had family members die, too. But never a child." God forbid that something happened to Rosie. Neena had once read that losing a child was the worst grief a person could ever go through.

"I just wanted to not have that pain from the time I woke up in the morning until I went to sleep at night." He scoffed. "At least when I *could* sleep, which wasn't much in those days."

"And what about Evangeline?" Had Gus killed himself, his beloved wife would have lost both her son *and* her husband. Had Gus considered that?

"Sometimes we could talk about it and sometimes we couldn't." He motioned toward his chest. "It was like the hurt was so deep, we couldn't let it out of us. Besides, there weren't any words that would describe it."

"Did Evangeline know you were considering suicide?"

Tears welled in his eyes. He shook his head. "I couldn't tell her. I thought about it for weeks, but I couldn't talk to her about it. I couldn't let her know that I might do that to her. That I might leave her, too."

"So what changed your mind?"

He gazed out the window, as if unsure he wanted to answer. Finally, he turned to face her. "John. John changed my mind."

She sat back, surprised by the answer, though she knew the two had met that night. "That was the first night you saw him."

Gus nodded. There was a faraway look in his eyes. "I had tucked a letter inside Evangeline's purse after she went to bed. And I was standing next to a marsh I used to hang out at when I was a kid." His fingers formed the shape of a gun. His hand rose to his head.

"And John appeared?"

Again, Gus nodded. "No one on earth even knew I was considering it. No one on earth could have stopped me. But he knew."

Neena's opinion of John shifted. He was no longer the distracting, annoying spirit. He had saved Gus's life. "But you can't hear him. How did you know that's why he was there?"

"I just kind of *felt* the caring. I knew what he was telling me, even though he didn't use any words." Gus extended his hand out in front of him. His eyes were unfocused as if his mind and body were back in 1999.

"He reached out and held my hand. He didn't talk, but I felt his skin. His presence. And I knew he cared. I knew he was telling me not to hurt myself."

Neena's hands rose to her mouth. She waited for Gus to continue.

"If John hadn't stopped me, I wouldn't have been around when Evangeline got sick. There wouldn't have been anyone to care for her." Again, his eyes filled with tears. "I needed to be here for that."

"She would have been devastated *then* if you'd killed yourself." Just like Neena had been devastated when Mama had left her. How she'd wished she'd spent more time with her. Cuddled in bed with her, even when Neena came home from college. Written down her cornbread recipe. Heard her sing along with Patsy Cline one more time.

Gus's eyes were wide. "She would have lost her husband and her only son in just a few months. But John saved me. John didn't let me do that to her."

Neena let Gus's words sink in. He hadn't been able to tell the love of his life—the person closest to him—that he was considering suicide. Not even her love could have saved him. If not for the intervention of an otherworldly spirit, Gus would have been gone years ago.

Did that same thing apply to Mama? Neena had never understood why Mama hadn't given her and Kevin an indication that she was about to leave them. But if Gus couldn't talk to Evangeline, then perhaps Mama had felt like she couldn't talk to them, either.

Then a different thought hit her. "Wait a minute." She sprang to her feet. "If John kept you from killing yourself, why won't you help him find Carolyn? You owe him th—"

Gus shook his head from side to side in a slow, wide sweep, emphasizing his point. "It ain't my place."

She put her hands on her hips. "He saved your life!"

Gus gave her an annoyed look. "I told you already. I'm not the one who can help him. I can't even hear him. And he's been waiting for *you*." He stabbed a gnarled pointer finger in her direction.

She lowered herself to the bucket again. Gus *had* told her that, but she hadn't believed him. She hadn't believed any of this unearthly nonsense at the time. But she was beginning to understand that John's world and this world were interwoven. Some unseen fabric she'd never sensed before.

Gus continued. "I knew the minute you arrived on the island that you were the one he'd been waiting for."

Her gaze searched his. "But how?"

He shrugged. "A connection, I guess. Between the two of us. Like two magnets that are pulled together by a force we can't see." He motioned to her with his head. "You felt it, too."

She nodded. She most certainly had. "But I have an article to write. And a boss who's trying to fire me. A boss who doesn't even know the difference between John and his father."

Gus scoffed and then stood. "I've got to get back to work. Claire's gonna wonder where I am as it is."

Neena stood, too, and pushed the bucket she'd been sitting on to the side.

He made his way to the door, then turned toward her. "You've got to decide what's most important."

"Paying my bills is most important." Rosie was most important.

A look of disappointment crossed Gus's face. "The man's been looking for his wife for *twenty-five years*."

"That isn't my fault." She felt childish the second the words had left her mouth, but she needed to keep an eye on *her* prize, not someone else's.

Gus lifted his chin in defiance. "No, it's not your fault. But it's your turn to save him."

Chapter Twenty-Two

Neena sat in the garden shed for several minutes after Gus left, contemplating his challenge to her. *Was* it her duty to help John find Carolyn? She hadn't asked for any of this. She hadn't agreed to anything other than to write an article about the twenty-fifth anniversary of their deaths, which she desperately needed to complete. And then John had shown up talking this nonsense about her having a "soul burden."

But was it really nonsense?

Dwight's reaction alone proved how her grief about Mama and Kevin had negatively impacted her. How much of a pall had that grief spread over the rest of her life? Maybe it was time to let it go. To realize that maybe she'd done her best with them. If people like Jewel and Ms. Sylvester could get addicted to drugs, then why did she hold herself responsible for what had happened to Kevin?

Maybe Neena *did* have a soul burden. Maybe all this guilt she'd carried around for so many years wasn't necessary. Maybe she *could* set it down, after all.

Yes, John had known exactly what she needed. And now it was her turn to help him.

But if she was going to chase around Cumberland Island looking for Carolyn, then she *really* needed to get her article finished first. She stood, took one final look around the shed—she probably wasn't supposed to be in here and likely would never return—and started the walk back to the inn.

She went to her room, mounded the multitude of pillows against the headboard and propped herself against them, her computer on her lap. Thank God the inn had such luxurious bedding.

But about forty-five minutes into her work session, the gauzy curtain framing the closed window fluttered. She stared at it for a moment, waiting for it to happen again. But no, maybe she was just imagining things. She needed to concentrate on her work. She had, after all, been looking down at her computer screen rather than out into the room.

She got back to work on the paragraph describing the church. Her strongest memory of being there was seeing John in the back pew, but of course, she couldn't include that in her article. Justin already thought she was half-crazy. She closed her eyes, envisioning the tiny chapel in her mind.

That's when she smelled the soap. Not the soap itself, but a manly, fresh-washed scent. Her eyes flew open to see John sitting in the high back chair near the fireplace. Why did he smell so clean? Did ghosts shower?

Younger Neena would have been all a-goo over that scent on such a handsome man, but now she drew in an impatient breath and forced herself not to roll her eyes.

"You're not very hospitable," he said.

"I'm trying to get my article finished."

"But you've decided to help me."

Further evidence that he could read her mind. "Yes, but saving my job has to come first." She rose on the pillows to get a look at his hands above the footboard. There was nothing in them. "No trinkets to leave in my dresser today?" *Thank God.*

He stood and paced the rug in front of the fireplace. "I want to hear your plan of attack."

"My plan of attack?"

"Your strategy." He had a "duh" look on his face. "For finding Carolyn. I've got some ideas, but I want to know your thoughts, too."

"Look, I realize how much you've helped me with everything I've been carrying around about my mom's and brother's deaths. But I can't think about how we'll find her until I get my work done."

He came to stand beside her, facing her computer screen. "Maybe I could help you. I ran a magazine once, you know."

Yes, she remembered. It had been called *George*. The iconic cover of model Cindy Crawford dressed as George Washington had gotten all kinds of buzz. She angled her laptop screen downward so he couldn't see it. "I don't need your help, but thank you."

"That's what you said before. That you didn't need my help." He turned to face her and flashed a victorious grin. "Turns out you were wrong."

"Were you always this annoying?"

"Most women found me charming." He had a teasing look on his face.

Her neck and cheeks heated. Since he could read her mind, did he know that she'd been one of those women? That she'd sometimes imagined outlandish tales about how her path might have crossed with his and they'd lived happily ever after—America's prince with a nobody from Jacksonville? "I know. *People* magazine's Sexiest Man Alive."

"1988." His mischievous grin conveyed that he didn't take the award too seriously.

"I barely paid attention." *Liar.* It was possible she still had that issue stashed in a box in her house somewhere.

"So how long until you're done with your work?"

"I don't know. I'm working as hard as I can, but I promise I'll help get a plan for finding Carolyn as soon as my article is complete." It irked her every time she thought of Justin. The smug little bastard.

John hesitated. "I hate to be a downer, but I know from experience that none of us really knows how long we'll be around. I want to try to find her before anything…bad happens."

She studied his face. Was he serious? "You're worried I might die before I help you find Carolyn?" She was propped up against a wall of cushy pillows, not careening down some rapids or scaling the face of a vertical cliff. He was being such a drama queen. "And I still don't know what makes me so important in finding her."

"You're the only person who's ever been able to hear me. That has to count for something, right? It seems like a good sign."

She rested her back against the headboard. What *could* that detail mean? And why her?

Her mattress sank as he sat on the bed next to her. How could a ghost always seem so *present*? His expression was both hopeful and cautious. "I'm hoping Carolyn can hear you, too."

She clasped her hands in front of her, begging him. "Look, I promise I'll help you, but please let me get my work done first."

He seemed to think about it for several seconds, then shrugged. "You're sure you don't want to tap into my magazine expertise?"

"Get out." She pointed to the door of her guest room, which in hindsight made no sense. John didn't need a door to exit.

He stood and wagged his finger in her direction. "Okay. I'm backing off for now, but I'm holding you to your word."

Within seconds, he transformed into tendrils of smoke, twisting like a slow-moving tornado. The bottom drawer of her dresser slid open on its own, and the funnel of smoke traveled that way, guiding itself inside.

Is that where he stayed when he wasn't visible to her? Had he been in there before? Again, her face heated as she thought about how many times she'd been naked in this room. Her fifty-six-year-old body was doughy and plump, especially compared to his younger, more fit physique, even though they'd once been contemporaries.

But she couldn't think about any of that right now. She knew of only one way John could help her bank account. And that was by having the anniversary of his death featured on the cover of *Coastal South Travel*.

***

After another hour perched against her headboard, Neena had made good progress toward finishing her article. But her mind had wandered, returning again and again to one question, despite her desire to work: How *could* she help John find Carolyn?

Like a person trying to solve a Rubik's cube, she turned the request at various angles in her mind.

If Carolyn hadn't appeared to her husband in twenty-five years, what could be done to draw her to Cumberland Island? Where might she have been for more than two decades?

Neena knew that not all faiths believed in the afterlife, but like John, Carolyn had been Catholic. Their wedding had been performed by the same priest who had delivered the eulogy for John's mother, Jackie Kennedy Onassis. Maybe, given that religious background, Carolyn's spirit would be "out there" somewhere.

Neena turned the Rubik's cube again, examining the question from a different angle.

If John could see Ms. Sylvester out in Boulder, Colorado, then could Carolyn's spirit see what was going on here, even if she spent much of her time elsewhere? Like maybe in and around New York City, where she grew up and later lived with John? Or in Boston, where she'd gone to college?

Did ghosts have a "home base" like people do? Neena made a mental note to ask John about that.

And why was it that only Neena could hear John speak? What did that mean? How could she use that to help him locate Carolyn?

She turned the Rubik's cube once again. Maybe next time she and John were together, she could use her phone to play the song they'd used for the first dance at their reception—"Forever in My Life," by Prince.

But she'd read once that it was the sense of smell that was most closely connected to memories. Like how the smell of mulled wine would always remind her of Christmases with Mama. Or how the scent of banana bread would always bring back memories of when they'd made it in Home Ec her sophomore year of high school.

So what smells might mean something to Carolyn? What scents might bring her to back to the island?

Gus had mentioned only one specific, food-related detail: Carolyn had loved Evangeline's apple fritters.

An idea popped into her mind. Perhaps they could lure Carolyn here with some of the fresh-baked pastries she adored? The idea seemed ridiculous, but then so was the fact that John F. Kennedy Jr. had disappeared into her dresser drawer an hour ago.

Neena set her laptop on the bed beside her and rose. Her story seemed to be at a bit of an impasse. She might as well pursue every angle she could think of while she was here on the island.

It was decided, then. She would ask Gus to get a batch of apple fritters from the kitchen. Perhaps she and John could take them to the church or to whatever part of the island had been Carolyn's favorite.

She glanced at the time on her phone, trying to remember the cadence of Gus's daily chores around the inn. Where might he be at this time of day?

She left her room and went out onto the wide veranda, hoping to find him on the grounds somewhere. Several of the inn's staff members were setting up what looked to be an outdoor dinner of some kind. There were more place settings than the inn had guests, so maybe some people were coming over just for the day? Or perhaps—like for John and Carolyn's wedding—guests stayed at both the IvyLena and the Greyfield?

Gus and a younger man Neena hadn't seen before were setting up an arbor of sorts. It was white and was set up under one of the largest live oaks. She took a seat in one of the porch's rocking chairs. She couldn't talk to Gus while he was with the other employee, so she'd wait here while they finished, then hope to get Gus alone.

Another employee pulled a truck near the arbor and began unloading white folding chairs from its bed. He set them into rows facing the arbor.

A warm, happy feeling slid through Neena's body. What a beautiful spot for a wedding.

Neena hoped the bride—whoever she was—knew how lucky she was to have such a magical spot for her ceremony and the reception that would follow. Neena could never afford such an elaborate event for Rosie, even on the mainland. But Neena would hopefully be back on her feet financially before her daughter met the man she wanted to marry. And God forbid that man ended up being Caleb.

A tingling sensation at the base of Neena's spine interrupted her intro-spection. She froze as it traveled up her nerve endings to the base of her skull, then stayed there, pulsing.

Oh, God. Not another panic attack.

She willed herself to remain calm, knowing her body had a mind of its own when an attack happened. But no—this felt different. Not the same as her other panic attacks. This didn't feel like it was about her at all.

Her gaze sought out Gus as a realization overcame her. This was about him. She was certain of it, but where was he?

Her heart raced. She stood and clung to the low concrete wall in front of her—the edge of the porch. She looked to the right and to the left, but there was no sign of him. She'd just started down the wide front steps—eager to find him—when he came around from the side of the inn, walking with the younger man he'd been working with on the arbor. The other man said something, then Gus threw back his head and laughed.

She studied him. He looked fine. Peppier than usual, actually. Maybe working with that young kid brought that out in him.

But if Gus was fine, then why did Neena have this overwhelming sense of dread about him? Why were her body and her intuition telling her that things were about to go horribly wrong?

The pair continued across the lawn toward the arbor, which was about a football field away from Neena. And still she stood, watching them. An older woman who was sitting on the porch gave Neena a curious look, but Neena couldn't concern herself with what people thought. Her instinct was telling her that something big—and bad—was about to happen.

Gus and the younger man reached the arbor, where Gus grasped one side of the arch in each of his hands. The other man pulled a hammer from a loop in his overalls and lightly tapped near the top of the structure. So they were reinforcing the arch, perhaps where the nails had gotten loose as it sat in storage somewhere. Not a big deal.

But that's not what it felt like to Neena. Something was going on with Gus. Something that felt like a *very big deal*.

She took another couple of steps down toward the lawn as she watched them.

Again, the younger man said something between them. Again, Gus laughed.

Gus moved to the other side of the arch and placed his hands—one on each side—just as he'd done before.

But before the younger man could raise his hammer to reinforce the nails, Gus collapsed to the ground.

Chapter Twenty-Three

"Someone call 911!" Neena yelled as she rushed down the steps and onto the front lawn of the inn. She ran toward Gus, who had collapsed one panic-filled second ago.

But how did an ambulance even come to the island? The paramedics would have to get on a boat and make the forty-five-minute trek over here. They'd likely bring their bags with them, but what about all the equipment they'd have to leave behind in the vehicle? The *life-saving* equipment they might need to treat their patients? To treat Gus?

She stopped running long enough to turn and yell back toward the guests on the porch. "Find out if there's a doctor here." Maybe one who lived on the island? Or a guest at the inn? Given how expensive it was to stay here, some portion of their clientele had to be doctors, right?

Her lungs begged for air and her legs were weak as she made her way across the massive lawn. She hadn't run that far since high school gym class. But still, she ran. She had to get to Gus.

When she finally reached him, she bent over, gasping, her hands on her knees. Below her, Gus's normally tanned skin had the color and waxiness of the vanilla bark she used to make Christmas candy. His head fell limply to one side, his tongue lolling inside his gaping mouth.

She laid a palm on his chest but couldn't feel it rise and fall. Desperation coursed through her like an electric current. He could *not* die. Not when he'd just come into her life.

She raised her head to the small gathering of employees that surrounded them. "Someone find a doctor! Call 911!"

The only CPR class she'd taken had been infant CPR more than twenty-three years ago when she was pregnant with Rosie. She barely remembered anything about it, but she did her best to press forcefully on his chest in a solid rhythm, trying to get him breathing again. She bent to whisper in his ear. "I'm here, Gus. It's Neena. I'm here with you."

"I'm a doctor," a woman said as she burst through the small gathering of employees who surrounded him. It was the youngish Black lady who'd had on the fuchsia dress last night, though today she wore casual hiking clothes. She lowered herself to the ground next to Gus.

Neena moved to her left, giving the woman full access to Gus's too-still body. The doctor immediately started CPR. Her motions were quick and efficient. Her actions got more aggressive, almost violent, but if this was what it took to keep Gus alive, then it needed to happen.

Neena was having trouble pulling air into her lungs. Her breaths were so shallow she felt like she, too, might be having some kind of medical emergency, but she wouldn't take any attention away from Gus. She sat completely still, as if her body knew that too large a movement might splinter the weak grasp he had on life.

"We need to give them some room," one of the employees said. He gently tugged on a coworker's arm and motioned to the others to get back to work, too.

Their anxious gazes stayed on Gus and the doctor, even as they took small, reluctant steps backwards, away from them. Neena could tell this wasn't only curiosity. Their expressions showed a love for this man. A deep concern for his well-being. A couple of them were crying.

Neena looked back at the man—now her friend—who lay on the ground. She needed to do something. She couldn't just sit there petrified while he suffered. Slowly, she lifted her hand and wove her fingers through his white hair—the only thing she could think to do. Rosie had loved it when Neena rubbed her head when she was little. Perhaps Gus would find some comfort in it, too.

He hadn't moved since he'd collapsed, which seemed like far too long ago.

The doctor continued to work feverishly, though the look on her face had become more stoic, somehow more clinical-looking.

After several more minutes, she sat back on her heels and took her hands off of Gus, a grim look on her face. "There's nothing more I can do."

"Is he dead?" one of the female employees asked in a meek, shaking voice.

The doctor gave one curt nod. "I'm afraid so."

Neena inhaled a sharp breath. Gus was dead?

The doctor looked up at a different employee. "Can you get something to cover him with until the EMTs gets here? Maybe a sheet or a tablecloth?"

The girl nodded somberly and turned to trudge toward the inn.

Neena's mind was like an inflatable raft being tossed around by the ocean. She had no sense of stability. No feeling that she was at all in control. "Did he have a heart attack?" she asked the doctor.

The woman placed a palm on each of her thighs and rose. Her husband supported her upper arm with his hand to help her. Sandy dirt clung to her knees. "We won't know for sure until they do an autopsy," she said.

Neena looked back at Gus's lifeless face. She couldn't imagine them cutting him open like a slab of meat. Was an autopsy really necessary for a man his age? Did it really matter why he'd passed away?

The only good news in all of this was that now he could see his sweet Evangeline again. He could see his son, Otis.

Neena's mind went to his daughters. He'd said they both lived near Atlanta. She hoped the inn knew how to reach them. She'd talk to Claire about that later.

The doctor looked to the gathering of employees. "How long does it generally take for the paramedics to get here?"

Most of them shrugged, an I-have-no-idea look on their faces. But one of them spoke. "It'll be a while."

"I'll stay with him," Neena said from where she still sat on the ground, cradling his head.

The doctor's gaze moved to her.

"I'll stay with him until they get here," Neena repeated. She couldn't imagine leaving his side. It would be difficult enough when the paramedics took him away.

He'd been her connection. Her first window into a magical world that she now somewhat accepted but still didn't fully understand. He'd taught her things that no one else could teach her.

And now he was gone.

***

Neena stood on the dock as the ferry—with two paramedics and with Gus in a body bag—pulled away. The afternoon sun glinted off the water as the hum of the boat's motor got softer and softer.

Claire put a hand on Neena's back. They were the only two people on the dock.

"He was a special guy," Claire said.

"He was indeed."

"You know, he rarely talked to guests. Kind of kept to himself, which was fine. It wasn't his job to interact with them. But he really seemed taken with you."

Neena turned her head to see Claire's face as she looked out over the water toward the ferry. She had a wistful expression.

Neena turned back toward the water. "It's like we had a...connection." She didn't want to say too much, but Claire already recognized there was something special between her and Gus. "Like we were kindred spirits."

"I'm really going to miss him."

"Me, too," Neena said. A beat of silence stretched between them. "Had he been sick?"

"Not that I know of, but I'm not sure he would have told me if he was."

No, he probably wouldn't have told anyone. Just like he hadn't told anyone about his near-suicide attempt. That was the kind of guy he'd been.

They stood watching the ferry for another minute or so, then Claire turned. "I've got to get back to the inn. Spend some time with the staff. I want to figure out a way we can have a little ceremony or something to honor his passing." She had already contacted his daughters, who were both headed down from Atlanta. She took a couple of steps from the railing. "You coming?"

Neena shook her head. "No. I'm going to stay here a while." The ferry was far out on the water, but she couldn't leave while the vessel holding Gus was still within sight.

Claire gave a kind smile. "Let me know if you need anything."

"I will," Neena said before she turned back toward the water.

Within minutes, the ferry had disappeared beyond the horizon. Neena moved to a bench on the dock, not yet ready to go back to the inn. The dock was solitary and quiet, except for the lapping of the water along the shoreline and the occasional call of a gull. The humidity caused beads of sweat to gather at her hairline.

She marveled to think that a man she'd known for only a few days had meant so much to her. How they'd had such a strong connection, even before they'd spoken a word to each other. It was like he'd been her gateway to John and all the lessons he'd had to teach her. Like the two of them had tag-teamed, forcing her to see the things she hadn't previously allowed herself to see.

Speaking of John, where had he been while all this was happening? She looked around her, but there was no sign of him. Had he seen everything that had gone on with Gus? Was he somehow loitering overhead or behind a live oak, watching everything that had unfolded on the front lawn?

Maybe he'd give her a brief reprieve—a bit of time to grieve Gus—before he expected her to start the search for Carolyn.

But something else niggled in the back of her brain. She really *could* be finished with her article, but she was hesitant to send it off to Justin in its present form. It was a good piece, but he was still likely to fire her, like he'd done the other older workers. No, this article needed to be outstanding to save her job. And she knew in her gut that it hadn't yet reached that standard. That it still needed something—that one detail or that one image—that would make it stand out from the other articles that were written about the famous couple and their private, exclusive event.

She glanced back to the horizon, where she'd last seen the ferry. She'd worry about John and Justin later. This moment, this quiet time, was about Gus.

She'd *known* he was in trouble, even before he'd known. He'd still been laughing with his coworker when she'd sensed that something was about to go horribly wrong.

And even though she'd known this in advance, she'd been unable to save him. The third painful time in her life that this had happened. But how was it that she'd sensed that something was about to go horribly wrong with Gus but had been blindsided by the deaths of her own mother and brother? It just didn't make sense. Even if she hadn't been able to save them, she should have sensed something was wrong and offered what comfort she could.

She stood and returned to the railing. She looked out over the water in the direction the ferry had gone. "Goodbye, Gus." Her lips trembled, but she didn't cry. She was still too numb. It still didn't feel real.

But as she stood there quietly, her mind seemed to have other plans. Her fingers gripped the railing as a sudden hot flash seared her skin. The thundering of her heart sounded like a massive herd of wild horses. She couldn't catch her breath.

Not here. Not now.

The horizon—so clear just a few moments ago—tipped sideways. The line between ocean and sky blurred, then disappeared into a jumble of blues and grays. She turned, knowing she needed to make it back to the bench before the panic attack was in full swing.

She took two steps.

And then the world went black.

Chapter Twenty-Four

Neena woke to Dwight's face hovering over her. The blue sky above him told her she was outside. But where?

She rolled to her side and curled up in a ball.

The unpainted wooden plank below her face.

The briny smell of brackish water.

The sound of water lapping below her.

She was at the dock. But she was so tired. She just needed to close her eyes for a few more minutes...

"Neena." Dwight spoke gently as he shook her shoulder. "Are you okay? Did you hit your head?" His fingers rose to her hair, gently moving along her scalp.

She squeezed her eyes closed. How long had she been here? How much had he seen of her panic attack?

"Neena, can you hear me?" His tone held more urgency. "Do I need to call an ambulance?"

"No ambulance." Her voice sounded like a gurgle. And that's how she felt—like she was underwater, fighting her way to the surface. But the planks of the dock were solid underneath her. Thank God she hadn't fallen into the river.

"Can I help you sit up?" Dwight said. "I want to make sure you're okay."

But her heart was still pounding, possibly loud enough for him to hear. She held up one finger—a signal for him to give her a minute. She lay on her side taking deep breaths, trying to get her frenetic body to resume its normal rhythms.

Dwight repeated supportive phrases while he rubbed her back.

You're doing fine.

Take all the time you need.

There's nothing here that's going to hurt you.

I'm here with you until you're better.

She was finally ready to open her eyes and sit up but dreaded that first look at his face. This was all so embarrassing. He was undoubtedly doubly glad they weren't going to see each other moving forward. Guys didn't want women who were high maintenance like this. Prone to fits and blackouts and whatever else this new anxiety disorder had in store for her.

She pushed herself up with her arms.

He snapped to attention. "Do you want to stay here on the dock's floor? Or sit on the bench?"

"Bench," she croaked as she closed her eyes. The sun was behind a cloud, but the brightness still hurt her eyes.

He gently helped her to the seat and sat beside her, leaning her against him for support.

"How did you find me?" Claire had left her on the dock alone, saying goodbye to Gus.

"I saw that you'd stayed with Gus's body until the paramedics got here. And then I saw you come down to the dock with them. I was worried about you."

Thank God he'd come down here. "Thank you." She'd never been more appreciative of someone's help.

He stroked her hair and kissed the top of her head—a caregiver's kiss, as opposed to the ones they'd shared earlier. "We can sit here as long as you need to."

His body was solid—the foundation she needed to get her bearings again. His presence comforted her. It felt good to be cared for, even by a man with whom she had no future.

After several minutes of silence, her body quivered less. Her heart rate had returned to normal. Her vision had cleared. But exhaustion felt like a heavy blanket pressing down on her, just like after her previous panic attacks. "I think I'm ready to go back now."

He helped her stand and wrapped his arm around her, supporting her as she took her first unsteady steps along the dock toward the shore. He stayed with her—going at her pace and stopping when she needed to—until they reached the inn.

He paused when they reached the foot of the wide staircase leading up to the veranda. "You ready for this?" he asked.

She closed her eyes and nodded.

"I could carry you up, if you want me to."

She managed to give him a wicked side-eye.

He held up a hand in surrender. "Okay. Maybe not."

"I'm ready," she said, as much to convince herself as to convince Dwight. Her legs were still weak, but she had to make it inside the inn. Mounting the stairs felt like pulling a truckload of dead weight up a major incline. She couldn't have done it without Dwight supporting her all the way.

"Rest here before you go to your room?" he asked when they'd finally reached the top and made it through the front door.

She nodded.

He helped her to a little upholstered bench that sat in the entry hall, near the wide staircase. After a couple of minutes of rest, he helped her up the stairs, through the library and to her room. Thank God he knew where it was. Thank God for the intimate setting of the IvyLena, where the handful of guests at least knew who each other was. Had she been in some big, impersonal hotel filled with strangers, she would have been left to fend for herself through a maze of elevators and long corridors.

He opened her bedroom door and helped her into her bed. She briefly wondered if there was anything embarrassing lying on the floor or draped over a chair, but she couldn't care about that now.

All she needed was to rest.

***

Neena awakened to a light knock. Before she could remember where she was, she heard a door open. Dwight's voice came from off to her right. "Mind if I come in?"

She pulled her hand out from below the covers and motioned him in.

"I made you some hot tea." He held out a steaming white mug.

She wiped a bit of slobber from the side of her mouth and sat up in bed. The mattress sank when he sat beside her and handed her the mug. He had on a dinner jacket. Was it that late already?

"Decaf," he said. "Chamomile, or something like that."

He pronounced it wrong, but she didn't say anything. Why correct a man who took such good care of her? "How long was I asleep?"

"About an hour. I checked on you once, but you were sound asleep, so I just left you alone."

"You checked on me?"

"Is that okay? I mean, one old man did stare at me when I came out of your room."

She grinned as she tried to take a sip from her mug. "It's fine. I appreciate it."

His demeanor got more serious. "Was that a panic attack? It was kind of scary."

She nodded.

"Gus really meant a lot to you."

"He did." But she still had no idea why her mind chose to give her a panic attack at that moment. Why then, as opposed to when she'd first seen John? Or when she thought someone had broken into her safe? Or when Gus had first died? It didn't seem to make any sense when it happened. "Hard to believe I only met him a few days ago."

Dwight looked pensive. "I get it, though. You don't have to know someone long for them to have a big impact on you. I had a counselor at my first sleepaway camp who I knew for exactly five days. He was the first guy who ever showed me that being a smart kid could be cool, you know?" Dwight looked toward the window and off in the distance, like he was remembering those days from decades ago. "I'll remember that guy forever. Brian Saunders." He grinned. "They called him B.S. for short."

She chuckled at the joke but was glad he understood how Gus could mean so much to her. "Maybe people come into our lives for very specific reasons sometimes."

He nodded. "And then they're gone."

"And then they're gone." *Like you.* She looked down into her tea to avoid his gaze.

He seemed to recognize the awkwardness of the moment, too. "It's a beautiful evening. Can I help you down to the porch?"

She frowned at him. "I'd rather the other guests didn't think I'm an invalid."

He chuckled. "How about I walk two steps behind in case you start to fall?"

She looked at the bedside table, trying to locate her phone. She had no idea what time it was, but the bedside table answered her question. Dinner would be served in twenty-eight minutes.

"Come on," he said. "I'll sit with you."

"Wouldn't you rather be in the living room, enjoying the hors d'oeuvres?"

"I'd rather make sure you're doing okay."

She shrugged and pushed the covers off her legs. "Then, sure," she said, though their togetherness jabbed at the tender spot left behind by his rejection. Each of them would soon fall into the "and then they were gone" category. But unlike Gus or Brian Saunders, Dwight didn't appear to have entered her life for anything other than heartache, even though he offered her some measure of comfort now. "Give me two minutes to change into my outfit for dinner?"

He motioned with his head to the room beside hers. "I'll wait in the library."

She got out of bed and changed clothes, brushed her teeth and her hair. She felt weak but much better than before her nap.

When she and Dwight settled into two side-by-side rocking chairs on the veranda, they sat for a long time without talking.

She let the sounds of the night envelop her—cicadas and hoot owls and the distant whinny of a wild horse. The rhythmic creak of Dwight's chair against the porch's floorboards and the otherwise stillness of the evening gave her a sense of peace. Her grief and her worries seemed like they were all part of a much larger universe. There was comfort in knowing that she was a tiny part of a much bigger world. That even though her heartbreaks felt monumental to her, they were all part of some giant master plan.

"Makes me want to live like this forever." Dwight's voice was low. Almost reverent. "Away from towns. Away from people."

"I know what you mean." But her real life included so many complications. A peacefulness like this was fleeting at best.

"Do you have a place like this where you can get away back in Jacksonville?" he asked.

She thought about his question. There were quite a few places where she could get out into nature. Sunrise at the beach, for starters. Or some of the nature trails she and Rosie used to enjoy. "I think the challenge is finding the time to just sit and *be*."

"You have to make the time. I mean, that's what guys do when they say they're going fishing for the day. They're going out in nature with nothing to do but sit in a boat all day."

She chuckled. "I'm not a fisherman. Fisherwoman. Fisherperson."

"But you need to make the time, especially after all you've been through these last few weeks. Don't you think?"

"You're right, but it's never as simple as it sounds."

The creaking of his chair quieted as he stopped rocking and leaned toward her. "You know why I eventually sold my business? Because I was tired of all the busyness. All the demands on my time. No amount of future earnings was worth not ever having a quiet moment to just sit and think."

"I don't have a business I can sell." Not even close.

"But that's not my point. My point is that you've been through a lot. You owe it to yourself to step away whenever you need to. Just tell yourself you've got a plan for the day—you're going fishing for the afternoon—then do whatever makes you feel at peace—taking a walk or sitting in a coffee shop people-watching or lying in bed watching Netflix or whatever. That's what I had to do after Brenda and I lost our daughter and when I was going through my divorce and when each of my parents died. I had to take time for myself. We all need time to heal in private. You know what I mean?"

She looked out over the massive front lawn, now cloaked in shadows, and beyond, to the river. She did believe that healing was a private matter. That different people approached it differently and that the amount of time needed varied from person to person.

But what struck her most about their conversation was that he was more introspective than other men she'd met. Or at least he was more willing to share his introspection. She liked that a lot, which made her even sadder that the two of them would part in a couple of days, never to see each other again.

But before she could respond to him, a bell chimed from inside the mansion. Time for dinner.

They each took a moment before they rose, as if neither wanted this moment to end.

"Would you like to join Carl and me at our table?" he asked.

She shook her head. "No, thank you. I appreciate you taking care of me today, but since we've already established that there's no...future..." She wasn't trying to get him to change his mind. She just didn't see the point in drawing out the inevitable.

"I get it." He stepped to the front door and opened it, then stood aside for her to enter the mansion first.

She touched his arm. "Thank you again for your help."

"No problem," he said as he followed her through the main entry hall toward the dining room at the back of the mansion.

She'd just settled herself at the large table when a tinkling of spoon-on-glass came from behind her. She turned to see Dwight standing. As usual, he and Carl were seated at a small table by themselves. Each of the other guests had stilled and turned to look at Dwight, too.

"Before we start dinner," he said. "I'd like to make a toast in Gus's memory. Sure, we didn't know him well. Some of us may not have even spoken a word to him, but any time a man lives to be that age and has seen what he's seen, he deserves to be honored." He held his glass higher. "To Gus."

"To Gus," the other guests said in unison as they raised their glasses.

There were several moments of reverent silence, then the doctor spoke. "I heard they're going to have some kind of little ceremony or circle of remembrance for the staff tonight." She looked toward a server who stood quietly nearby. The server nodded—a confirmation of what the doctor had heard—then reached up and ran her forefinger under her eye. She held her lips tightly together, as if willing herself not to cry.

Neena was glad that Gus's coworkers would honor him in this way. That those who'd worked with him for so many years would take the time to reminisce about what he'd meant to them. Perhaps she and John could do the same, since they'd both known him in such a unique way.

But her attention now was on Dwight. He wasn't a particularly gregarious guy. He hadn't made it a point to get to know or even converse with the other guests during his stay, but he'd stepped up when something important had happened. Like he knew what mattered most. His quiet confidence portrayed dignity and respect.

He was definitely the kind of guy that Neena could have gotten attached to. She would have liked to have explored where their relationship could have gone. But instead, she wouldn't see him again once she left the island.

She wouldn't have thought it was possible after Gus's death, but watching Dwight now made her heart ache even more.

Chapter Twenty-Five

Neena closed her eyes and rested her head against the truck's headrest as the vehicle rattled down Main Road. Though she'd been desperately tired after last night's panic attack, her night had been restless. She'd had repeated bouts of wakefulness, when she hadn't been able to get Gus's death off her mind.

John had appeared in her room as the sun was coming up that morning, and the two of them had come up with a list of ideas on how to find Carolyn. Where on the island she would most likely appear, based on John's recollection of what she'd enjoyed during the week of the wedding.

They'd agreed to meet at the church as soon as Neena could figure out how to get there. She definitely hadn't felt strong enough to bike that far. Not after everything that had happened yesterday.

She'd thought about her article on and off all night. It was technically complete, but she still wasn't sure it shined the way she wanted it to. The way she *needed* it to. Something in her gut had told her to get her mind off it for a bit and allow her subconscious to noodle around on its own. Or maybe helping John this morning would give her some new insight. Some bit of helpful information, though it would have to be something she could corroborate with someone who was, well, *alive*.

"You sure you want me to just leave you here?"

Neena's eyes popped open when the gardener spoke. The truck was pulling around the side of Beulah Alberty's house in The Settlement. The tiny church was right in front of them.

"It's got no lights and no air conditioning, ya know?" the woman said.

"That's why I came early in the day." Neena pasted on a fake smile. She had cajoled the gardener to take her there privately, apart from the daily tour given by the inn's naturalist. There'd be no way to explain to others what she and John had planned to do here. And she certainly didn't need any witnesses. "Besides, I've got all I need." She held up her water and her notepad, but in reality, her phone was the most important thing she'd brought with her.

The truck came to a stop, and Neena opened the door to get out.

"See you in an hour," the woman said.

"Thank you," Neena jumped down from the tall work vehicle and waited for the gardener's truck to pull away. Her heart beat faster as she anticipated what might happen inside. She patted her pocket again, making sure her phone was still there.

She walked the twenty or so yards to the church and crept up the stairs. She scolded herself for doing so. She was doing nothing wrong. It was kept unlocked so people like her could visit, but thank God no one else was here now.

She inched the door open and stepped inside. The warm air was a bit stale—a testament to the few visitors who came here—but still, she closed the door behind her. She wasn't sure if she would hear others approaching the church, and she didn't want anyone to witness what she was about to do.

She took another step forward and glanced around the single room. Each of the eight pews sat empty. The front of the church looked exactly how it had when she was there before. No sign of John, but surely if Carolyn showed up, John would, too.

Still, Neena walked to the center of the room and pulled her phone from her pocket. She pulled up her music streaming app and punched the button to play the song John and Carolyn had first danced to as husband and wife. Prince's distinctive voice filled the church with "Forever in My Life."

She moved slowly in a circle holding the phone above her head with an outstretched arm, like an offering to the gods of some sort. She closed her eyes, trying to imagine first the wedding ceremony, then the beautiful couple swaying in each other's arms during their first dance at the reception. What a charmed life they'd led. A life so different from Neena's. So different from Rosie's.

Behind her, a female spoke. "Ma'am? Is it okay if we're in here?"

Neena immediately lowered the phone and spun to where the voice had come from. A pair of what looked to be day hikers stood near the open doorway. Neena hadn't heard them enter over the music. She reached down and silenced her phone. "Oh. Yes. Sorry. I'm a journalist writing an article about the twenty-fifth anniversary of the death of John F. Kennedy Jr. and his wife. I was just...trying to imagine their wedding."

"Did they have music in here?" the forty-something woman asked.

Her male companion spoke up, correcting her. "It doesn't even have electricity."

The woman motioned toward Neena. "*She's* got music in here."

"Spotify didn't exist when JFK Jr. got married," he said. "The *internet* barely existed then."

"Can we go up to the pulpit?" the woman asked Neena.

Neena nodded and stepped aside, giving them room to pass by her. She understood the awe she saw in the woman's demeanor as she stepped onto the raised area at the front of the church. Neena had had it on her first visit here, too. Hell, she *still* had it. This tiny place was part of American history.

"My family visited Dallas when I was a kid—the grassy knoll and the book depository and all that," the woman said.

The man snorted. "Be grateful you're not a Kennedy. Their life expectancy is pretty low."

Neena hoped John hadn't heard that unsavory comment. All she wanted was for this couple to leave. To get back to her business at hand. To carry out the plan she and John had agreed to the night before.

The woman now stood behind the pulpit, looking out over the pews. "I wish our wedding had been intimate like this."

The man snorted again. "Like your mom would have ever gone for that."

The woman stepped from behind the pulpit and down the couple of steps as she spoke to Neena. "You would have thought *I* was marrying a Kennedy the way my mom acted about our wedding."

The man took on a cocky posture. "You got something better than a Kennedy."

The woman rolled her eyes good-naturedly.

Neena stayed silent, not wanting to draw them into any conversation that might elongate their stay. She had limited time before the gardener returned to get her.

The man walked toward the door. "Okay, babe, you've seen it now. Let's go find some more horses."

"You and those damn horses," the woman said, but she, too, walked toward the entrance of the church. She turned back toward Neena once she'd reached it. "We'll let you get back to"—she circled her hand in the air, indicating the center of the church, where she'd first seen Neena—"whatever it was you were doing."

The man grunted—or maybe hid a laugh?—then tromped down the steps outside, his wife trailing behind him.

Neena rushed to the door and quietly closed it. She didn't want anything she did to call the couple's attention back to her or the church.

When she turned back to the room, John stood in the center aisle, near the front of the church.

"That guy's an asshole," John said.

Neena breathed a sigh of relief. "I thought you'd never get here."

"I saw them coming and knew we wouldn't really have time—"

Irritation flared inside her. "You saw them coming but didn't warn me to put my phone down and stop spinning in circles in the middle of the room? Now who's the asshole?"

He grinned. "It was kind of cute, actually." He motioned to her phone. "Now play the song again. Let's see if we can get her to come here."

Neena pulled her phone from her pocket and once again started the song. Like she had done earlier, he stood in the center aisle with his eyes closed, though he stood stationary instead of spinning in those ridiculous circles she'd made.

She stepped quietly to one of the pews and sat down, her phone resting on her lap so John could still hear the music. She wanted to give him as much privacy as possible but still be nearby. This was about him and his bride. Neena was just the bystander with the cell phone that could play their song.

She wondered if the word "forever" brought him pain—because of the plane crash so soon after their wedding or perhaps because he hadn't seen his wife in more than two decades. There had been no "forever" for this couple—at least not yet, anyway.

She glanced up to check on him. He swayed slightly, his head and shoulders moving in sync with the rhythm. Was he remembering the feel of her body pressed against his as they'd danced to this song? The sense of excitement they must have felt at having pulled off their secret wedding? The way they'd managed to celebrate their love in such a joyful, private manner?

Neena had read that the constant presence of paparazzi had put a strain on their marriage. John had grown up with it, but it was new—and stressful—to Carolyn. A private wedding would have been quite the victory, considering those circumstances.

The song ended, and Neena picked up her phone to play it again. This would be the eighth time through it.

"Don't," John said, his voice terse.

She looked up from her screen to his grief-stricken face. She raised her eyebrows, questioning him, her finger still poised to play it again.

He looked despondent as he plopped down in the pew opposite her, on other side of the aisle. "It's not working." He placed his elbows on his knees and his face in his palms.

Her heart broke for him. He wanted so desperately to find the woman he loved. What might Neena have felt like had a man ever loved her so completely? But today wasn't about her. It was about John and Carolyn.

She held her phone out to him. "Do you want to go try it at the Greyfield Inn?" After all, that was where the first dance had taken place. Much like the IvyLena, only registered guests were allowed on the Greyfield property, but maybe John could go there on his own?

That would give her time to go back to the IvyLena and look over her article one more time, hoping some new inspiration hit her for how to improve it. Yes, it could be sent to Justin in its current state, but she'd be happier if it had a bit more spark to it.

John shook his head. "The church was more special to her than the reception." He was silent for a moment, then he sat back in the pew and looked at Neena. "She had me bring her back here later that night, you know?"

"Back to the church?"

He smiled sadly. "She wanted to see it again when she wasn't so nervous. When she could take it all in without a bunch of people staring at her."

"So you came back...later?" The wedding took place at dusk, so it would have been dark then.

He nodded. "We snuck away from the reception for a little while. I asked Gus to drive us back here—he worked at the IvyLena but was pulling a shift at the Greyfield that night. We lit the candles and she stood there at the door." He turned to look to the spot where she would have stood then. "Still in her wedding dress—looking the most beautiful I'd ever seen her." A wistful look filled his eyes.

Neena remained silent, letting him relive the memory.

He turned again to face forward as he spoke. "And then we walked to the front and stood at the altar."

"Where was Gus while all this was going on?"

John jabbed a thumb behind him. "He waited outside. Having a cigarette, I think. He used to smoke in those days."

Neena had never smelled a bit of smoke on him. She wondered when he'd quit. So many things had changed—about Gus, about John, about her, about the world—in the years since the wedding.

"We weren't here long," John said. "We didn't want the people at the reception to think we'd gone missing, but she got what she wanted. A few quiet moments here, just the two of us." His voice shook with emotion. "It was almost better than the wedding."

Neena rose and went to comfort him. She couldn't hug him because of how he sat in the pew, so she knelt beside him and placed a hand on his knee. It was as solid, as *real*, as any knee she'd ever felt. And when he placed his hand over hers, it was large and warm.

"She was a gorgeous bride," Neena said.

"Yes, she was." His gaze was fixed on where they would have stood at the front of the church.

Neena bumped his leg with her shoulder. "And the groom wasn't bad, either."

He looked at her and chuckled.

"Do you think Gus ever told anyone that story?" she asked. He'd been so protective about not talking about individual guests when she'd interviewed him.

"Nah. He was too classy for that. And, besides, they'd all signed confidentiality agreements."

Her knees creaked as she rose. "I still don't think he would have told anyone, even without the agreement."

"I don't, either."

"So, what do you want to try next?" They'd discussed several options as they'd formulated their plan at dawn that morning. But which one would he choose? She had almost exactly twenty-four hours before she had to catch tomorrow morning's ferry back to the mainland, so they needed to get on it.

Gus had collapsed and died before she could ask him to get her some apple fritters, so she hadn't even mentioned that idea to John. She'd checked at breakfast, but there hadn't been any in the pastry basket at the coffee station. Granted, there were delicious-looking peach turnovers and blueberry tarts, but none of the fritters Carolyn had loved.

"You want to come to the Greyfield with me? Try playing the song there?" he said, giving in to her earlier suggestion.

"Registered guests only." She would *not* risk getting caught trespassing while she was on the island. "I'll loan you my phone to take with you."

"If that doesn't work, we'll go find some horses on the beach. Maybe she's there, watching them."

So, they had a plan, however hopeless it seemed. Neena looked at her phone. 9:52 a.m. "My ride back will be here in eight minutes. Let me show you how to use this thing." iPhones, after all, hadn't existed during his lifetime. She taught him how to punch in her passcode, navigate to her music app, and play the song. Curiosity and wonder filled his eyes as he took in everything she taught him.

A few minutes later, she hustled toward the back of the church, ready to meet the gardener for her ride back to the IvyLena. Neena was just about to reach the door when she heard his voice. "Hey," he called to her.

She turned.

He was now standing in the center aisle. "That story I told you about us coming back here after the wedding?"

"Yeah?"

"Everyone who took part in that is now dead."

She looked at him, puzzled. What was he getting at? "And?"

"If you include it in your magazine article, who's going to refute it?"

Chapter Twenty-Six

John had tried playing the Prince song at the Greyfield Inn after he and Neena had left the church, but Carolyn did not appear.

He and Neena had reconvened for a trip to the beach. Still no luck when they played the song there.

Now they sat in a couple of Adirondack chairs tucked close to the IvyLena's foundation so other guests couldn't see Neena talking to...well...an empty chair.

John's arms and legs draped over the chair—a picture of defeat. His eyes showed pure heartbreak. "I was so certain you were the missing ingredient," he said to Neena. "The one thing that would finally allow me to find her."

Neena wondered if his pain was similar to what she'd felt ever since Mama's death. Kevin's death was still too new for her to really understand what it was all about—like an open wound that was still tender to the touch. She suspected John's loss of Carolyn was different, though. There must be something about having found that person who really understood you. Who *chose* to spend their life with you, rather than it being predetermined because of family bonds.

Neena wasn't resentful that she'd never had a love like that. She was proud of her independence. Of the life she'd built. Of the happiness she had on those rare occasions when she could block her empty bank account from her mind. But she'd always had a niggling doubt about what she'd missed out on. What it might feel like to have little intimate secrets with someone who'd promised to never leave.

"It's times like this that I really wish I could have a beer," John said.

Neena turned toward him. "You don't drink...once you're...you know?"

He laughed. "You can say it. I know I'm dead."

"And you don't drink in the afterlife?"

He shook his head. "Or eat."

"What food do you miss the most?"

He thought for a minute, then a slow smile spread across his face. "When I was a kid, we had a cook who made the best spaghetti and meatballs."

"I used to love my mom's spaghetti, too."

They sat silently for a few minutes, each lost in their own memories. A light breeze floated through the trees, ruffling both her hair *and* John's.

Finally, he spoke. "Can you use that part in your story? The part about how Carolyn and I went back to the church during the reception?"

She shook her head. "I need to attribute it to a source." She gave him the side-eye. "And it can't be a dead guy."

He shrugged. "So Gus told you before he died. Seems like a simple solution to me."

"Except he didn't." Her voice was more emphatic than she intended.

"And who's going to know that?" he asked.

"I pride myself on my journalistic integrity. Surely you knew about that concept when you were running your own magazine."

He gave a resigned nod. "Yeah. I get it. Integrity was one of the things most important to me—in all parts of my life. My mom had stressed it to us just about every day starting when we were still in diapers."

Neena knew the influence a single mother had over her young children. Her own mother had raised Neena and Kevin by herself for most of their lives. But at least Neena had vague memories of her dad, who'd abandoned them when she was seven or eight.

She hated that John had never gotten to know his own father. That his mother had to do all the child-rearing, even though there were likely nannies and countless Kennedy relatives around. That he was raised as a fatherless son. Her heart broke for him just a little bit more. "I'd have to tell my editor how I got that information. And I don't know how I'd do that." Justin had already tried to send a replacement to the island because he thought she was unstable. Telling him she'd talked to a ghost while she was there was out of the question.

John gave a mischievous smile. "It would be a great anecdote for your article, though."

She smiled back. "Yes, it would."

He leaned forward, as if he'd just had a new idea. "What about that crazy guy who lives in that gatehouse along Main Road?"

"What about him?"

"He saw us drive back to the church, you know."

Neena sucked in a breath. "On the night of your wedding?"

"Stood right in the middle of the road so we couldn't pass and—" But before John finished his sentence, he was gone.

Neena glanced around, trying to figure out what had just happened. What had John sensed that caused him to disappear?

"Neena?" Dwight had apparently come from around the corner of the inn.

"Dwight. Hi." She turned toward him, hoping he hadn't seen her talking to an empty chair.

He frowned. "What are you doing down here all by yourself?"

She shrugged. "Just enjoying some alone time. I'm leaving tomorrow, so I'm trying to soak it all in." The second the words were out of her mouth, she realized how desperate they sounded. She was *not* trying to lure Dwight back with threats that she'd soon be gone.

"Yeah, I get it." He looked out over the front lawn. Two brown horses now grazed under the low-slung branches of the gigantic live oak. "It's a beautiful place."

"When are you and Carl leaving?"

"Wednesday morning. He's got an afternoon flight out of Savannah."

"It's good y'all got to spend time together." She hated this small talk. She had no idea if Dwight had enjoyed his time with his brother, especially given Carl's work schedule and that damn misguided conversation about the Grand Hotel.

"I really wish things could have turned out differently between us," he said.

They could have, she wanted to scream, but didn't. She made a little sound in the back of her throat. "Yeah. Me, too."

An uncomfortable silence stretched between them, with her still sitting in her chair and him standing nearby. She wasn't sure where to look or what to do or how to act. She wasn't sure if she wanted this moment to end or for it to never end. Because if he was nearby, then at least there was some hope that he might decide to look past her grief to see the real her.

Finally, he spoke. "I guess I'll give you back your alone time."

"Have a safe trip home," she said.

As she watched him walk away, she tried not to imagine what might have developed between them.

"Looks like I'm not the only one missing out on something." John's voice came from beside her. She turned her head to see that he now occupied the nearby chair.

"It's hard to miss out on something you never really had. Besides, I'll get over him." At least she hoped she would.

John took several moments to answer. He was as solemn as she'd ever seen him. "I guess that's the difference about our situations. I'll never get over Carolyn." His eyes misted. "I'll never stop looking for her."

Chapter Twenty-Seven

Neena would have to figure out later how to thank the gardener for driving her—yet again—to the other end of the island. This time, however, the gardener would wait nearby, her truck visible from Boone Calhoun's front porch so the reclusive man would know Neena hadn't arrived there alone. That there would be witnesses, should he try to harm Neena.

"He's never given anyone an interview, you know," the gardener said as she slowed to a stop at the gatehouse that hugged the side of Main Road.

Neena ran her sweaty palms down the front of her shorts. "Well, maybe I'll be the first."

The gardener hitched her chin toward a wide spot in the road about twenty feet ahead. "I'll turn around and park down there so any other cars can get by me. You sure you're going to be all right?"

Neena snorted. She had no idea what would happen when she knocked on Boone Calhoun's front door, but she would be as careful as possible. That damn Justin better appreciate what she was doing to get this article written.

She opened the door of the truck and stepped out. Behind her, the gardener pulled away slowly. She had already done a three-point turn and inched onto the shoulder up ahead—facing the gatehouse—by the time Neena took her first step onto Boone's long, narrow front porch.

"Go away!" a male voice barked from inside once Neena had knocked.

"I want to ask what you saw the night of the Kennedy wedding," Neena called through the door. Since her time here was likely limited, she needed to get straight to the point.

The door swung open, and Boone stood there, an angry look on his face. He might have been an imposing figure at one time, but his tall frame now looked weak and stooped. He wore a baggy olive-colored T-shirt over dirty, torn jeans. His thin white hair was pulled back into a ponytail. "Did you not hear what I said? Go. Away." He said the last two words slowly and loudly as if Neena might be dense.

"Were you at home the night of the Kennedy wedding?"

The man's menacing laugh made Neena even more nervous than when she'd arrived. "Lady, I haven't been off the island since I moved here in the early nineties," he said.

Neena wished she could write a story about such an eccentric person, but that was a project for another day. "So did you see much of the wedding festivities?" Surely even a recluse like Boone would have been curious about the world's most famous bachelor.

Boone started to shut the door, but Neena laid her hand on it.

"It must have been nice, being in on a secret like that," she said.

"Wasn't much of a secret. Most of the island knew."

"But not the people on the mainland. Not the paparazzi." Neena continued to press on the door, forcing it to stay open. "And an event like that doesn't happen very often, especially in a place this remote."

Boone scoffed. "Thank God for that. I moved to this island for a reason."

But Boone's gaze was now on something on the ground off to Neena's right. She turned to see what he was looking at as Boone rushed past her and bent to study a plant in the garden bed that abutted one end of the porch.

"Damn rabbits," he said as he fingered the greenery.

At least he was outside now, no longer shutting the door in Neena's face.

"The *Washington Post* wrote that you waved to the wedding guests as they drove by your house in open-air jeeps," she said.

Boone had moved on to examine a plant in one of the huge planters on the porch. "Yeah, well, the *Washington Post* wasn't on the island that day, so how would they know?"

"And later that night, you stood in the middle of the road, blocking a different jeep when John and Carolyn tried to return to the church."

Boone stilled, his back still to Neena. "I don't know what you're talking about."

But his reaction had said otherwise. "That's the part you didn't tell the *Post* about. That John and Carolyn went back to the church during the reception." Neena was guessing here, but she needed to say something—anything—to get Boone talking.

He bent to pick up a watering can. He still hadn't looked in Neena's direction.

"I'm just trying to confirm some facts," she said.

He stood and glared at her. "I return to my original statement: go away."

She needed to take another approach. "Look, I don't work for a big publication like the *Post*. I work for a small magazine out of Jacksonville. I'm just trying to write an article and pay my bills and—"

"Three hundred people a day." Boone's demeanor had grown even more agitated.

"What?"

"Three hundred people a day. That's how many the National Park Service lets on this island a day."

Neena had no idea why he'd switched to this topic, but perhaps she could gain his trust by following along. "Do you think that many come here each day? Or are there days, like when it's really cold in the winter, when hardly anyone visits?"

He gave another maniacal laugh. "Oh, those are the people you *really* have to worry about. The ones who are willing to brave the cold wind across the sound when it's forty degrees out—those are the ones who are the scariest."

She used a soothing tone, hoping to calm his agitation. "Why are they scary?"

Boone paced the porch. "Because they'd go to any length to find me. To figure out what I'm doing out here. How I'm living my life."

"Maybe they just want to see the island."

He spun to face Neena, planting both of his feet on the weather-beaten floorboards of the porch. His knuckles were white where he gripped the watering can. "That's where you're wrong. They *say* they want to see the island, the church, but I know why they're here."

"Look, I don't care who you used to be or how you're living your life. I just want to know about the night of the Kennedy wedding. That's what my article is about."

He gritted his teeth and looked for a second like he might say something, then shook his head and stepped off the porch, disappearing around the corner of the house. He hadn't told her again to go away, and it *did* seem as if he was about to talk. But following him along the side of the house would mean she'd be out of the gardener's view.

Neena quickly glanced toward the truck parked about twenty feet away. The gardener appeared to be looking down at her phone. Neena wished she was more attentive. What if Neena had another panic attack? What if she passed out or couldn't breathe? No telling what Boone would do if Neena became even more vulnerable than she already was.

But she'd come here to do a job, and she was determined to do it. She followed Boone along the far wall of the weather-worn house. She passed a window that gave her a glance of the spartan furnishings inside.

At the back of the house, they reached a lean-to that had been tacked on to the structure. A pegboard under the awning held all kinds of tools—shovels and awls and hammers. Any number of items that Boone could use to harm Neena.

Thoughts of Rosie flashed through her mind. Rosie was too young to lose her mother. Neena knew. She'd been adrift for so long after losing her own mother at about Rosie's age.

In a quick, almost violent motion, Boone turned toward Neena. His feet were spread wide. He held the watering can aloft, like he might strike her with it. "I knew you were one of them the minute I saw you."

She didn't care who "them" was. She just wanted out of there before anything bad happened to her.

He rushed toward her and screamed in her face. "Tell me who sent you."

Neena backed up as far as she could before her back hit a piece of plywood resting across two sawhorses. "My editor sent me. I work for *Coastal South Travel*. I'm writing an article on the Kennedys."

"And I'm supposed to believe that?"

"I just want to verify that they went back to the church that night."

He got so close to Neena that the length of their bodies touched. His hot, tangy breath rushed over Neena's face as he spoke in a menacing whisper. "So you can write about the crazy guy who stood in the middle of the road and stopped them? So you can cause even more people to come spy on me?" He waved his arm in the general direction of The Settlement. "And besides, Gus made me promise not to tell anyone what they were up to."

Neena's knees went weak. *She had it.* Confirmation that Gus and John and Carolyn had gone to the church that night. This was what she needed to include that detail in her article.

Boone backed away and began to pace in front of Neena. The entire lean-to was the size of a walk-in closet, yet they were both under its roof.

"Those people invaded my space. The night of the wedding was like...an attack. And the other people...they been coming ever since." Boone moved in short, jerky motions that made him look like a frightened bird.

In such close quarters—and since Neena now had what she'd come for—she was able to focus on the man's face.

Neena had been afraid of him ever since Hiram had said he toted a gun, but now she was unsure what she saw in Boone's expression.

Was it the aggression she'd expected when she'd arrived here?

Or was it fear?

Chapter Twenty-Eight

Neena continued to watch as Boone paced under the lean-to's roof. She considered the level of fear that Boone must live with—that he'd been living with for years. That must be exhausting, to always have his senses on high alert. To constantly feel threatened. To never get to relax and just *be*.

Neena's own experience with mental illness had nearly sucked the life out of her—and hers was short-lived compared to his.

Suddenly, Neena wanted to reach out to this man. To provide comfort. "I really do think the people who come here want to see the island and the church where the Kennedy wedding took place. I don't think they're here to spy on you."

Boone brushed roughly at the side of his face over and over again. Neena assumed it was some sort of nervous habit brought about by his agitation.

"You don't know anything about what's really going on," he said. "About how many people come here to...invade my privacy."

Neena took a step forward. "I know what it's like...to feel out of control. I was in a mental health unit not long ago. I still have panic attacks. I'm still...recovering." Or maybe she'd never recover. It was too early to tell. She now accepted that John wasn't a hallucination, but there were so many ways in which she needed to regain her confidence and resilience.

Boone cowered to the other side of the small enclosure. "I'm not ever going to one of those places. I'm not ever going to a hospital or an institution or a—"

"I'm not saying you have to. I'm saying that…I understand at least a little about how you feel."

He shook his head violently. "No one—"

The air was sliced by the loud blare of the truck's horn. Neena turned toward the noise and took a step outside the lean-to, far enough to see that the nose of the vehicle was now next to the porch. The gardener had apparently pulled closer but was likely afraid to get out to find where Neena had gone.

And while Neena had once been scared of Boone, she now felt sorry for him. She wished the gardener would give them more time to talk. More time for her to perhaps convince Boone to get some help.

"I don't want anyone else near me." Boone's voice shook with fear. "Go. Just go." And with that, he dashed around the far corner of the house.

Neena followed him until he hobbled up onto the front porch and disappeared inside the house. The door slammed shut. The sound of multiple locks clicking into place told Neena their conversation was now over.

***

A mix of emotions swirled inside Neena as she walked toward the dock the following morning, ready for her departure from Cumberland Island. She was proud of the article she'd written. The crowning jewel, of course, was John's information about the secret trip back to the church that no other reporter had ever written about. But even without it, she'd dug deep to discover new behind-the-scenes information about the fairytale wedding that had captivated the nation more than two decades ago.

She hated to leave the island. It was such a special place to her. A place that, in many ways, had changed her life. She turned and stopped, looking at the IvyLena one more time before heading farther down the dirt road. Once the wide path rounded toward the dock, the mansion would be out of view.

She could return to the island for a day trip, but it was highly unlikely she'd ever get to stay at the inn again. At several hundred dollars a night, it was well beyond her means—and probably always would be. Day-trippers couldn't even enter the private grounds of the inn, so even if she did return, she wouldn't be able to go inside. To once again feel the history and ambiance of this special place.

Even if she'd never encountered John or Gus, the place would have been extraordinary, but they had each made her experience so much richer. So unique. So *personal*. Leaving the island also meant leaving each of them behind, as well.

She took in the veranda, where she and Dwight had sat in rocking chairs as they got to know each other. What would it have been like to sit with him on another front porch somewhere, the two of them growing old together? She'd tried to convince herself that she was only attached to the *possibility* of a relationship with him, but she knew in her heart that they'd had a real connection. She'd felt more comfortable with him than with any other man she'd ever met.

She forced herself to look away from the veranda—to not dwell on something she couldn't have—but that made her feel even worse. She imagined John, sitting in one of the Adirondack chairs overlooking the river, as his search continued for his missing wife. What an honor it was to have met him. To have been a witness to his charm and playfulness and innate sense of dignity. They'd said their goodbyes when he'd appeared in her room the night before. He really had seemed to appreciate how she'd tried to help him, but in the end, they hadn't found Carolyn. Their mission had failed, and now Neena was leaving him—alone and heartbroken and not knowing when the next person might show up who could help him in his search. With her and Gus both gone, he was at least temporarily without a direct connection to the living world.

Her eyes misted as she glanced to the spot on the front lawn where she'd last seen Gus alive. Hopefully he was already with Evangeline, not searching for his wife the way John was.

There'd been a period of time when Mama had insisted the family go to a nearby Methodist church, but since Neena had left that religion behind, she was no longer sure what she believed about the afterlife. She made a mental note to think about that when she had quiet time at home alone.

For now, though, she needed to get to the ferry. She moved her gaze from left to right, taking in the grounds. Four horses grazed on the expansive lawn. At the far edge, she could barely see where the road turned into the forest—the road she and Dwight had taken during their walk.

She took a deep breath, then turned and made her way to the dock.

"Good morning," said one of two male employees who were on the ferry, preparing it for the short trip to the mainland. He pointed to a rubber mat that sat at the foot of the small stairs that would take her onto the vessel. The mat had a small reservoir of water on it. "Please clean the sand off your feet before you come aboard."

She did as she was told, swishing her sandals in the shallow puddle before taking his hand and stepping onto the ferry.

"Please make sure we got everything out of your room we were supposed to get." He pointed to the single suitcase tucked under one of the benches near the back of the ferry.

She wondered whose job it had been to retrieve it from her room now that Gus was gone. "That's all I had. Am I the only one headed back today?"

He winked. "A private excursion just for you."

The other employee turned and joined in their conversation. "Very exclusive. Pick any seat you'd like."

She settled onto a wooden bench that faced the back of the ferry, outside the small, tent-like structure that housed the controls of the boat. She wanted to enjoy the view of the marsh and water one last time as they headed back to shore.

The second man pulled the rubber things that kept the boat from bumping the dock inside the vessel as they prepared to take off. Slowly, the vessel swung around into the middle of the river and chugged along the shoreline.

A great egret rose from the grasses as they went by, its long wings an expanse of white against the bright blue sky. The marsh grasses were her favorite color of chartreuse, interrupted by an occasional twisted trunk of a dead tree—driftwood in the making.

The wind from the boat blew her hair into her face as she scanned the surface of the water for dolphins. She reached into her purse to search for an elastic band, but her hand instead hit something that crinkled. Cellophane, maybe? She looked inside, trying to think of what it might be. But when she pulled it out, her mouth fell open.

A small clear bag containing two toasty-brown pastries.

Evangeline's Apple Fritters, according to the little stick-on label affixed to the outside of the sealed bag. The label also held the IvyLena name and logo. She glanced toward the two employees in the tented area at the front of the boat. Did they see her surprise at what she'd found? But they stood chatting, their backs to her while one of them steered them through the water.

She instinctively looked to the sky, the bright sun heating her skin, and said a silent "Thank you" to Gus. Though she'd never had the chance to ask him for them, she knew in her heart they were a gift from him. She closed her eyes, letting the memory of him wash over her.

When she opened her eyes again, a woman sat on the bench across from her, not even three feet away. Neena gasped as her brain registered who it was.

Carolyn Bessette-Kennedy.

Her blond hair was pulled back, though the wind caused the baby hairs around her face to move in a frenetic dance. She wore burnt orange capri-length leggings and a formfitting T-shirt—the same kind of casual attire any other guest would wear at the inn. A daypack sat beside her on the bench seat.

Carolyn pulled her sunglasses up and placed them on top of her head. "Would you mind if I had one of those?"

But Neena could only stare. She couldn't get her body to move or her mouth to open.

Carolyn gave an understanding smile. "Your apple fritters." She nodded toward Neena's lap. "Would you mind sharing one? They were my favorite."

Neena fumbled the bag before finally lifting it and holding it toward Carolyn. "I got them for you." Her throat was so constricted she could barely speak.

Carolyn seemed pleased with that response. She gently took the bag from Neena's hands and opened it, pulling one of the delicate pastries from inside.

Neena finally felt like she could talk. "We've been looking for you."

Carolyn's gaze rose. There was a tiny crumb on her bottom lip. "We?"

"John and me. He's been desperate to find you." How could this woman—this ghost?—not know her husband had been searching for her all these years?

Carolyn's face brightened. She shifted forward on the bench. "You've seen John?"

Neena nodded. "I have," she said, as his musky, fresh-washed scent floated in on the sea air.

Chapter Twenty-Nine

Neena sat silently—waiting expectantly—on the ferry that was taking her from Cumberland Island back to the mainland. That musky, fresh scent always signaled John's arrival. She watched Carolyn's face, wanting to see it—the moment the woman laid eyes on the husband she hadn't seen in twenty-five years.

Neena felt a presence beside her—an arm brushing against hers—but still, she kept her gaze on Carolyn's face.

The woman's eyes widened as she looked at the bench next to Neena. The musky scent grew stronger.

Carolyn's hands rose to her mouth as her eyes welled with tears. "John."

Only once the two had seen each other was Neena willing to move. She scooted over on the bench, angling her body so she could take in both John, who was beside her, and Carolyn, who sat on the bench across from him.

"I've been looking all over for you." He took her hands and held them in the space between their knees.

"I thought..." Carolyn seemed to be having trouble getting over the surprise of seeing her husband again. "I thought I'd never get to see you again." She set the apple fritter she'd been holding on the seat beside her.

The pair stood in unison and moved toward each other, their body-to-body contact as real as any embrace Neena had ever seen. Their hands traveled over each other's arms and torso and face, as if testing to make sure that what they were seeing was really there. John wiped the tiny crumb of apple fritter off Carolyn's lips as he traced them with his forefinger.

The jarring of the boat got harder as it skidded over the water. John and Carolyn wobbled from the motion, then laughed. They sat down on the bench opposite Neena, as if there was ever any question about them not sitting side by side now that they'd found each other. John pulled his wife's legs onto his lap so that she was turned, facing him.

Carolyn's eyes searched John's face. "I can't believe you're really here." Her voice cracked with emotion.

He lowered his mouth to hers and the couple shared their first kiss in more than two decades—a slow, luxurious gesture filled with love and longing and tenderness.

Neena knew this was a private, intimate moment, but she couldn't bring herself to look away. For some reason she couldn't explain, she had been brought into this search for Carolyn, this reunion. She was supposed to be a part of it.

John leaned back to look at his wife's face, but still clung to her. The smile had disappeared from his face, replaced with a look of remorse. "I am so, so sorry for what happened to you and Lauren."

A puzzled look crossed Carolyn's face. "And you, too. You died there, too."

John bowed his head. "Yes, but I should have been able to save us."

Neena wondered if John said that because of what had happened in the cockpit that night or because he knew the National Transportation Safety Board had ruled the crash as "pilot error."

Carolyn placed a finger under his chin and raised his head. Her hand moved so that her palm rested gently on his cheek. "It was our time to die." She looked into John's eyes as if trying to make sure he understood her point.

"Your poor parents. They lost two daughters at the same time," he said.

She nodded. "I look in on them all the time. They both had a really hard time dealing with it, but I think they've finally accepted it."

The pair sat silently for a few moments as if contemplating the impact their deaths had on the people around them. The wind whipped their hair and clothing as they clung to each other.

Carolyn's palm was still on John's cheek. "I do *not* blame you for what happened."

John's expression was hard to read—a combination of confusion and potential relief. "How could it not be my fault? I was at the controls that night."

"And you've been stuck here on earth, right?"

He nodded.

"And I've moved on to a different place than you have. A place of peace. It's like"—she seemed to search for words—"like your shame and self-blame have kept you here." She gave him a sympathetic smile. "So let go. Forgive yourself."

A glimmer of hope passed through his eyes. "And that will allow us to spend time together?"

She smiled and nodded.

"You really believe that?" His voice shook.

She leaned toward him, emphasizing her point. "I don't just believe it. I *know* it."

He grinned and ran a hand through his hair. His look of relief made his already-handsome face even more attractive. More open. Less worried. More carefree than Neena had ever seen it. "I wish I would have known all this for the last twenty-five years," he said.

She laid her pointer finger on his nose. "I wish you had, too."

Neena choked back tears. Maybe that's what she'd needed all along—to cast off her shame and self-blame. To forgive herself.

"I've been searching for you, too," Carolyn said. "And now I know why I couldn't find you."

He lowered his face to his hands, as if the emotion was too much to bear. "I thought...I thought we wouldn't be together again."

She gently pulled his hands away from his face. "I want to spend *all* my time with you."

He closed his eyes and let out a deep breath, then drew her into another embrace. "Now that I've found you, I'm not ever going to let you go."

Neena sat back and studied their bodies instead of just their faces. Their forms had started to become less and less opaque.

"We should say goodbye to your friend," Carolyn said without breaking eye contact with John.

He seemed to have to force himself to look away from the bride he'd been searching for for so long. "I can't thank you enough. You've returned my treasure to me." He looked at Carolyn and smiled, then returned his attention to Neena. "I hope I've been able to help you in some small way in return."

She had trouble speaking. This man had done so much for her. She would be forever indebted to him. "You've given me something equally as valuable. Even if I did think all your talk about my 'soul burden' was a bunch of crap."

They both laughed.

He released Carolyn and moved to the other bench to sit next to Neena. His embrace was as warm and solid as any real human. His musky scent surrounded her. She laid her head on his chest—just briefly—as she tried to soak in everything she wanted to remember about this moment.

"Goodbye, John," she said when he'd released her.

His brown eyes were filled with the same sorrow she felt. "Goodbye, Neena."

"I won't see you again, will I?" she asked.

He shook his head. "Probably not."

She nodded to indicate Carolyn. "Go catch up on the last twenty-five years."

As much as it hurt to see him go, Neena would—of course—rather he be with his wife than with her. Neena may not have ever found true love, but they certainly had. They both deserved their happiness.

CHAPTER THIRTY

Neena sat back on the bench as the ferry skittered across the water toward the mainland. John and Carolyn were finally together, but they'd disappeared soon after John's goodbye to Neena. They'd been locked in an embrace as their last visible traces floated away on the sea breeze.

Now alone amid the vast beauty of the wetlands, Neena was happy the couple was together, but her heart ached at the notion that John and Gus were both gone. Were plans underway for Gus's funeral? Had his daughters both arrived from the Atlanta area?

As the ferry got farther and farther away from the fairytale of Cumberland Island, reality began to set in. She would soon step back into her regular life.

She tried to prepare herself for the possibility—the probability—that Justin would soon cut her loose from *Coastal South Travel*. No more assignments from her bread-and-butter account would make it even more imperative that she work to get new assignments from other publications. Despite the whirlwind of fantastical activity that had happened over the last few days, her bank account was still in the same sad shape as when she'd first arrived on the island.

She looked out toward the marsh grasses and wondered where John and Carolyn were now. How they'd begin to make up for the time they'd spent apart. He certainly had been diligent in searching for her all those years. If Neena died today, who would she seek out with such desperation?

She sat back and contemplated that question. Yes, she'd want to see Mama and Kevin, but Rosie would be her priority. Neena would want to be as close to her daughter as possible, to check in on her often, even if they inhabited two different worlds. To watch her grow into the woman she was meant to become.

As much as Mama and Kevin had meant to Neena—and as much as her guilt over their deaths had shaped her life—Rosie was the person who really had her heart.

Why had she spent so much time obsessing over the past when her relationship with her daughter—right here and right now—was in such bad shape? She needed to get their relationship back on track. Yes, Neena's job was important, but nothing was more vital to her than her daughter.

She would spend her drive time thinking about how to mend those fences, but for now, the ferry was pulling into the dock in St Marys. One of the men walked around the railing, pushing the bumpers—is that what they were called?—over the edge so the vessel wouldn't scrape against the dock. The other employee expertly maneuvered the boat into place.

The first man turned to her. "If you want to go get your car, we'll bring your suitcase up to the curb and meet you there."

"Thank you," she said as she fished her keys out of her purse. The IvyLena Inn had, again, thought of every detail.

She'd retrieved her small SUV, had her suitcase tucked in the back cargo hold, and had just gotten onto I-95 headed south when her cell phone rang.

An 843 number she didn't recognize. She pressed the button on her steering wheel to answer.

"Hi. It's Dwight." His beautiful Southern drawl filled her car via Bluetooth. "Claire said you left this morning."

"My story was written. It was time for me to go home."

"I was hoping to talk to you before you left."

Both his rejection and his comfort during her panic attack after Gus's death flashed through her mind. She wasn't yet sure what to make of this call. "Oh?"

"I wanted to apologize. I shouldn't have been so quick to...push you away."

She was silent for a few beats, letting his words sink in. "And what caused this change of heart?"

"Well, first, it's been a long time since I met someone like you. Someone who makes me comfortable. Who makes me want to spend all day just talking to them. And it seemed a shame to have that connection but not spend time getting to know you."

But that had been the case when he'd first dumped her. Could she use the word "dumped" if they'd never really been a couple? It had sure felt like being dumped.

He continued. "And then Gus died and that reminded me of the...finality of things. I don't want to be an old man one day who always wondered what could have happened with that wonderful woman he'd met on Cumberland Island."

"So this is all about you not wanting to have any regrets?" She was being cautious. She didn't like that the focus was all on him.

"Yes, but mainly I've felt bad about what I did to you. I keep seeing that look on your face out on the porch swing when I told you I couldn't see you anymore."

"So this is a pity call." She was tempted to take him back, but she was going to make him work for it.

"No!"

"Then what's the bottom line?"

"I want to see you again. I want to give us a chance."

"My brother died only a few weeks ago. There will still be times when I'm wallowing in grief. And I'm not going to hide who I am or how I'm feeling." She wouldn't do that for Dwight. She wouldn't do it for any man.

"I'm not asking you to do that."

"And you think you can handle it?"

"I think we'll both be going through hard stuff. You'll be grieving your brother and I'll be figuring out how to...take a chance. How to risk getting hurt again."

Maybe he had a point. Maybe addressing their emotional baggage could set them both free.

He continued. "But I think you're going to be worth it."

She chuckled. "You *think* I might be worth it?"

"You have to admit, we don't know a lot about each other." His voice, too, had a congenial tone.

"What if I end up—I don't know—putting mayonnaise on my French fries or something horrible like that?"

He laughed. "I can think of worse things."

"What if I insist on watching the Hallmark Channel every time we're together? Or what if I own seventeen hamsters? Or—"

"I'm willing to take my chances." His good humor came across in his tone. "So what do you say? Can we give this a try?"

Her heart gave a little pitter-patter like it had when Randy O'Donnell had asked her to prom decades earlier. "I'll commit to taking it slowly."

"I can live with that. I'll call in a couple of days once we're both back home and settled in. Does that work for you?"

A warm feeling filled her chest, despite the car's AC blowing at full blast. "It does."

"You should be home in—what?—a couple of hours?"

"That would be the case if I was headed home, but I'm taking a little detour." She hadn't realized until now that she'd made the decision, but the universe seemed to be pulling her in a different direction, away from Jacksonville.

"Oh?" His voice was laced with curiosity, but he didn't say anything else, like he didn't want to be too nosy so early in their relationship. "Don't you have to get your story handed in?"

"I can send it in from Gainesville," she said. "I'm going to see my daughter."

Chapter Thirty-One

Neena dialed Rosie's phone number when she was about fifteen minutes from the campus of the University of Florida. Her daughter was the one person who was welcome unannounced at her house at any time, but Neena otherwise hated drop-in guests. She wasn't going to do that to her daughter.

"Hello?" Rosie's tone was neither warm nor hospitable.

"Hey, what are you up to right now?"

"Right this minute? Loading the dishwasher." The hesitancy in her voice indicated that she knew something was up.

"Mind if I drop by in just a bit? I just hit the outskirts of Gainesville."

"Why are you here?" There was now even more wariness in Rosie's voice.

"I'll explain when I get there. So I can stop by?"

Rosie let out a dramatic sigh. "Do I have a choice?"

"Not really. See you in a few." Neena punched the button on her dashboard to hang up the phone, then pulled over to punch Rosie's address into her GPS. She'd only been there a few times because most of their visits were when Rosie had come home to Jacksonville.

Neena glanced at the clock and did a quick calculation in her head. The timing still worked out okay. She'd drive to Rosie's, have a conversation with her, then log onto Rosie's internet to send her article to Justin.

A quarter of an hour later, Neena knocked on the apartment door.

The door opened with a jerk, and Rosie leaned against the door jamb, blocking the entrance. "If this is going to be a reprimand for breaking into the safe, you should have just called me," she said.

"Are you going to invite me in?"

"Are you going to bitch at me for breaking into the safe?"

Neena gave her the I'm-trying-to-be-patient mom look she'd given her so many times over the years but didn't say anything. Finally, Rosie relented and turned her back on Neena. She walked into the living room without inviting Neena in.

Neena followed her inside, anyway. She'd already come this far, and there were things she needed to say to her daughter—things that she should have said a long time ago.

Rosie made her way into the tiny kitchen and popped a pod into the coffee machine. "So why are you here?"

Neena hesitated for a moment. She'd rehearsed these words on her drive here, but even so, actually saying them out loud wasn't easy. "I wanted to apologize. I didn't mean to mislead you about the will. My mother had told me how she wanted you to use that money, and I thought the document actually said that." It had been a conversation in Mama's kitchen, similar to the one they were having now—one of a handful of important conversations that were still so clear in her mind, even years after they'd taken place.

Rosie opened the overhead cabinet and took a mug down. "And I'm supposed to believe that? If I hadn't seen the will myself, I never would have known...you never would have told me—"

"I wasn't trying to lie to you. I really thought that was what it said."

Rosie punched the start button on the machine a little harder than she needed to. "So you came to apologize. Apology accepted." Her tone was impatient. "Is there anything else?"

Neena took a deep breath. Though Rosie was ready for a fight, Neena's goal was to remain as calm, as understanding, as possible. "You need to realize that even though you're twenty-three years old, I still want to protect you. To keep you safe. To not see you ever get hurt—physically, emotionally, financially."

Rosie's gaze was on the coffee spurting into the mug, but Neena could tell she was listening intently.

Neena continued. "It's what moms do. It's what they'll always do." She paused, willing herself to push on through this conversation. "But I now realize that I would have hated someone trying to tell me what to do—how to live my life—when I was your age. So, I'm sorry. I'll try to be less controlling." Her experiences on the island had shown her that she couldn't be responsible for the lives of other adults, including her daughter. "You'll always be my baby, but I'll keep reminding myself what a smart and savvy young woman you are."

Rosie finally turned to face her. Her expression was a mixture of hopefulness and skepticism. "So it's okay if I go to Paris with Caleb?"

"Is that what you want to do?"

"Yes."

"Well, it's your money and your time, so you get to decide how you'll spend them."

Rosie's eyebrows rose. "Seriously?"

Neena nodded, a smile on her face. She loved making her daughter happy.

A grin tickled at the edge of Rosie's lips. "What caused this change of heart? Especially when you've been so convinced that going to Europe with him would ruin my life?"

But there was no way Neena would tell Rosie about John or Carolyn or her mysterious connection with Gus. Maybe she would one day, when there was less doubt about her mental stability. "I had a lot of time to think while I was on Cumberland Island."

Rosie's grin broadened. "And you finally realized I'm an adult?" she teased.

Neena hated to dampen the happiness of the moment, but she needed to say everything she'd come to say. She slid her fingers along the edge of the countertop as she decided how to start. "I finally realized that I can't hold myself responsible for what other people do." An image of Kevin's body on her guest room bed flashed through her mind. "I mean, I tried to help Kevin. I provided him with a place to stay, a way to get away from the life and the people he hung out with back in Charlotte." She fanned her hand in front of her tear-filled eyes, determined not to interrupt the conversation with a crying jag. "But in the end, he—or the drugs—made the decisions. I have to realize I did my best. I can't hold myself responsible."

Rosie came around the counter and wrapped her arms around Neena as she sat at the counter. She rested her head on her mother's shoulder.

Neena continued. "I'm sorry that I've held on to you so tightly. That I've tried to control you, even as an adult. It's like you've paid the price for me wanting to make sure everything turns out okay. I guess I've been this way for a long time. I mean, after my mother's death...I just always felt like I should have done more. Like I should have been able to save her."

"And like you should have been able to save Uncle Kevin, too," Rosie said, still hugging her mother.

Neena nodded.

"Neither of those were your fault, you know," Rosie said.

Neena nodded, unable to speak. She understood that now. Her experience on Cumberland Island had shown her that she needed to forgive herself. That we can't control the things other adults do, even those closest to us. All we can do is love them as best we know how. And that's what she planned to do with Rosie from now on.

"And whatever dumb decisions I make in the future?" Rosie joked. "Those aren't your fault either."

Neena barked out a short laugh. She would do her best to let Rosie make her own decisions. The trick, of course, would be to let her daughter make her own mistakes, but not ones that were too big or too far-reaching.

Rosie pulled back so she could look Neena in the face. "You know, the older I get, the more I realize how much you did for me growing up. I mean, now that I'm out on my own, I realize how expensive things are. Raising a child has to cost a ton of money. And yet you bought us a house and you paid for my gymnastic lessons, even though I was really bad at it. And remember that time in high school when I wanted those expensive designer jeans? You told your friend, Wendy, that you couldn't go out to dinner with the girls and I knew it was because you were saving for those stupid jeans. I didn't have the heart to tell you I didn't even like the way they fit me once I got them."

Neena was crying now. She'd never realized how much Rosie had actually *seen* what Neena had done for her. "Then can I have my ninety bucks back, please?" she teased through her tears.

"And remember when you paid for that really expensive trip for me to go to Washington, DC, with the safety patrol? One of the moms who chaperoned was a speech-language pathologist. That was the first I'd heard of that job, and it sounded so...noble. Getting to help other people learn how to communicate? That's way better than being a spreadsheet jockey in a cubicle somewhere. That trip made me discover what I wanted to do when I got to be an adult. And I never would have met that lady if you hadn't saved up to send me on that trip."

How had Neena not heard this story before? She wished she could thank that woman, and all the other women who had been good role models for Rosie over the years.

"You've been a *good* mother," Rosie said. "And you've prepared me for...whatever happens in the future."

The tears streamed down Neena's face even more than before. "Thank you. I needed to hear that."

Rosie bumped her with her hip. "I can't believe you ever had any doubt."

Chapter Thirty-Two

Six Weeks Later

The rented boat bounced along the waves, jarring Neena's body each time it skipped across another swell in the Atlantic. She cradled a small wooden box under each arm, like a fullback protecting a pair of footballs from would-be tacklers who tried to strip them loose.

She'd always loved the way the sun glistened off the water. The way the vastness of the ocean calmed her. But her nerves were on edge today. She was finally doing something she could have done—should have done—years ago.

Dwight placed a hand on her knee while he kept his other hand on the steering wheel. "It should get smoother once we're away from the shore." He shouted so that he could be heard over the sound of the boat's motor.

She smiled, not sure if she was more nervous about the rough ride or the mission they were on.

So much had changed since her return from Cumberland Island. She now had weekly phone calls with Ms. Sylvester, who seemed to be doing better now and insisted she call her "Vicki," though that would never seem natural to Neena.

Neena would likely never hear of Ethan or Jewel or Emma again, though she wanted to believe each would find peace in their life. It was a reminder of how brief encounters—a smile, a comment, even an overheard story in a coffee shop—can change the trajectory of someone's path. She wondered whose lives she'd touched in that fashion and vowed to try to recognize those brief moments moving forward. To use them to lift people up whenever she could.

Rosie had left two days ago for Paris, with Caleb in tow. He'd been kinder to her while Neena was in Gainesville for their graduation. Had treated his mother well during the celebration meal they'd had at a local restaurant with his parents. His high school-aged sister seemed to adore him. Neena had decided to try to see him in a different light, though she was still unconvinced he was the right man for Rosie. But her daughter was an adult, and Neena needed to let her be in charge of her own life.

"This is far enough," she shouted to Dwight.

He turned his head to look at her. "You sure?"

Neena nodded. She appreciated his patience through all of this. He'd even insisted on paying the fee to rent the boat, though their business today had nothing to do with him.

He dialed back on the boat's speed and slowed the vessel to a stop. They were both silent for a few minutes as it bobbed in the water. He seemed to sense she wasn't quite ready.

"Your mom would be proud, you know," he finally said. "Of you, of Rosie, of how famous you've become." He flashed her a teasing smile.

She smacked him on the knee. He'd been ribbing her about her recent "fame" since her article on Cumberland Island had gone viral, earning her recognition from traditional journalists and social media influencers alike. The print issue had sold more copies than any other issue in the history of *Coastal South Travel*. Interview requests were coming in from local TV stations all along the Atlantic coast, from Jacksonville to Boston.

And best of all: an invitation to appear on a nationwide NPR program. The segment would be recorded the day after tomorrow.

"Yeah. About that," she said. "I've been holding out on a little news."

His eyebrows rose. "Oh, yeah?"

"Justin asked me to join the magazine full time."

Dwight's smile rivaled the shimmer of the water behind him. Her heart warmed. He really did seem to want what was best for her.

"Like as a regular staff member?" he asked.

She nodded, happy to share this news with someone other than Rosie. But there was more. "And I also got a job offer from *Travel + Leisure*."

He gave her a quizzical look. "That's one of the big ones in the industry, right?"

She was sure she had a ridiculous grin on her face. She could hardly believe it herself. "One of the biggest." She still couldn't believe her article had caught their eye.

"So what are you going to do?"

"Well, I'm leading Justin on a bit, but considering he fires everyone over the age of forty—"

Dwight chuckled. "He doesn't have a chance, does he?"

"It's *Travel + Leisure*! I mean, what travel writer *wouldn't* want to go to work for them?"

"Do you get to stay in Jacksonville?" He seemed a bit worried that maybe she'd move too far away.

"They want me to stay somewhere in the Southeast, so Jacksonville is fine."

He raised his hand in a high-five motion.

She slapped her palm on his. "They've been looking for the right person to cover the region, and they think I'm the one. The editor-in-chief actually called me herself."

"A call? Not an email or a direct message on LinkedIn?"

"Terribly old-fashioned, isn't it?" She smiled at the knowledge that she'd soon no longer be reliant on the twenty-something upstart now running *Coastal South Travel*.

"Make sure you're getting what you're worth," Dwight said.

"Oh, for sure. And this means a salary and health insurance and…I mean, I could still be laid off at any time, regardless of which corporation I work for. But it sure feels good to have a little stability for once." The steady income would help her pay down her hospital bills and maybe even allow her to save a bit more than she was used to.

She still couldn't believe her article had been so well received, especially the part about how John and Carolyn had gone back to the church during the reception. Americans seemed to always clamor to hear more about the Kennedy family.

She'd done her best to not sully Gus's name or draw unnecessary attention to Boone Calhoun in her article. She'd written that "only a handful of people knew about the late-night return to the church—the driver who'd taken them there, one resident who lives along the road that runs the length of the island, and anyone John and Carolyn may have told." Sure, she'd had to tell Justin that Boone had confirmed the information, but she wouldn't ever tell anyone else. A good journalist doesn't reveal her sources, whether they are dead or alive.

Dwight's voice interrupted her thoughts. "Have you told *Travel + Leisure* that you're definitely taking the job?"

Her gaze moved from the horizon to him. "I'm waiting for the official offer letter. Then I'll wish Justin good luck in reaching the younger audience he craves so much, and I'll go on to work for an older, more established competitor. Some people appreciate *older* and *more established*."

Dwight laughed, but Neena grew more serious.

"You ready for this?" she asked.

He gave one short dip of his head. "I'm ready."

She stood, a wooden box in each hand. "One at a time? Or both together?"

"It's your call."

She nodded and handed him the newer of the two boxes. She held the other one—the one containing Mama's ashes—in both hands as she walked to the front of the boat. She stood for a moment, allowing the happy memories from her childhood to waft over her—the sound of Mama's laughter, the softness of her skin, the proud look on her face as she straightened Neena's graduation cap right before Neena turned to join her classmates for the high school processional.

Neena would still have those memories tucked inside her. She would hopefully always have them. But there was a finality to today. She was finally putting Mama to rest. She stood with her face to the ocean breeze, wanting to remember this day for the rest of her life. Wanting to feel Mama's presence here.

Finally, she opened the lid and turned the box over, watching as the tiny khaki-colored particles scattered across the water below. Tears ran down her face as she said goodbye to the mother who—Neena now recognized—had loved her as best she could. As best she knew how. Life was hard, even without the mental illness Mama had wrestled with. A younger Neena had wanted to place blame—on Mama, on herself—but out here, as she let Mama go free into the vast ocean, she was filled with a sense of grace. Grace for herself. Grace for Mama. John and Gus had given Neena that gift, and for that she would be forever grateful.

She closed the box and turned toward Dwight, who held out the other wooden container. He had a somber look on his face, like he understood the gravity of the situation. Today had actually been his idea. He was considering something similar for the ashes he had from his stillborn child. He'd told Neena that Cumberland Island had taught him the importance of moving beyond his sadness and grief. They'd had a lot of late-night conversations about how the experiences of the past had shaped them...and how they wanted to live their lives as a result of the lessons they'd learned.

They exchanged boxes and she again turned toward the ocean, ready to bid farewell to the brother who had been the only remaining vestige of her childhood, of where she'd come from and who she'd once been. Though she and Kevin had been adults for a long time, making their way in the world, that invisible thread had always linked them together, regardless of where they were. She wished his life had turned out differently. Wished that whatever had haunted him—whatever had driven him to find refuge in drugs—had been easier for him to understand and to deal with.

She mourned his death, but also understood that the strongest thread of her life now connected her to Rosie, the child currently making her way in the world. Like Mama and Kevin and Neena, Rosie was now making decisions on her own. Learning the tough ways of the world and the hard lessons of life. Neena could only hope that she'd prepared her daughter as best she could—to love and receive love. To be grateful for the beauty around her. To make decisions that would keep her safe and warm and well-fed and happy.

Neena opened the box containing Kevin's ashes and let them scatter over the ocean, following Mama to wherever the currents would take them. Her shoulders shook as tears flowed freely down her face.

"Are you okay?" Dwight asked quietly from his place in the driver's seat.

She nodded. "I just need a tissue."

He squeezed her hand briefly as she passed by him, making her way to the back of the boat where she'd stored her purse inside a built-in storage compartment.

She opened the lid of the bench seat and reached inside her bag. But instead of feeling the soft packet of tissues she'd tucked inside her purse earlier that morning, something else crinkled at her touch. The sound of cellophane?

With her hands still hidden inside the bench seat, she grasped the small package and pulled it out—a gift in a fancy clear package, a little larger than a sandwich bag—two apple fritters, the size and shape of those she'd shared with Carolyn. The wrapper was held closed by a small, logoed sticker that read the IvyLena Inn. A warm sensation coursed through her body, like the sought-after hug of a beloved relative. She didn't know if this gift was from John or Gus or the universe in general, but maybe it didn't matter.

What mattered was that Mama and Kevin were now free. That Neena had shed the guilt of believing she should have been able to save them.

She looked out over the horizon—thanking John, thanking Gus—then tucked the small package back inside her purse, got the tissues out, and closed the lid of the bench seat.

Maybe she'd tell Dwight about all of this one day, but for now, it was her secret. A secret she shared with Gus and John. Two extraordinary men who had helped her understand how to set herself free.

***

Thank you for reading *Neena Lee Is Seeing Things*. Please consider leaving a review on at least one website and/or telling a friend about the book.

Please also sign up for my newsletter at SheilaAthens.com. My next book, *Mae Van Dorn's Perfect Storm*, will be out in late summer/early fall of 2024.

Acknowledgements

Many people have helped tremendously along this book's journey into the world, including book coach/story guru/author Susan DeFreitas, #1 Amazon charts bestselling author and master certified author coach Camille Pagan, New York Times and USA Today bestselling author Karen White, and Wall Street Journal and USA Today bestselling author Pamela Kelley.

Other author friends have provided insight and support along the way, including Carla Damron, D.L. Williams, Valerie Bowman, Madeline Martin, Kathryn Dodson, Leeann Treese, Janet Rundquist, Kelly Elizabeth Huston and Paulette Stout.

I love my writer peeps, especially those who feed my need for writerly discussions and insight. Many thanks to the ladies of the bungalow, the writer hikers, the Women's Fiction Writers Association, and the authors of the Clubhouse Author Conference. They all know who they are!

Thanks to beta readers RA Cook (a wonderful children's author herself), Aryn Bloom, Jillian Deese, and Lisa Barge for their insight into how to make Neena's story stronger.

I'd also like to thank Jeannie Mitchell and Ulrike Bittenbinder—people from my "real life" who have helped support this writing gig in their own unique ways.

Finally, thanks to all the readers who have read this book, and especially to those who have passed it on via word of mouth or online reviews. You have **my heartfelt appreciation** for helping Neena's story reach others.